Love Knows No Boundaries II
Karma Unleashed

Coffee

Lock Down Publications
Presents
Love Knows No Boundaries II
Karma Unleashed
A Novel by *Coffee*

Coffee

Lock Down Publications
P.O. Box 1482
Pine Lake, Ga 30072-1482

First Edition November 2014
Printed in the United States of America

This is a work of fiction. Names, characters, places, and incidents either are products of the author's imagination or are used fictitiously. Any similarity to actual events or locales or persons, living or dead, is entirely coincidental.

Cover design and layout by: **Dynasty's Cover Me**
Book interior design by: **Shawn Walker**
Edited by: **Shawn Walker**

4

Stay Connected with Us!

Text **LOCKDOWN** to 22828 to stay up-to-date with new releases, sneak peaks, contests and more...

Thank you!

Submission Guideline.

Submit the first three chapters of your completed manuscript to ldpsubmissions@gmail.com, subject line: Your book's title. The manuscript must be in a .doc file and sent as an attachment. Document should be in Times New Roman, double spaced and in size 12 font. Also, provide your synopsis and full contact information. If sending multiple submissions, they must each be in a separate email.

Have a story but no way to send it electronically? You can still submit to LDP/Ca$h Presents. Send in the first three chapters, written or typed, of your completed manuscript to:

LDP: Submissions Dept
Po Box 1482
Pine Lake, Ga 30072

DO NOT send original manuscript. Must be a duplicate.

Provide your synopsis and a cover letter containing your full contact information.

Thanks for considering LDP and Ca$h Presents.

~Acknowledgements~

First and above all, I want to acknowledge my mother, **Mary**. I have officially learned the statement, *A Mother's Love* encompasses much. If I could time travel, I would be the best child ever. NO smack talk, NO procrastinating when you said move, NO tears of any kind on my account. But all I have is *now* and in moving forward, I want to show you just how much you and your unwavering love means to me. I truly only want to succeed so I can bless your days here. I love you from the bottom up.

This book is written in appreciation to each of my **readers.** I do this for you. Every project I ever touch will *always* be about you. Vaguely spoken, but the depth runs deep.

To **Ca$h** and my entire **Lock Down Publications** team, I couldn't imagine a better literary family to be a part of. I love all of you! We move as one!

To a beautiful soul who is the guardian angel of a Queen I know. **Khiya**, may your wings *always* cover your mommy.

My brother, **Nola**, you had been instrumental during my creative process. You have been my muse through life as well as this book. Mucho, *mucho* gracias!

And lastly, *my rock*. Never had I met a person as complete as you. I endeavor to walk in the light you so generously shine on me. With each beat…

~Dedication~

This entire book is dedicated to my daddy, *Emile*.

October 2, 2014
An open letter

I will forever feel a certain level of guilt for being so enthralled in my own life that I forgot about yours. My *slow to reach for the phone* act wasn't an indication of how much love I have for you. I just stupidly allowed my world to overshadow the one that we shared. I apologize for every time I made you feel unimportant or unloved with my non actions. I know you know I love you and the great news is, I know you love me, too. I'm just so hurt, Daddy, and I *am* to blame. I'm sure you'll tell me not to be so hard on myself and I wish I could, but I should have honored you more. I should have made you a priority, but I took your time here for granted. And that was because you were my undefeated Superman. There was no sickness you couldn't overcome. I believed that and now that thoughtless belief has me in tears, full of grief with a massive headache and an even heavier heart.

I don't remember if I'd ever told you, but you were an amazing man! Your personality and confidence was admirable. I was proud to show you off and say, "That's my daddy!" You were full of wisdom, intelligence, brightly comical.

And you were my personal savior. I remember how you came to my rescue so brave and valiant when my apartment got broken into in 2005. And when my ex threatened to steal the breath from my body, you were prepared to lay him to rest first. I am my daddy's baby.

The lyrics below is *Joy* by Chrisette Michele. It was your ringtone for each time you called my cell phone. Now imagine me singing this to you.

Walked down the sidewalk.
Starin' at your feet.
Wishin' my steps were longer.

So, by your sides I could keep.

Hold your hand much bigger.
Never wanted mine to grow.
So, I could always feel perfect.
Inside your palms just so.

No one loves me just like you do.
No one knows me just like you do.
No one can compare to the way my eyes fit in yours.
You'll always be my father, and I'll always be your joy.

I love you, Daddy. Forever and ever!

Sincerely,
Your lil' girl

Rest in Paradise
11/30/47-10/1/14

Coffee

Chapter 1

"**O**pen up this muthafucka!" Tracie anxiously demanded of Minnie, standing outside of her house. She leaned on the door with both hands, pressing her ear against it to check sound from within. But she was unable to hear anything with the exception of the downpour of rain and the boisterous thunder that boomed around her.

Minnie was in her dark bedroom carefully, yet swiftly, patting the objects on her dresser blindly searching for the house key to unlock the front door. She was gearing up to unleash the dragon the unknown woman was summoning.

An uneasy knot formed in her stomach when she tried to make sense of what was happening, but she had not a clue. The more pounding she heard the more her adrenaline spiked and she had become desperate to put an end to whatever madness was on the other side.

Tracie's bad nerves forced her body to quake, and it didn't help that she was cold and drenched to her socks. "Minnie!" She impatiently screamed for the umpteenth time.

"Oh, I'm coming," Minnie said loud enough for no one.

After a few minutes of sightless probing, Minnie held the key between her fingers and speedily walked back up front. She fumbled the key into the hole and when she unlocked it, the sheer force of the door crashing open against her made her stumble backwards.

"Aaahhhh!" Minnie fearfully screamed at the burly image that huskily stood before her. Unable to process anything but saving her own life, she threw the hardest right bow she could muster moments before she followed up with the left.

G'Corey took a serious hit with the first blow, but he blocked the second one as he went to place her in a bear hug. She struggled wildly to get a loose but to no avail.

"Let go of me," she pleaded. "Helpppp!" She called out at the top of her lungs, kicking her dangling feet.

"Minnie! Minnie!" G'Corey sharply blurted. He called her name once more and this time it registered that the alleged attacker was her rescuer, her husband. He let her go slowly, she wrapped her arms around him and began sobbing. "It's okay. I'm here," he consoled, rubbing her back with one hand while massaging his jaw with the other.

"I'm—sorry." She hyperventilated through her cry.

"Why did you start swinging on me?" G'Corey wiped off the facial moisture that blanketed her flushed skin.

"Somebody was ruthlessly banging on the door." Her chest heaved up and down repeatedly as she attempted to regulate her breathing.

"This door?" G'Corey pointed in its direction as he asked in false shock.

Yes, *this* door," she spoke agitatedly. "Some woman was calling my name, threatening that I let her in."

"What the fuck?" G'Corey grimaced. He reached into the bag of supplies he had dropped on the floor the moment he was assaulted by his wife and pulled out the flashlight. He escorted Minnie into their bedroom. "Get in bed and wait for me here."

"Where are you going?"

"To check around the house and up the block to see if I can find who you talking 'bout," he spoke in a protective tone as he turned the flashlight on.

"I'm coming with you." Minnie resisted him steering her into bed. She wanted to confront the female herself. She was anxious to know what was so important that would cause a woman to abandon the safety of her own home to come out to hers in riotous weather and stir a commotion.

"No, you not." He placed his hand on her stomach. "You gon' take care of this lil' one while I go peep things out."

She looked down at her belly to acknowledge her growing bud. *My baby*, she thought. Minnie's emotions were all over the place. On one hand, she wanted to disregard the pregnancy speech, but then again she couldn't. G'Corey wasn't able to see her eyes lower into slits, but he could hear her huffing in protest. "Okay," she said in a monotone voice.

He kissed her forehead, bolted out of the front door and secured the locks. Minnie sat on the edge of the bed, rubbing her trembling hands over her face. Too many disturbing thoughts raced through her mind.

G'Corey stepped into the alley alongside his house and shined his light where Tracie was laying sprawled faced down on the concrete.

He picked up her slack body and threw her over his shoulder. He sprinted up the street, turned a couple of corners and allowed Tracie to slip from his grasp and fall haphazardly to the ground.

"Aaarghh," Tracie groaned as she regained consciousness.

"Wake yo punk ass all the way up, so you can remember this shit right c'here." G'Corey stood over her as she dizzily propped up on her hands and knees, looking up at him pleadingly.

The *grrr* in G'Corey's voice was ominous. Her slick tongue nor street fighting skills would be enough to get her out of this altercation unscathed. Her gut told her that she had gone too far this time, so she braced herself for the evitable.

Twenty minutes had elapsed when Minnie heard G'Corey come inside. She jumped up and met him in the living room. "What happened? Did you see her? Who was she?" Minnie spat the questions out rapidly.

"Nothing happened and I saw no one." G'Corey began undressing out of his wet clothes.

Minnie shook her head in disbelief and folded her arms. "Uhn. Uhn. Something's not right. That girl was intent on breaking down my door. She wouldn't have just given up and disappeared into thin air."

"Maybe she realized she had the wrong house. You ever thought about that?"

"G'Corey," she said with the sharpness of a tack, "I *heard* her say my name, repeatedly."

"Baby," he chuckled to minimize the intensity the conversation was heading in.

"There's nothing funny about this," Minnie warned.

G'Corey blew out really hard. "Look, I can only vouch for what I saw, ya heard me. And I didn't see nothing. I wish I would have, though. I don't appreciate some strange bitch bringing drama to our door."

"Humph." Minnie was very annoyed at the lack of answers she had to her unsettling questions. "She was out there far too long to just up and split *and* to do it conveniently before you arrived. But let's say she

Coffee

did. It's still a problem because she kept calling my name. She wanted me. But. For. What?" She asked in an accusatory manner.

G'Corey fumbled through drawers, feeling for a change of clothes. *Fuck*, he thought. "You know Mildred lives a few houses down. Obviously, she thought she stayed here and was tryna get that broad's attention." He attempted to create doubt. "That young ass lil' girl stay in mess."

She smacked her teeth, "Mildred and Minnie sounds nothing alike."

"It does if she called her *Milly*," he lamely countered. Seeing that his response did nothing to allay her suspicions, G'Corey quickly changed tactics. "Listen, baby, I don't know what the hell happened. But it feels like you putting me on trial for some shit I know nothing about. If you want to, we can hit these streets together, but whoever lil' one was, she probably long gone, nah."

Minnie threw her head back exhaustedly, letting out a sigh. "I'm going to bed," was her defeated response.

***

"I'm happy you decided to come over." Janessa pulled Elias into her home. She placed a hand behind his head, drawing his face closer to hers as she kissed him softly on his cheek. "Aww, you're soaked. Take off your clothes, baby," she instructed.

Elias didn't budge at her words. He was still seething on the inside. Janessa shook her head and rested her candle on the credenza when she realized he wasn't complying.

"You're so spoiled," she giggled. She began stripping him of everything. Once Janessa was done, she took his wet items into her hallway bathroom and hung them over the shower rod so they could air dry. She went back up front where he stood with his arm folded across his chest supporting the arm that allowed him to rub his goatee, contemplatively. "What's the matter with you? You haven't said one word."

"I'm straight," he answered, flatly.

She handed him a dry towel, "Doesn't sound too convincing, but okay," Janessa frowned a little, but whatever thoughts held his mind

14

hostage weren't going to be an issue by the time she was finished with him.

Janessa led Elias into her bedroom, in the back of her house. He sat on her bed and she lit more candles to both illuminate the darkness and set a mood.

"I'm gonna open a window so we can get some fresh air in here. We're gonna need it." Janessa made small talk as he remained deathly quiet. "Tough room. Geez Louise," she joked until she took a more serious approach.

She stood directly in front of him and pushed him onto his back. Removing the towel he draped around his waist, she exposed his exquisiteness.

Janessa didn't coin the name *Juicy J* for nothing. Her head game earned her that title, so if he refused to use his words, she would make him offer up his moans.

Janessa's mouth watered as she eyed his package. Hovering above it, she spat on the head of his dick and voraciously enveloped as much of him as she could. She glided her tongue ring from the base of his dick up and along the trail of his pulsating vein until she reached the bulbous head. He didn't say a peep, but the sound of his toes cracking under the command of her sexual suction sent her into overdrive. Janessa then propped up on all four, still latched on as she began playing with her passion fruit.

"Umm," Janessa whimpered between the slurping and slopping on his steel.

Any other night, Elias would have gone ape on Janessa behind the work she was giving, but he was distracted.

"Aaaahhh," Elias finally bellowed. He was aggravated that he couldn't focus on the big booty before him. He concentrated a little more, grabbing her hair with both hands as she slow necked him. Janessa smirked. Elias grimaced. It wasn't working. His mind was set on instant replay.

"You forfeited your spot... I'll call you."
La'Tasha didn't bat a lash or blink an eye before she swiftly shut the door in his face.

"I'll call you?" Elias repeated as his eyebrows creased further into the bridge of his nose. He stood in shock at how she played him like a scrub. "You cold-blooded bitch!" he said aloud as he attempted to process what just happened—to him.

Elias held an old Western stare at her house unsure if he should kick the muthafucka in and choke the shit out of her like his first mind suggested. He thought long and hard and was seconds away from doing just that until his phone rang.

"What?" Elias rushed.

"Hey, baby. What you doing?" Janessa sensually spoke into the receiver, ignoring the shortness in his voice.

Her question made him truly question what the hell he was really about to do. He was on his way to committing character suicide had his train of thought not been derailed.

"This ain't playa," he admonished, looking down at himself reproachfully.

"Excuse me?" Janessa wasn't following him.

"That wasn't for you," he dryly made clear.

"Then tell me what is," she resumed her sexual innuendos.

Elias was hot under the collar, but he managed to utter the three words she craved hearing, "Get it ready," he ordered before hanging up. He looked at La'Tasha's place, disgustingly so, one last time before he walked into the thick of rain and back into his truck.

By the time Elias placed himself in the now, Janessa was straddled on top of him.

"You like my up and down, baby?" she cooed as she drew her breasts inward and flickered her candy licker erotically across her bullet sized nipples.

Elias said nothing, but instead secured both hands around her waist and aggressively pumped hard inside of her tenderoni. He was going to screw her until he could no longer envision La'Tasha.

Chapter 2

It was 3:41AM and Sleepy hadn't been able to sleep. Acacia was profoundly on his mind. The desperate plea in the last voicemail she had left sat heavily on his chest.

"Sleepy, I am so sad, but I understand why you refuse to talk to me. It hurts so, so, so bad, but I get it. I don't know what to say other than I apologize, and that I love you. I may have a messed up way of showing it, but you know I do. And if there is any part of you that still loves me, please come home so we can talk. Please?" She paused to suppress her cry, *"Please."*

Sleepy listened to Acacia's message repeatedly and each time he had, he heard more of the pain drip from her heartfelt words. Hearing the vulnerability in her voice reminded him that she could be soft, and he missed *that* side of her.

He rose from off of the sofa bed he occupied in Javier's living room and opened the front door. He stood in the doorway with his hands extended above his head, holding onto the edge of the door seal as he looked at the downpour. He thought to show up at their place, but the flooded streets wouldn't allow him to leave. He shut the door and plopped back onto the bed and wondered how she was holding up. Was she asleep or up thinking of him? Did she really learn her lesson? Was she able to change her ways like she said she would? Too many questions that would all be soon answered. Sleepy was ready to make up—hopefully for good this time.

***

"Ms. Terry," Nurse Wynter addressed Tracie as she entered her room at Mercy Hospital. "These two gentlemen would like to speak to you. Will that be alright?" She smiled.

"I don't—aaahhhh," she grabbed at her aching throat, "know nothing." Tracie denied immediately.

Wynter checked her blood pressure. "Just tell them what you do know, okay?" She stepped out of the room to give them privacy.

Tracie rolled her eyes, but stopped mid-way when the pressure from having received a major blow which shattered her socket caused an instant headache. "Shit!" She rested her hand over the eye draping.

The uniformed policemen approached her bed. "Good morning, ma'am. I'm Officer Womack and this is my partner, Officer Gentry. We just want to ask you a few questions."

She spoke slowly. "I don't know who did it or why. What's left to ask?" Tracie slowly sat up in her bed, wincing at the striking pain in her abdomen.

The policemen looked to one another before Officer Womack continued. "We're here to assist you and potentially arrest the person responsible for harming you. Can you confirm that you stay on Hullen?"

"Umm hmm," she answered unenthusiastically.

He jotted notes onto his pad. "You were a good ways from home. What were you doing in this area?"

"I don't remember."

"Did you get a good look at your attacker?" The other officer interjected.

"No."

"Do you know anyone who would want to cause you harm?" Officer Womack zeroed in on the eye that wasn't bandaged with the hopes of gauging the sincerity in her response.

"No!" Tracie snapped, looking down and then away.

The men retreated a few feet back and spoke amongst themselves. Tracie could hear them express their disbelief. Her lips began quivering with anger because she wanted to be left alone and they were harassing her with questions she'd never answer truthfully.

"You know more than what you're telling," Officer Gentry bluntly accused. "You're just like the rest of these young girls who will prove, at the expense of their life, their loyalty to a man who could give a shit less. You were beat within an inch of your life and you're still going to claim that you know nothing?"

"That's what I said," Tracie glared at him. "Now, are we done?"

Officer Gentry shook his head and directed his comments to his partner. "She knows who did this. She wasn't raped or robbed. The attack wasn't random. It was premeditated." He turned toward Tracie.

18

"Look at you," he scoffed. "You have a fractured nose, two cracked ribs, and ligature marks around your neck, yet you still wish to protect him?"

Tracie cradled the palm of one hand inside of the other and gently rolled her tongue over her loose teeth. "I'll give you a name." Tracie took a soap opera pause before speaking again. "His first name is *Fuck,* and his last name is *You.*"

"Un-fuckin-believable," Officer Gentry blurted in disgust. "I'm out of here." He waved her off and stormed out of the room and into the hall, leaving his partner to conclude the investigation on his own.

"Shouldn't you be following him?" Tracie looked at the policeman and then to the door.

He reached into his shirt pocket to pull out his card as he stood next to her. He relaxed his shoulders and spoke in a fatherly tone. "You know I had a daughter your age just as stubborn as she wanted to be." Tracie rested her head back onto the pillows and stared uninterestedly off into nothingness, but he continued. "She refused to tell me, or anyone for that matter, that the man she loved was the one responsible for the abuse she suffered. I begged her to let me help her, but she never allowed me. Eventually, it all came to end on the day I was able to arrest that son of a bitch."

"Your point?" Tracie smartly questioned while readdressing her attention back to him.

He blinked back the tears. The death of his daughter happened years ago, but the pain itself never died. "Let me help *you.* Call me when you remember." He placed the card in her hand and held it in her palm a few seconds longer than needed. Without another spoken word, he walked out.

Tracie sighed in a small breath as she looked around the room and embraced the familiarity of being in cold hospital rooms that stemmed from ass whippings, courtesy of G'Corey, that had gone too far. Having a moment to herself, she reflected on what took place some hours ago.

Tracie stood on the doorstep, banging with great urgency when she saw headlights approaching her at a creep speed. She turned all the way around to face the person she assumed was G'Corey when the car parked directly in front of the house she was at. She abandoned her mission to get inside and replaced it with seeing if the person stepping out of the car was her man. By the time she was able to identify it was him, he had delivered a swift uppercut so devastating that the next thing she recalled was coming into consciousness on the neutral grounds on Jefferson Davis Hwy.

"Wake yo punk ass all the way up, so you can remember this shit right c'here."

"G'Corey, let me explain," Tracie tried to stand to her feet, but was too dazed to do so.

"Fuck that! I've warned you 'bout playin' with me. Now, I'ma show you why playin' with Minnie is bad for your health."

G'Corey viciously kicked Tracie in the abdomen with the boot of his Timberland.

"Ooff," she blew out as she rolled over onto her back instinctually bear hugging her stomach. "Our baby," she wailed.

"Baby? I'ma stomp that bitch out yo pussy." He raised his foot to send it crashing down squarely on the center of her belly, but she managed to move, catching his foot at the same time and causing him to lose his balance. "Muthafucka," he scolded as he fell backwards.

Tracie mustered the strength to rise to her feet despite the throbbing contracting pain in her stomach that forced her to lurch forward. G'Corey sprang up and in an infuriated rush he fought her like she was a man. He showed her no mercy even up to the point where she took his hits without shielding herself from them.

When he grew tired of punching her, he lifted her up by the neck and began cutting off her circulation. Tracie clawed at his hands, chocking for air, and begging he free her from his grip with her protruding eyes.

"Next time, I'll kill you, bitch." G'Corey dropped her battered body on the muddy grass seconds before he took off running.

Tracie slipped in and out of consciousness at that point. Therefore, the memory of what happened between the time she heard G'Corey's final threatening words and the beeping of the machines that monitored her were a blur.

Tears streamed from her eyes as her heart broke. G'Corey's actions were despicable. She knew he was dead ass wrong, but she reasoned some men needed a little more love than others so she was still willing to show him hers. G'Corey was destined to come around. She was sure of it.

Tracie was so caught up in the nightmarish recalls of last night that she hadn't realized she was no longer alone. She dried her cheeks and hardened her face. "What?"

Wynter sensed her defensiveness and proceeded with caution. "It's not even eight o'clock and already you've been bombarded with doctors and police, but I just wanted to give you a bit of good news." Tracie stared flatly. "Tests have confirmed that while you'll need plenty of bed rest to heal, your baby is stable. Even at nine weeks, the fetus is strong." She smiled her cheeks into her eyes and told her that she'd check back later, exiting as quietly as she came in.

Tracie bowed her head and rejoiced while rubbing her stomach. "We're not giving up on daddy. Ever."

***

"Ummm, Papi, you feel so damn good," Acacia dug her fingers into his back.

He mechanically swerved inside of her wet plushes, causing the tiny hairs on her body to stand at attention. Acacia was lost in emotion as he sent the strongest strokes through her valley.

"Hmmm. Ooohhh. Aahhh," were the soft lyrics she sang as he pushed his way further inside of her love.

An hour had past, she'd came repeatedly, but he hadn't. Caffeine must have been his blood source because he was nonstop.

"I'm gonna fuck you like I'll never see you again." He aggressively growled in her ear as he hit her spot vigorously.

She smiled at the naughty notion of his statement and continued throwing back the work he was giving.

The harmony between the squeak in the bed springs and her own high pitches drowned out the creek of the front door opening.

The unlocked door raised immediate suspicion as Sleepy entered, closing it behind him and cautiously looking around. He took notice of a travel bag without peering inside, but wondered if Acacia had plans of leaving somewhere.

"Acacia?" Sleepy firmly called out as he stepped further inside, curiously looking about. He walked over to the coffee table and counted the open bottles of Gin and shook his head, disappointingly so. *Damn, four. How many days had you been drinking, Ma?* "Acacia?" He stepped over the blanket on the floor.

Acacia froze at the sound of her name, but *he* didn't. He kept breaking her down with each push. She wasn't sure who she was hearing, but she needed *him* to stop so she could focus.

"Acacia?" Sleepy called out, peeping into the kitchen, then into the den area and now closer than before his steps and his voice could be heard clearer.

She quietly, but rowdily pushed *him* off of her. *What the hell is going on? If that's Sleepy out there,* she thought. "Who the fuck are you?"

Still inside of her, Sleepy's identical twin brother whispered mischievously, "Diego."

"What the hell?" she mouthed, mushing his face and forcing him to raise completely off of her. She frantically scooted back and away from him, covering her mouth at the realization of what just took place. Acacia bolted out of the bed quietly, scurrying to find her panties and t-shirt that were haplessly thrown around the room.

Diego boldly stood, stroking his hard flesh unaffected by the call of his brother's nearing voice. Acacia tripped over herself, gathering his clothes and shoes off of the floor and shoving them into his chest as she backed him in the direction of the closet. She pulled at the knob, but snapped her neck back toward the sound of her name being called, yet again. Diego smiled sinisterly as if he had nothing to lose by them being caught.

"Acacia?" Sleepy opened their bedroom door and was caught off guard.

She wasn't there and the room was untouched. He looked around only to survey that things looked exactly the way he left them months ago when he was last there. He spun around and headed for the guest bedroom, the only other conceivable place she'd be.

Acacia's lips trembled with fury. "Get the fuck in there and don't say shit!" she spoke on a hard whisper. Diego resisted her stuffing him into the tight space and stumbled backwards.

The click of the door knob turning forced sweat to pop across her forehead.

Shit! Acacia's eyes darted to Diego's shirt lingering on the headboard. She forcefully pushed the closet shut and dived on to the bed, taking the shirt with her.

"Acacia," Sleepy widely opened the door, pausing when he looked at the fear painted on her face. "Why are you looking like that?"

Acacia quickly and inconspicuously hid the shirt under the covers, then spoke with a shortness of breath. "That's because you scared me. I wasn't expecting anyone to come barging in," she spoke truthfully. Then she got up from the bed and walked over to him. She didn't know how to react seeing him back home, so she stood in front of him looking confused.

"Why do you look nervous?" He questioned firmly.

"I—I don't know," she stuttered. "I don't know if I should be happy you're here or if I should feel guarded because of it." She looked up at him fretfully.

Acacia felt most uncomfortable standing half naked in the same room with one man whom she was unsure would remain quiet and another man whom she loved with everything in her. Sleepy reached out and allowed the back of his hand to glide gently across her face before he cupped her cheek, stroking his thumb across the smoothness of her skin. Acacia closed her eyes sweetly and held his hand against her face. For a moment, she almost forgot she was standing in the middle of a twilight zone as she relished in his touch. Sleepy smiled as he pulled her into his arms and wrapped her in his embrace.

Tears pushed out of her eyes at the smell of his familiar scent that she didn't identify on the man she assumed was Sleepy when she gave him her soul. *How could I not know?* Her cries became louder, against her will, as she saw flashes of last night and that morning's sexual fest with his brother.

"I'm here, now." Sleepy comforted, stroking the top of her head, repeatedly. He pulled her away from him, holding her at arm's length.

"We're gonna have a long talk because I'm here to work it out with you, if that's possible. Is it?" He dropped his head to look into her lowered eyes.

She squeezed her eyes tightly and shook her head *yes*. Sleepy knew Acacia would be emotional, but he wasn't prepared for the storm of tears that seemingly came from out of nowhere. But he charged it to her feeling overwhelmed at the opportunity she only begged for hundreds of times through countless messages.

"Come with me." He took her hand to lead her into the bathroom.

She resisted a little as she reached for her shorts that were hanging from a knob on the dresser. "One moment," she spoke weakly. She slid into her clothes, rejoined hands and then followed Sleepy's lead out of the guest room, but not before looking back to see a crack in the closet door reminding her of Diego's presence.

Chapter 3

Samiyah stood helpless, watching two men she loved fight over their love for her. "Stop them!" She pleaded to random men on the scene, but no one intervened. She tried to diffuse the brawl herself, but ended up being unintentionally, but violently pushed to the concrete. If the fight didn't end soon, the men were bound to get the attention of the distracted police.

The crowd grew bigger as spectators appeared. Suddenly, one woman screamed and pointed, "He's got a gun!"

Samiyah's eyes bulged out of her sockets. She stood to her feet, waving her hands wildly. "Stop! No!" She went around the circle begging. "Somebody, stop them, please."

Cedric never left home without his Glock .40. The security company he owned required he didn't, but it still worried Samiyah when she saw it strapped to his waist because she didn't know how far he would go.

The brawl continued for a minute more before an older, but army-fit gentleman succumbed to Samiyah's petitioning and pulled Gerran, the wildest street fighter of the two, off with the help of another brother. In a domino effect, a couple of guys did the same with Cedric, keeping him at bay.

"Calm down, Youngblood." The older man told Gerran when he tried to buck out of his hold.

"Get off me!" Cedric shifted past the two man barricade that blocked him once Gerran was hauled away. The push of his weight forced him to stumble forward, bumping the men who restrained him out of his way. Straight ahead he saw the small incisions of Gerran's eyes trained on him as he was still being suppressed by the gentleman. Off to the right of him was Samiyah, crying liberally. Then his eyes shifted to the two policemen walking in his direction.

"Five-O coming dis way." A teenaged boy called out while perched on his bike.

Old School released his hold on Gerran and straighten the crumple of his shirt, patting him on the shoulder. "The fight's over." He advised him as the police drew near.

Coffee

Cedric abandoned his impulse to resume their match to check on Samiyah. He headed over to where she squatted with her head buried into her hands. "Are you alright, sweetie?" He tried to lift her chin.

She looked out of the corner of her eye to see if Gerran was watching and he indeed was. His lips curled tightly as he looked on and watched Cedric comfort her.

Cedric doubted Gerran was willing to jump stupid in front of One-Time and risk the paddy wagon ride downtown to Tulane and Broad. But Cedric kept his peripheral trained on him just in case he decided to get out of pocket.

One policeman stood in the center of the mini crowd that was still assembled, rotating slowly in a three hundred and sixty degree turn and asked, "Are there any amongst you who are residents of Building S? We need to speak with you." He scouted the crowd for tenants.

Cedric glared at Gerran, keeping his stare hawked on him as he audibly called out, "Yea, *my* girlfriend rents one of the units."

Samiyah's eyes shot up at Cedric when he boasted his claims on her, and the abysmal feeling that clutched her stomach refused her the ability to look over and measure Gerran's reaction to hearing it. She already knew it was frightening.

Gerran scoffed, looking down his nose. He saw enough to know enough, but he was too stuck to move.

The officer asked Samiyah a few questions and jotted down her information. Once he collected all that he needed, he and his partner walked over to another victim rocking back and forth on the hood of a car, distraught over her loss.

Samiyah had the most uncomfortable rumble in her belly. Whenever her nerves went on the fritz, she would have an uncontrollable urge to use the bathroom. Caught red handed and in front of watchful eyes had her in need of a toilet, badly.

"Let's go, sweetie," Cedric spoke clearly enough for anyone within earshot to hear. He gathered Samiyah in his embrace and basically carried her weakened body in the direction to his car.

Gerran allowed them to walk a few feet away before he shouted, "Samiyah! Stop!"

Samiyah jumped at his command and grabbed at her abdomen as if it would stop the bad case of bubble guts on the brink of liberating themselves. Cedric attempted to motivate her stride, but she didn't budge.

"Samiyah?" Cedric released his grip around her shoulder and stood in front of her. "Samiyah?" Bewilderment registered in his gaze toward her.

She couldn't respond. She couldn't even look up to face him, but she *could* cry. Her face contorted into a painful ball, her lips quivered with a fearful shake, and snot began a slow sneak out of her nostrils. Cedric looked past Samiyah and noticed the smug expression plastered across Gerran's grill. Cedric boiled over in anger at his girl's unwillingness to put one foot in front of the other as he tried to encourage her steps once more.

"I'm sorry," she spoke faintly.

"What?" He questioned her to repeat herself, although he heard exactly what she had said.

Samiyah dropped her head, shamefully.

Cedric tilted his head back and let out a hard breath as a favored cliché rolled through his mind and off his tongue. "Fool me once, shame on you." He shook his finger at her as her eyes strayed away from his disciplinary pointing. "Fool me twice, shame on me, ya heard me." There was so much to say, but he declined to play a fool another second. He spit on the sidewalk alongside them, booted up Gerran and then Samiyah before he took that walk of shame.

Samiyah wanted to run behind Cedric and explain that this moment was complicated, but he wouldn't listen, at least not now. And she couldn't risk pissing Gerran off more than she had, so she stood idle. Samiyah didn't move straightaway, she had to compose herself because if Gerran was still behind her, like she was sure he was, then she needed to be ready.

She used the inside of her shirt to wipe the emotional mess her face produced before she awkwardly and slowly turned to face Gerran's direction. *He's still here.* She felt too many emotions to settle upon whether that was a good or a bad thing.

She looked pitiful, but her external display didn't begin to scratch the surface on how embarrassed and low down she felt, inwardly.

Samiyah clasped her hands together and rested them against her lips as she walked over to him, guardedly. She had no idea what to say and the more she attempted to come up with the perfect apologetic intro, it all sounded like babble in her brain.

"I—da—I—don't," Samiyah swallowed hard and started over. "I don't know what to say," she spoke truthfully.

Gerran shook his head in disgust. "Say nothing," he gritted.

"Huh?" Her mouth hung slightly open, but no other words followed.

His head and heart pounded with the knock of an 808 and the more he stared at her was the more he wanted to physically harm her. His hand trembled with the need to discharge the building fury within. He parted his lips to speak, but he angrily changed his mind.

He thought better of his actions and turned around taking a few steps before Samiyah blurted, "Gerran, you can't leave me." She managed to say through uneven pitch.

He looked back with contempt emitting off of him. "Watch me," he growled.

Samiyah walked up behind him and reached out for his elbow, but he animatedly rejected her touch. She seized her movement and looked on regretfully as he walked with the purpose to put distance between them. She was stunned to the point that she didn't notice she wasn't breathing until she choked for air.

Samiyah stood alone in the middle of a crowded driveway, realizing that she'd lost everything she had in the blink of an eye.

He's gone, and he's gone. No job and no home.

Suddenly, the stretched out baby t-shirt strangled her circulation. She became overheated and flushed. Samiyah gasped. Her legs were no longer able to support her and she collapsed, crumpling to the ground beneath her.

***

Sleepy retrieved a wash cloth out of the linen closet and ran cold water on it, wringing the towel of excess water. He began wiping Acacia's flushed face. "What has you so upset, Ma?" Sleepy also took note of her bouncing knee. "I won't shut you down. I'm here to listen."

An internal war was waged between the side of her that wanted to tell the truth and the side that wanted to pretend Diego didn't happen.

Of all the statements she could have made or questions she could have asked, she chose the most alarming one. "Why you never told me your brother was your twin?"

"What?" Sleepy was taken aback. He choked on how he would answer her because his mind became clustered with too many questions of his own. *How did she know that? Have they been talking and why? Did he come by?* Then his mind shifted to the unlocked door. The bag at the entrance. And the shock on Acacia's face when he opened the bedroom door. "Did Diego come by? Is he here now?" The second the questions left his lips he spun out of the bathroom and headed back into the bedroom.

Acacia knew she was fucked up now. She shot up and followed behind him virtually walking on his heels. "Papi, wait!"

Sleepy said nothing. He was inside of the room so quickly it appeared he morphed himself there. He threw the hanging comforter on top of the mattress and checked underneath the bed. He then scrambled to his feet.

"What are you doing?" Acacia held her hands up, but reluctantly stepped out of his way as he made a beeline to the already opened closet door. He shifted through the hanging coats and saw nothing. Acacia took a deep breath of relief but almost choked when she heard a knock on the front door followed by *his* voice.

"Acacia?" Diego's deep voice resounded throughout the house and penetrated her ear drums as if he was right up on her. He stood in the doorway with his head peeped inside.

Acacia tensed up and looked blatantly suspicious. She dared to move or even acknowledge the call of her name. Sleepy grimaced as he whipped his head in the direction of the voice he recognized immediately. *Diego!*

Diego opened the door fully to step inside but before he could cross the threshold, Sleepy had ran from the back of the house and charged him with a football tackle. The speed and strength behind him sent Diego flying backwards and off of the porch. Diego hit the ground on his back first and Sleepy fell off to the side of him. Sleepy quickly scrambled over to his brother and climbed on top of him. Seeing Diego at his house, unwarranted, brought up all of the unresolved issues Sleepy had with him over his ex-fiancé, Janel.

"My brother home?" Diego asked Janel from the outside of her first level duplex.

"No. He's working the late shift. He'll be home in the morning. Come back, later."

She went to shut the door, but Diego blocked it with his foot. "Aye, Janel, let me crash here tonight, yo."

She looked at him from the slit of her cracked door still restrained from the latching chain. "I don't believe that's a good idea."

"What'chu mean, Jay?" He over exaggerated the lick of his lips. He looked at his watch. It was 10:30PM. "You really gonna make me wait on a slow ass bus, just to catch the ferry to Manhattan, then the 4 train way out to the Bronx? You buggin', Ma."

"I'm not fuckin' with you like that, Diego. It's really not a good idea."

"I promise to be on my best behavior." He drew an X over his heart with two fingers, kissed his tips, and sent it to the sky. "Come on, Ma."

She didn't trust him. More importantly, she didn't trust herself. Although both her fiancé and soon to be brother-in-law looked identical from head to toe, that's where the similarities stopped. Sleepy was the sweet type. He was everything a girl needed for the happily ever afters. While Diego was the dangerous one. He was everything that misled a woman into feeling that one night stands were the new American Dream.

Diego had a 'take charge' attitude that was so damn irresistible. The only repellent known to keep a girl faithful was for her man to be present when Diego was because he had the ability to make every female's no mean yes.

Janel smacked her lips, sighed, and then rolled her eyes before she closed the door. Ten seconds later, Diego heard the door creek open and saw the wave of her hand telling him to come inside.

After she locked up, she left him in the living room and retreated into the kitchen. He removed his jacket and New York fitted cap and sat on the sofa briefly before he too found his way in the kitchen.

Janel was slicing fruit for her late night snack when she noticed him in the doorway. "What?"

He held his hands in the air. "I've been told I'm good with these." He wiggled his long fingers. "Do you need help?"

"No, thank you. I can manage."

Diego leaned against the seal of the door as he admired her exotic African features. She stood five feet nine inches, long legs that ran the length of the Hudson River. Her coffee skin tone was drinkable, her natural crown of hair that rested on her head was almost bigger than her doll face, but it added to her flyness.

He walked behind her sweeping up against her softly as he stood next to her leaning up against the sink. He inhaled her. "You smell like mangos, Ma."

"You would too if you were cutting them." She pointed the knife to the large fruit.

He chuckled, "You know a forbidden fruit taste better than that shit."

She paused in mid slice. "Is this the reason you come here? To try me, Diego? This ring," she held up the back of her left hand, "means I'm off limits." Janel's breathing changed slightly as she commenced to slicing her fruits faster. She felt nervous and she needed to secure herself inside of her locked bedroom.

"Nah," he denied his intentions with his words.

"Umm hmmm," she remarked with disbelief.

Diego smiled at her 'round the way girl' demeanor and touched the nape of her neck. She jumped at his touch and nicked herself with the knife, "Aaahhhh," Janel sucked and then shook her hand to ward off the throbbing sensation of her cut index finger.

Diego reached for her hand and she tugged it back. "Chill, Ma. Let me see." His gold bottom grill gleamed as each word left his juicy *lips. Her blood started seeping out of the cut, so she relinquished her pull and allowed him to examine it. He ran some cool water, placing her hand underneath it for a few seconds. He then planted a sensual kiss on her fingertip before he devoured it inside of his mouth.*

"Diego, stop," she sounded unconvincing. "Stop!" This time she spoke to herself as she jerked her hand back.

"Stop fuckin' around." He sexily growled in a way that turned her on.

She backed up so far she ran into the wall as he met up with her and pressed his body against hers. She held her hand up. "I'm engaged—to your brother." She looked up at his beautiful brown eyes.

Diego placed her ring finger inside of his warm mouth and sucked her engagement ring off. He centered it on the tip of his tongue and blew it out, causing it to drop to the floor. "I don't see no ring."

Her ya ya started doing summersaults in her pajama shorts without her permission.

Diego stared her in her eyes intently as if he was trying to determine who she was. He zoned in closer to her mouth and could feel the cool of her breath against his skin. He brushed across her lips and they parted. He smiled, she closed her eyes and then he devoured her tongue.

It had been several months since Sleepy was able to sleep at night alongside Janel. His hours at the construction company changed, forcing him to make it home just in time to see her leave for her job at Intermediate School 49 on Warren St. He looked down at his watch and smiled when he saw it was half an hour before midnight. Janel would still be up listening to Coltrane and sparking a doobie.

He whiffed the flowers he had picked up from Food Emporium leaving out of Manhattan. It was his way of giving his ex-bachelor pad the feminine touch Janel complained it lacked.

He got off of the bus and reached for his cell phone to call her. He had a three block walk before he reached home, but she would never expect that.

"Imagine the surprise on her face," Sleepy thought.

"Get dressed, Diego. You got to go." Janel put on her tank top.
"It was that bad?" He joked.
"No! It was that good, but you gotta go." She began handing him his belongings when she heard Sleepy's ringtone chime from her cell phone. A lump formed in her throat and suddenly that one night stand didn't compare to the happy she had with Sleepy.
"Quit spazzin', yo. Sleep is at work 'til morning."
"Doesn't matter. I knew it was a bad fuckin' idea letting you in." She started pushing him out of their bedroom and down the hall into the front room.
"You're gonna send me on my way like I'm a herb?"
Janel said nothing. All she could think about was getting him out of the house, calling Sleepy and blazing one to settle her guilty conscious. When she swung her door open to push a reluctant Diego out, she saw Sleepy's smile turn to a scowl from the bottom of the porch steps.
Diego hadn't noticed Sleepy yet because he was still facing Janel while zippering his jeans. Her eyes widened to the size of saucers and the few words that weren't suffocated in her throat came out of her mouth in a gurgling sound. The minute Diego turned to face the cause of Janel's shock he was greeted by Sleepy's fist.

Sleepy straddled his body and punched him in the nose before Diego had the chance to block the hit.

Acacia watched on as they rolled back and forth on her lawn, both wrestling for the upper hand. She stood back wishing her hangover was the cause of her double vision, but that wasn't the case. There were two men tussling before her and the sad truth was she had sexed them both.

Coffee

Chapter 4

Minnie lay in bed staring at her digital clock flash the incorrect time. The electricity was back on. *Thank God*, she thought. She reached for her watch, that was also on the nightstand and saw that it was 9:15 a.m. She could tell that she had fallen asleep, but she wasn't sure when it happened or how long she'd slept. Minnie looked over her shoulder to see G'Corey was wide awake and watching her.

"Good morning," he said the moment their eyes connected.

She turned back to face her side and then sat up with her back toward him. "Good morning." Her voice was flat.

G'Corey didn't say anything more as he rolled onto his back and rested his hands behind his head looking up at the canopy over their bed. He knew his wife's mild manner wouldn't allow her to spill the volcanic eruption burning the lining of her esophagus, but her cold shoulder scorched just the same. He spent hours contemplating how he would go about righting the wrongs of everything he'd done. The close call with Tracie letting the cat out of the bag was the last straw. There was no more room for games. He needed to bring the New Year in as a new man.

He glanced over at Minnie shifting through the clothes basket and he admired her, all of her. Reflective moments made his eyes twitch with regret as he continued to gawk at her. *She's so undeserving of your shit, dawg*, he punished himself.

Minnie reached down to pick up her shirt that fell to the floor when she noticed his eyes were glued to her derriere. In no mood to give him anything to lust over, she put on her extra fluff robe that was amongst the laundry.

The mystery woman and her Houdini act had left a foul taste in her mouth.

G'Corey readjusted his lay in bed and smirked at the symbolism behind her cotton candy housecoat. She always used it as some sort of protective shield.

"Leave it on," he told Minnie as she was about to turn the light off. She never removed her robe until it was pitch dark.

"Why?" She questioned almost in tears.

"I don't just want to feel you. I want to see you." G'Corey stroked his raging bull through his boxers.

"You're just trying to embarrass me." Minnie broke down into a full fledge cry.

G'Corey sprung out of bed and wrapped her inside of his arms. "Why would I do a stupid thing like that? I love your body." He caressed her back.

"Impossible!" she said almost immediately after he professed his truth, sucking back her tears.

He pressed his hard dick against her stomach. "You really don't think I do?"

"That only means your libido works, not that you love my—"

"Shhh," he silenced her foolishness. She attempted to break his hold, but he held her tighter. "I'll tell you as many times as I need to, ya heard me. But I think you sexy and that even trumps what you think."

She smacked her lips and shook her head. Suddenly, G'Corey began rocking his body side to side taking her body into his rhythm.

"What are you doing?" Minnie questioned the obvious dance they began.

"Don't go changing to try and please me," G'Corey closed his eyes.

Minnie looked up at him singing horribly. "Is that Billy Joel you're—"

He raised his voice over hers. "You never let me down before…" She softened and relaxed under the croon of his voice, smiling at his attempt to make her feel good about herself. "…I love you just the way you are." G'Corey stepped back from her and noticed her eyes were closed for a brief second and then she opened them slowly. He gently placed his hands in the cross of her robe and loosened it. Minnie thought to resist, but fought herself not to. He guided his hands over her exposed breasts and up to her shoulders, allowing the robe to fall to her feet. G'Corey hungrily smiled at her which made her nervous and adored at the same time. Then he repeated in speech, "I love you just the way you are," before he turned off the lights.

Minnie brought out the grown man in a thuggah. In the past he was too full of cum to see it, but these days his vision was becoming clearer. It was time to pay her back for her love with his *undivided* love.

Just then, in that moment, the proverbial light bulb went off inside of his head. *Fuckin' right,* he thought.

***

When Samiyah came into consciousness, she was being assisted into a seating position by an older gentlemen.

"What happened?" She felt disoriented. She looked at her nightmare surroundings known as her reality and it all came back to her. "Oh, shit!"

Mr. Johnson, her downstairs neighbor, remained kneeled beside her. "You alright?"

"Far from it." She stood to her feet, dusting herself off. "But, I'll be okay."

Mr. Johnson looked up at their building. "All of this happened as a result of a curtain catching afire from a damn candle during last night's black out." He shook his head in frustration.

"Seriously?" She smacked her lips. They silently looked at the rubble remaining of their home before Samiyah broke the quiet still. "You have somewhere to go?"

"Nah, I'm a lonely man. No wife. No kids. No friends. No place to go." He lowered his eyes to shield the hurt in them, but he still managed to see the tremble of Samiyah's lip, "I know you're not worried about this old man," he attempted to joke.

Samiyah didn't answer. She simply walked into his space and caught him off guard with a hug. It was to comfort him, but she needed one as well. "You'll be okay," she assured. He took a deep breath and hugged her back.

After they shared a brief moment of tenderness, she backed away wiping her eyes. "Thanks, I needed that," Mr. Johnson admitted.

She forced a smile for encouragement. "So did I."

Mr. Johnson had lived downstairs from her for a few years and she did her best to keep her distance from him because of his insatiable flirting, but now she was saddened to know this would more than likely be the last time she saw him.

He ran his handkerchief over his balding and graying hair before he slipped it into his back pocket. "Take care of yourself—My-Mya." He faintly smiled, hoping she didn't blast him for saying her name like that.

Samiyah felt no need to correct him this time. "You do the same— Eddie."

He gingerly gazed at her. Not with the usual lust, but with the endearing look he'd give a friend. He waved bye and disappeared amongst the throng of people, becoming the third man that morning she had watched walk out of her life.

***

"Ummm," Janessa yawned and animatedly stretched her arms wide. When the back of her hand kissed the cool indention on the pillow and not the side of Elias' face, she knew he wasn't in the bathroom but instead gone. She sat up and looked over to the empty spot. "Good morning and good bye to you, too."

***

Elias sat on his sofa staring at the crotch of his pants, imagining Janessa in her reverse cowgirl position. Lil' mama definitely knew how to ride a pony without falling off. *She did that,* he thought. A devilish grin crept on his face, but was replaced just as quickly with a mean mug.

"Aaarghh," he groaned. His freaky flashbacks kept getting interrupted with stank ass scenes of La'Tasha.

"Fuck this! I'm 'bout to blow this bitch down." Elias reached for his phone. He had to get some shit off of his chest. Ole boy from last night should have pulled out of her scandalous ass by now, so there should be no reason she didn't answer his call to receive the cursing out she rightfully deserved. He scrolled through his contacts until he came across her name.

I'm deleting this muthafucka when I'm done, he made a mental note.

He pressed the call button, but an incoming call from Samiyah came through first.

He blew into the phone when she said *hello*. The diesel on his chest was too heavy to hold a conversation with his round. "In the middle of something, what's up?" he answered.

"Where do I begin?" She muffled her cries so she could talk.

Elias changed his attitude when he heard distress in her voice. "What's the matter, Yah?" She tried to respond, but only murmurs left her lips. He waited for her to speak, but she couldn't. He became alarmed, "Where you at?"

"My apartments," she managed a timely response.

He knew the sound of trouble when he heard it. "Stay there. I'm on my way." Elias hung up the phone and jetted out of the door. La'Tasha became a secondary thought.

In less than half an hour, he pulled into Lake Wind East. The smell of charred wood and ringlets of gray smoke floated in the air. *Fuck!* He whispered as his head swiveled from side to side checking out the disarray in the complex. He parked his truck in an available spot a few buildings down from hers. Her section was still blocked off from traffic for obvious reasons. When Elias saw her building burned to the ground, he stopped in his tracks and ran his hand over his face.

"Ain't this a bitch?" Elias grimaced.

"Tell me about it." A woman standing next to him holding a baby on her hip agreed as she shook her head.

Elias took off walking, searching for Samiyah.

He found her sitting on the pavement with her arms wrapped around her legs with her chin resting on top of her knees. Her stare was blank, so she didn't realize Elias was approaching until he spoke.

"Give me your hand," he extended his. She looked up at him with doe eyes and the damn that held back the well of tears broke. She stretched out her hand to meet his and he lifted her into his arms. The instant her face cradled against his chest she cried so hard she soaked his shirt.

Minutes had passed when he finally broke their embrace. "Dry your eyes." He ran the palm of his hand over one side of her face as she did the other. "Are you cool enough to follow me back to my place?"

"Ugghh," Samiyah threw her head back. "That's a whole 'notha story. It's over at Cedric's house."

"How did you get here, then?"

"I'm gonna need a 32 oz. daiquiri with a few shots of Ever Clear before I utter one word of this fucked up situation I'm in."

"Say no more."

***

Diego didn't want to rumble with his brother, so he refused to throw a punch. But it made no difference to Sleepy, he was enraged. The proof was in the pounding. The sound of Sleepy's boney knuckles hammering away at Diego's pretty boy face made a cinematic sound. Diego was eating a good amount of those licks while shielding others.

The gash above his eye was minor but the blood pouring from it was misleading. It shocked Acacia into action.

"Sleepy, you're gonna kill him if you don't stop," Acacia warned. She didn't want to save Diego exactly, she just didn't want Sleepy serving time in Angola State Penitentiary for manslaughter. She came off of the porch and forcefully grabbed Sleepy around his neck and under his arm, pulling him away, barely. They clumsily fell backwards. She hugged him securely and whispered in his ear, "It's not worth it, Papi. He's not worth it."

Diego sat up and looked down at the crimson colored stains that decorated his shirtless body and sweats.

The mere sight of him drove Sleepy insane, but since they were face to face he had to ask, again. "Did you sleep with Janel?" Sleepy was breathing hard in between his words.

Acacia looked at Sleepy sideways with the *what the hell* look, but her guilty conscious wouldn't allow her to question him.

Diego gave him the same answer he provided five years ago. "No. What you saw that night was me shutting my fly after I took a leak."

"I despise a fuckin' liar." Sleepy spat the instant he heard his denial. He scurried to his feet, freeing himself from Acacia's hold. He hopped up his porch steps, two at a time, until he was inside. He retrieved the bag he assumed was Diego's by the door and tossed it onto the lawn. "Stay the *fuck* out of my life!" Sleepy pushed both hands through the air to exaggerate his emotions. "Let's go, Acacia." He summoned her in a drill sergeant manner.

Acacia did as he requested, walking into his extended arm.

"Sleep," Diego called out, but his brother ignored him. He took a hard breath. "Yo, Sleep. I'm dyin', yo," Diego blurted.

That got Sleepy's attention. He turned around. "You're what?" He looked at him with disbelief.

"I'm sick, son."

Those words replayed in Acacia's mind like a skipped record. *I'm sick, I'm sick…* Then without thought she gave shrilling volume to the silent question screaming to be asked in her head. Her hand covered her chest in a frightful fashion. "You got AIDS?"

Coffee

Chapter 5

Minnie was submerged neck deep in a hot bubble bath. Her scented candles were lit, and her small water proof radio that was set to AM 940 played a gospel melody. She closed her eyes and began humming along with CeCe Winan. She tried to center her thoughts on God and not the Devil that was at her door, but she couldn't drown her out.

Matter of fact, last night's episode resurfaced other negative memories Minnie had suppressed.

"Are you okay, baby? Tell me what happened," Minnie asked her boyfriend, G'Corey, of two months.

G'Corey massaged his injured shoulder that was rested in a sling. "Some fool rear ended me and sent me crashing into the steering wheel. But insurance will cover the damages to your bumper, so don't worry about that. Aaaahhh," he groaned in pain as he shifted positions.

"Oh, baby, I'm not. I'm concerned about you." She looked at her usually strong bear of a man mutate into a helpless cub. "Let me get you out of these clothes and into bed. You need to rest."

She stripped G'Corey down to his boxers and eased him under the covers. She kissed him on his lips, then collected his clothes to deposit them into his dirty clothes hamper.

"Your bathroom is a mess. When was the last time you cleaned it?" She stepped into the hallway to hear his answer.

"I'ma busy man, ya dig. Some things gotta hit the back burner."

Minnie shook her head at his typical dude mentality. Before tossing his jeans into the basket, she reached in the pockets to pull out its contents so they didn't accidently get washed. There was a Popeye's receipt and a smashed piece of gum, she threw those away. She then came across a folded paper with a stapled card attached. She reviewed it to see if it was important. It was the accident form from State Farm. She saw that his name was listed under 'Driver', but what shocked her was the female's name alongside it.

She marched into his bedroom and stood at the foot of the bed.

"What's up, bae?" G'Corey sensed her energy had changed.

"You tell me. Who the hell is Jenny Wilson?" She held out the insurance sheet.

Shit! G'Corey thought. He forgot he had that in his pants.

Jenny "Juggernaut" Wilson was his on-call freak. She had the best head game in the tri-state area and if her punani was in competition at the Olympics, she'd be on that winner's platform. So, when she called G'Corey and told him that she was in need of his Mr. Goodbar he found it fitting to supply her demand.

Minnie was a good girl, indeed. She had some bullshit ninety day rule and refused to panty drop. But it was G'Corey's belief that no brother should have to walk around with blue balls on the strength of a pussy policy.

"Oh, Jenny. That's my thuggah, Charles', ole lady. I was dropping her off in Gert Town, at his crib, when I got into that accident."

"Why didn't he get her?"

"Baby, I don't know. His hands were tied."

"Why didn't you mention her?"

"What was there to say? Look, my potna asked me to scoop her up since I was 'round that way."

Minnie looked at the location listed on the form, "S. Carrollton Ave. What business you had uptown when you were supposed to be taking my car someplace downtown?"

"Damn! A thuggah can't do no spur of the moment type shit? What? I only have a ten mile radius allotted from the designated area if I drive your car? Man, look here, you can take your keys, ya heard me and leave if you gon' drill me. I told you who the broad was but you still asking all them questions."

Minnie was blown away by his callous attitude. That was an ugly side she'd never seen before. She looked around the room as if she was in search of something while trying to articulate her devastated feelings. But because she couldn't formulate a Christian thought, she bit her tongue. Her eyelids batted at a thousand miles per second until a gush of tears rolled freely.

Minnie gathered her things and headed toward the door.

Fuck! G'Corey mouthed before he jetted out of the bed to stop her. He couldn't let his foul up bubble over into his good thing.

44

"I'm sorry for that outburst. I'm cranky and that was the pain medicine talking. Baby, I didn't bring Jenny up because I didn't want you to feel what you are feeling now." Minnie remained silent with her head dropped, sniffling back tears.

They stood at his door as he made a phone call to Charles to have him verify that his lie. It was man law to take a charge even if you were innocent, so Charles knew the play.

That night ended the way all others had. His words won over her uncertainties.

Her eyes tightened and her mouth balled into a knot as vexation found its form across her face. The stress reliever concoction of chamomile and lavender Epson salt did little to relax her. Minnie needed answers. There was no peace to be found in a string of mysteries.

By the time Minnie opened her eyes, G'Corey was sitting on the edge of the tub. His presence startled her, causing her to slightly splash water all about. He chuckled and reached for her loofah.

"What are you doing?" She swayed the bubbles toward her to cover her breast.

"What it look like?" He lifted the sponge. "I'm gonna wash your back."

"I want to be alone with my thoughts if that's alright," she spoke sweetly with a drizzle of sarcasm.

"A'ight." He handed her the loofah and then dried off his hands. "I'll be in the kitchen."

After thirty minutes, Minnie emerged out of the bathroom wearing a pair of jogging pants and her oversized Janet Jackson's Velvet Rope Tour t-shirt from her concert in '98. She fanned her hand in front of her face to see and breathe past the smoke.

"You're just in time for breakfast." G'Corey opened the back door and window to allow fresh air inside.

"They're burnt." She unenthusiastically lifted her pancakes.

"Nah, those are my Cajun cakes. Try 'em." G'Corey smiled at his creation.

Minnie really didn't have an appetite. "I'm not hungry," she confessed.

Coffee

"You may not be, but my lil' one is. Here, eat this banana." He handed her one from the fruit bowl.

It made no sense to take out her frustrations on her bud, so she ate the breakfast he gave her but in another room.

G'Corey knew that Minnie associated last night with him, although she had no proof to make the connection. He also knew suspicion wasn't fact, but he didn't need his wife doubting anything relative to their marriage. He needed to up the ante. His run of the mill attempt at putting a smile on her face didn't cut the mustard. He looked down at his runny eggs and threw them away in the trash. He had another idea.

He walked into the living room where a T.D. Jakes' sermon was watching her. "Bae, get dressed."

"Why?"

"Because I want to take you somewhere." G'Corey sat on the edge of the coffee table directly in her line of vision.

"I'm comfortable like this," she contested.

He sighed, "Have it your way, just come with me."

Minnie wasn't sure why she was taking things out on him, but some part of her felt like she was rolling over yet again and it didn't sit well with her. She stared at him a few seconds more before she unhurriedly got up.

He smiled uncontrollably as he watched her retreat into the bedroom to get her Reebox tennis shoes from out of the closet. He rubbed his hands in a mischievous manner at his plan to put a permanent smile on her face.

***

Elias and Samiyah sat parked in his truck in Joe Brown Park after they had left the Daiquiri Shop on Crowder Blvd. She recapped the entire story of her morning, leaving nothing out.

"Damn, you got my head smokin', ya heard me. This some *Young and the Restless* type shit." He shook his head as he absorbed her pain.

"Eli, I don't know what to do." Samiyah leaned forward, crying into her hands. Elias rubbed her back in a circular motion with one hand as he massaged the bridge of his nose with his free one.

46

"The one thing you don't have to worry about is where you gon' stay. I got you, and whatever else you need. Right now, we're going to get your car from by ya boy house."

"I'm not ready to face him," Samiyah said nervously, sitting back upright.

"You gotta, bay-bae. The sooner the better."

Samiyah thought how she endured last night's storm just to get thrust into a shit storm of her own the next day. "This got me all the way fucked up."

"That might be true, but you a soulja. You got dis," he encouraged. Her river continued to flow in two streams down her face. "Stop crying. You not cute when you do that, no," he clowned, attempting to change up her frown.

She laughed through her tears. "Don't do me that," she weakly smiled.

Silence danced between them for a few minutes until Elias interrupted their quiet time. "Where does dude stay?"

Samiyah knew she had to face him, although she was in no hurry. "In Lake View on Canal Blvd."

"Word? You can smell when a thuggah got cake, huh bruh?" *Canal Blvd*, he repeated. "I didn't know Cedric was stackin' like that."

"Ummm hmmm," Samiyah nodded her head. "He's a total package and he's gonna make some girl happy. It just won't be my retarded self."

Elias started his engine to pull off and begin the trek to Cedric's place. Samiyah leaned her forehead against the window as she tried to prepare herself for the verbal battle to come.

***

Sleepy looked at Acacia with a stone face the moment the question left her lips that made her tuck her tail between her legs. She apologized almost immediately.

"Hell no! I don't got that gangsta, Ma." Diego said, referring to the HIV virus. Hearing that, Acacia felt instant relief. Diego reached for his bag, stood to his feet and turned to Sleepy. "Can we talk, inside?"

"Inside or out, who said I want to talk?" spat Sleepy.

"Come on, yo. Your heart too warm to be cold."

Diego was right, his brother wasn't cold-hearted. Although it had been Sleepy's plan to go the rest of his life without speaking to him, he couldn't in good conscious know Diego was dying and still slap his hands away.

"How do I know you're telling the truth?" Sleepy questioned the validity of his claim.

He dropped his head, then looked up. "Ask the family. Ask mama. Call whoever you like. They all know," Diego offered.

Sleepy began feeling mixed emotions. In the face of death, was his hatred toward his brother, over an affair with his first love, worth holding on to?

He didn't want to be welcoming, but he couldn't turn his back— not on this. "Come inside," Sleepy said reluctantly.

Diego took humble steps toward the entrance of the house. As he approached, a chilling inner voice whispered in Sleepy's ear. Sleepy extended his hand, stopping him in his tracks. "When did you show up here?"

"Late last night," Diego answered.

"You slept with my woman?" Sleepy didn't beat around any bushes.

Woman? Acacia smiled inwardly at the title, but frowned at how it was being used.

"Nah," Diego denied.

"I don't know why I asked you. Your word ain't shit," Sleepy concluded.

"I swear I didn't. I crashed on the sofa and then when morning hit, I went for a morning jog. But you trust your girl, don't you? Just ask her." Diego pointed his finger over to Acacia.

This Puto, she thought. Acacia felt her intestines push into the upper cavity of her chest.

Sleepy did just that. He faced her and firmly stated, "Acacia, don't lie to me. Did he talk his way into your shorts? Did you two have sex?"

Her mouth gaped open and the thump of her heart echoed down in her toes. She was having an out of body experience. She imagined tiny images of herself on either shoulder debating their points on what her answer should be. Truly, the answer was simple. All she needed to do was say it.

Yes, but I thought he was you, she mentally practiced her response.

She assumed if they were going to have a shot at making the relationship work, she shouldn't go in with a dark cloud hovering over her head. The moment to speak was now.

She answered meekly, "No." Clearing her throat and jerking her neck back in shock, she repeated with more authority, "No! Why would you ask me that?" Her courage to speak the truth crumbled under the fear that Sleepy would inadvertently look at her differently.

Sleepy consolingly rubbed both of her arms up and down simultaneously. "That stripper at Rico's party took advantage of my high, and shit happened that never should have which is why I told you. And all I'm saying is if that happened to you," Sleepy clenched his jaw, "I would understand that Diego was the fuck up behind it." He waited a moment before he continued, "But know my understanding will not supersede *this* moment."

Acacia had a chance to redeem herself. To not go down in relationship history as being the woman to cower away from setting the record straight. But all she did was purse her lips and stare at him with the *I already told you* look.

"I believe you." Sleepy hugged her and kissed the top of her head. After a few seconds of embrace, they headed inside. Sleepy stopped short of entering and turned around to see Diego still standing in the place where he stopped him. "Are you coming?"

Coffee

Chapter 6

Elias pulled up alongside the curb of Cedric's home. "What's your game plan?" He leaned his head back onto the headrest looking over at Samiyah.

She looked down at her nails as she fiddled with them, letting out a sigh, "To not hurt him more than I already have." Samiyah then stared out of her window and at his two story home. "Humph," she grunted.

"What?" Elias looked out of her window too.

"I was just thinking about our relationship in the beginning. We were friends, and I told him that's what we should have remained. Bad shit always happens when two people who shouldn't cross lines do it anyway. But I gave into the possibilities and now look at the mess." She took Elias' hand and pressed it against her chest, holding it in place. "You feel my heartbeat?"

He nodded his head *yes*. Her heart was racing and the longer she procrastinated the faster it sped.

"It's now or never," she said aloud.

"Need me to wait on you?"

Samiyah removed his hand off of her breast, closed her eyes and kissed his knuckles. "Nah, you can leave. But thank you for always having my back."

"No doubt," he smiled her way.

She pulled the door handle and the lock popped up. Opening the door, she placed a foot on his running board. "I'll call you before I come by to make sure you're home."

"No need. I'll be waiting on you, ya heard me."

"I dig that. I love you," she spoke sweetly.

"Fa'sho. I love you, too."

Samiyah walked halfway up the driveway before she turned around to wave Elias off.

She walked up to the front door and was just about ready to knock on the door when she heard music blaring from inside. Curious to identify what he was listening to, she pressed her ear against the door. Her heart sunk into her stomach when she heard The Spinners tell him how *it takes a fool to learn that love don't love nobody.*

***

"Why are we at the Esplanade Mall?" Minnie asked the moment she saw him turn into the parking lot of Kenner's shopping center.

"You'll see in a minute," he smiled, looking at confusion resonate across her face.

"I'm not dressed for this." Minnie looked at her unfashionable gear.

"You the one who wanted to be hard headed. I asked you to change, but that ain't what you wanted," he reminded her.

"I look like a troll and you got me around all these people," she spoke distastefully of herself.

"Go 'head and pout now, big baby. But in a hot minute I'ma make you shine," he boasted.

Minnie didn't know what that meant, but she was sure to find out.

After he parked, they went through Macy's entrance. He opened both set of doors and once inside, he proudly grabbed her hand and walked her to the designation she still had yet to know.

G'Corey glanced down at his favorite watch. "This can't be right."

"What's wrong?" Minnie questioned.

He tapped on the glass face. "I need a new battery or something. The hands aren't moving." He saw a jewelry store up ahead. "Bae, have a seat here." He directed her to a nearby bench. "Let me run up in Zales real fast and see if they'll change that out for me real quick."

"Alright," Minnie agreed with no fuss.

G'Corey zipped off into the store and Minnie pulled out her cell phone to call Samiyah. Her phone rang a few times before her voicemail picked up. She hung up electing not to leave a message. Instead, she sent a text.

2:42PM: Hey. I haven't talked to you since yesterday morning. Are you alright? Hope so. I'm not exactly sure how I feel. In the mall with G'Corey but I need to talk to you at some point today.

Minutes later, her phone alert sounded. She thought it was Samiyah messaging her back, but it was her husband.

2:54PM: Come in here. Short a couple of dollars.

Minnie didn't respond to the message, she simply walked inside of the store. She reached into her wallet and pulled out whatever cash she had on her to give to him.

He turned to face her as he stood at the register, "It's twenty. I'm short two dollars." She handed him a five. "Thank you, baby," he pecked her on the lips and offered her a seat at the countertop as he waited on his watch repair.

"Welcome to Zales. My name is Sheletha. Are you looking for anything in particular today?" The sales manager happily asked.

"No, thank you. I'm just waiting on my husband," Minnie pointed over to him.

"Well, if anything grabs your attention, let me know," she smiled.

Twenty minutes had passed. Minnie was generally the patient type, but she didn't understand what was taking so long. As she walked up on him, he turned around to face her. "G'Corey what's taking—"

G'Corey dropped down on one knee and extended an opened crushed velvet box toward her. She covered her mouth to suppress her yelp when she saw a six carat princess cut bridal set sparkle like Texas stars.

"I bet you're wondering what's going on," G'Corey said, smiling generously at his blushing wife.

She shook her head up and down, dropping her hand to speak. "What are you doing? It's not our anniversary."

"I know that, woman," he smiled, looking up at her. "I just wanted to do something special, ya heard me. And what better way to say I love you than to upgrade the symbol of our love?"

"Awww," Sheletha sang in the background, tilting her head and covering her breastplate.

"May I?" He reached for Minnie's left hand, twisted the three carat marquis cut off and slid the other ring bling on.

Her hand trembled with excitement as he secured the expensive rock on her finger. Tears of happiness slid down her face and those dreadful feelings from earlier began to dissipate.

"I love you," Minnie beamed.

"You better do more than love me, tonight." G'Corey doubled raised his eyebrows. He stood to his feet and kissed her romantically.

A small gathering of women who entered the store began clapping at their display of affection. The echo of applause startled Minnie out of her enchantment as she turned to face the direction of the sound. She smiled graciously as they smiled back at her. G'Corey bear hugged her from behind as she held onto his arms, rocking slightly side to side.

Although her shabby outfit hadn't changed into Cinderella's gown, Minnie felt like the belle of the ball in front of those cooing ladies and G'Corey was *her* prince charming.

"Mr. Daniels," Sheletha read his name off of his credit card. "Sorry to interrupt. I just wanted to hand you your receipt along with your Visa."

"You good and thank you for all your help," G'Corey shook her hand.

"My pleasure," she waved goodbye as they headed out of her store.

He draped his arm around Minnie's neck and she wrapped her arm around his waist, smiling at her new diamond.

"So, I got one mo' thing in mind," G'Corey stated.

"You do? Well, can I go home and change out of these clothes first?"

"Uh, we can go home, fa'sho, but you don't need clothes where I'ma take you."

***

Samiyah sat on the patio furniture in deep thought. She told herself that after the song concluded she'd go inside, but he played the same song on repeat for an hour. It didn't appear he was coming out of the zone he was in no time soon, so she uncrossed her leg and stood to her feet. It was time to face the music. Samiyah slid the key inside of the lock and pushed the door open once she heard the locks disengage.

She walked in the living room where he was slouched on the sofa with his leg crossed in the figure of a four, smoking a blunt and chasing it with a fifth of Hennessey.

Cedric didn't notice Samiyah standing there. He had his eyes closed as he swayed his head side to side to the beat of the music.

Sometimes a girl will come and go/ You reach for love, but life won't let you know/ That in the end, you'll still be lovin' her/ But then she's gone, you're all alone, he sang in broken pitch.

Samiyah felt asthmatic watching the man she loved more than her actions showed break down before her eyes. Tears coated her face at the sappy sight of his hurt. She bridged her hands over her mouth and nose to simultaneously wipe them across her cheeks in separate directions.

"Cedric," she faintly called out for him, but he didn't hear her. She didn't have the strength to raise her voice any higher, so she walked over to the stereo and turned it off.

"What the—" Cedric shot up to his feet. He was jerked from his somber state by the abrupt silencing of his music.

"Can we talk?" Samiyah asked.

Cedric stared at her for an uncomfortable amount of time. She felt uneasy standing there before him waiting on him to respond. He lowered his eyes and examined his blunt before he took a pull from it. "There's nothing to say." He choked on his exhale, taking a seat back onto his sofa.

"I know you're—"

"You don't know shit, ya heard me," Cedric spoke evenly as he cut her off. "Do yourself a solid. Clear out your drawer, grab your shit out the closet and anything else you may have lying around this muthafucka and leave." Samiyah opened her mouth to speak. "Quietly," he added.

Cedric's demeanor was icy. The quiet of his love always made her feel at home, but now she felt like a stranger. She knew why and she couldn't help but mourn for the loss of what was and will never be again.

She turned to retreat into the bedroom to silently gather her belongings, but she couldn't. Not without at least apologizing. She about-faced. "I'm sorry," her voice quaked. "I don't want you mad at me and I never meant to play you." Her eyes begged for a response as the last words of her brief speech left her lips.

Cedric looked off and shook his head side to side. *Why is she talking?* he thought. The longer she stood there looking remorseful was the angrier he was becoming. He wanted to go slap off, but decided to suppress his colorful tongue.

"Save your apologies for Gerran, they may have a chance with him," he stated coldly. "And *you* didn't play me, sweetie. I played myself fucking around with a confused woman. So, what I look like being mad at you? I just learned the hard way that I can't *fuck* with you. So, again I say, get your shit and get out. And don't forget to leave my key."

"Wow," was Samiyah's only response.

She pitifully turned around and excused herself to the back of the house where her things were. The thirty feet walk to his bedroom felt like more like thirty miles. Every step she took felt slowed down by the weight of her guilt and pain.

She stood at the doorway and inhaled his Gucci cologne that lightly lingered in his room. She looked at the bed they were just in last night. He laid across her breast as she stroked his back with the tips of her finger.

If I would have known that was going to be the last time we made love, I would have cherished it more, she thought.

Clearly Cedric had been through the break-up ritual. There was a box along with some garbage bags already on the bed.

She began unloading the one drawer she occupied, whisked a few outfits she had hanging up, and scooped the few pair of shoes of hers that were next to his.

There were pictures of them around the room she was sure he would discard. She walked over to the one of her sleeping.

"Why are you framing that?" Samiyah felt embarrassed.

"It's a beautiful pic, ya heard me. And I'ma keep it right c'here," he placed it on the nightstand alongside his bed, *"for the nights you not here, so I can always wake up next to you, ya dig?"*

"I dig," Samiyah giggled before he set the picture down and assaulted her with juicy kisses.

Samiyah covered her mouth, shook her head in disappointment and muffled her cries. Everything held memories. From the wall he pressed her against when they had wild sex, to the floor she slept on next to him when he threw his back out. She had a sensory overload just from being in his room, alone. It was too much.

She grabbed the picture of her sitting on his lap sideways with his arms wrapped around her waist, kissing her neck. That would be the memorabilia she'd keep of the way they were.

"Bye room," she regretfully whispered as she stepped out.

With her things in hand, she stopped off in his office. Next to his computer was a pen and pad. She wrote down a note. She inhaled and exhaled before walking back up front. She dropped her things in the hallway by the door and walked over to Cedric.

"Here's your key." She extended it to him. He blew out hard took it from her. "I love you, Cedric. I always will."

He stared at her with less contempt than before, but with disdain nonetheless. "Take care."

Her eyes clamped shut, but it still didn't stop the unstoppable gush of tears. Cedric was hurt, but he kept that bottled in. Samiyah turned around to leave, grabbing her belongings. She left, leaving the yellow post-it note on the inside of the door.

When he heard his door shut, he ran his thumb and index fingers across his misty eyes. His nerves caused his leg to shake at rapid speed. He wanted to rush outside, take her in his arms and forcefully kiss her. Have the greatest make-up sex that'll make her vow to be his, alone. But it was best that she leave and be gone forever.

Cedric walked over to the blinds that overlooked his front lawn and saw her pulling out of his driveway slowly as if she was waiting for him to do what his mind semi suggested. However, he watched her disappear down his street.

He went to lock the front door when he saw the sticky attached to it. It read: *If I would have met you first…*

"Fuck!" He belted in an angry boom. He missed her already.

Cedric's energy zapped from his body at the thought that it was officially over. His heart broke and it felt too heavy for his chest, he needed to sit back down.

Coffee

He plopped on the sofa, took a hard swallow of the brown, and turned the stereo back to the same song, hiking the volume up louder than before. Cedric massaged his tightened chest and dropped his head.

I'll always love you, too.

Chapter 7

"Talk," Sleepy sat on the love seat across from Diego sitting on the sofa.

Diego sat leaning forward with his elbows planted on his thighs and his hands steepled under his chin. He blew out hard before he spoke. "Fuckin' health is goin' to shits. I have kidney failure and it's pretty fuckin' bad. Doctors said if I don't get a transplant soon, I will need dialysis to sustain living, yo."

"A *transplant*? Sleepy repeated skeptically. "Let me get this straight. You flew down here to ask me if I will do a test match and possibly be your donor?"

"Nah. Hell nah, son. I came down here to make peace with you, bro. Too many years went by without us talking, and I wanted to change that." He shook his head remorsefully. "There's nothing like seeing an expiration on your life that'll make you rethink some shit. Like what's important, nah what I mean?"

Sleepy briefly reminisced on better days between them. Growing up they were thick as thieves, but that had altered and he didn't know when or how the temperature between them changed. They'd went from sharing the same bed, same clothes, and most times same thoughts to living as if the same blood didn't course through both of their bodies.

"Why didn't you just call?" Sleepy inquired.

"Would you have answered?" He answered his question with a question.

Sleepy blew out hard and massaged his goatee, pensively. "Nah, I wouldn't have." He shook his head *no,* running his hands from the top of his head and down over his face. "I'ma be real. It'll fuck me up if something happened to you, but I can't just forgive you because you dropped some heavy shit on me."

"I know it ain't done like that, yo. I'ma give you some time to wrap this around your thinker. I'll hold up at a Best Western or something for a few days or so." He shuffled through his bag for a pen and something to write on. He scribbled on the back of his plane ticket. "Here," he reached it to Sleepy, "take my number. Call me when you ready to talk."

"Humph." Sleepy considered leaving him hanging, but took the paper from him.

Diego then shuffled through his bag and rummaged for a wife beater to put on. Once he located one, he threw it over his shoulder. "Is it a'ight if I use your bathroom before I bounce?"

Sleepy nodded his head, "Follow me."

Acacia emerged out of the hallway where she had been nervously eavesdropping on their conversation. To play it off, she walked into the living room to remove the empty bottles of alcohol that decorated the coffee table. Sleepy walked past her to lead the way for his brother. As Diego approached her, he looked at her seductively from bottom to top. She felt uneasy as he sexually sized her up, so Acacia cut her eyes at him wearing an unmistakable sneer. But he blew a quick kiss her way in response to her thrown daggers.

She looks so damn cute when she mad, Diego thought.

Once Diego closed the door to the bathroom, he examined his face for damages. The cut over his eye would leave a nasty scar, but the bruising and swelling would go down in a couple of days. He retrieved a wash cloth from the linen closet and began removing the stained blood from off of himself. After he cleaned off what was visible, he turned around to throw the towel in the clothes hamper behind him.

Diego spotted a pair of her panties and couldn't resist the urge to pick them up. He smiled as he dangled her stripy red boy shorts, whirling it around his finger. He caught a familiar whiff that made his eyes roll to the back of his head. Their lustful encounter wouldn't be their last if he had anything to do with it. Tucking her underwear in between the waistband of his boxers and sweat pants as a souvenir, he headed out.

Diego stepped out and into the hallway. When he walked up front, he heard their voices lower as he approached. He stepped around them and grabbed his bag, "I'm out, yo." He placed his thumb and pinky to his ear in the shape of a phone, "Hit me up."

Sleepy nodded. "A'ight," he spoke swiftly, almost blowing him off.

Diego threw his head back at Acacia, "Thanks for being welcoming. Be easy, yo."

Acacia's facial expression hid her revulsion, but her eyes read a different story. "Goodbye." She walked up to him to close and lock the door. She thought she would feel instant relief with Diego out of their house, but she felt just as uncomfortable. Now, they were alone. Him. Her. And her veiled shame.

"Come here." He called her over to sit next to him on the sofa.

The weight of the world felt like they rested upon her feet because her steps toward him were heavy. She looked into his brown eyes and wanted to confess for the third time, but instead she sat quietly and allowed a small smile to dance across her lips.

Sleepy looked at her and picked back up where he had left off before the issues with his brother. "As I was saying, I've been missing the hell out of you. I love you. But what I don't love is that green eyed monster inside you."

"I know, Papi. I don't like that part of me either," she admitted.

"Do you want us to work, Acacia?" He questioned. "I'm talking about no more of this breaking up shit," he clarified.

"More than you know," she blinked back tears.

"If that's the case, you can't keep allowing your feelings to run you. You can't blow up behind every incident that looks foul. You gotta be able to trust me even if you don't trust the other person." He paused for a second to gather his thoughts. "Perfect example. The first flash that went through my mind when I heard and saw my brother was that he sexed you. I could have easily killed him with my hands." He balled up his bruised knuckles, bringing them to his face. "I trust Diego so little that *his* word needs to come with a signed notary, Father O'Malley's blessings along with the angel Michael appearing in the flesh with a message. But I believe *you*, so when you said nothing happened. I accepted that nothing happened, at your word. Do you see how trust goes a long way?"

Acacia hung her head low. At that moment, she didn't deserve his confidence in her. "I've never let go of my past hurts from anybody including the one incident with you and I'm sorry." She began whimpering as she fought back the tears. "It's just the ugly part of me that do messed up things I end up regretting. But it's not the core of me, I swear." In an inhale, she sucked in a deep breath, then released it. "I do trust you. I just never forgave myself for being so believing in others that I'll work overtime to make sure I don't get fucked over again. I don't want to lose you and I'll do anything to keep you in my life this time. You got to believe me."

Sleepy pulled Acacia into his arms. He inhaled her and nostalgia overwhelmed his senses. He missed the smell of the apricot scented shampoo she used to wash her hair with daily and the jasmine soap that lingered on her skin. The feel of her body pressed against his made him realize how she was his perfect fit.

He kissed her collar bone. "I love you, Ma."

She lifted her head off of his shoulder. "I love you, too."

He looked into her eyes. Her lashes were wet with tears. He kissed one eyelid sweetly and then the next before he covered her mouth with his. He felt his nature stir in his jeans and he knew it was time to put an end to his longing.

In the middle of their kiss, he used his body to begin pushing her backwards onto her back. His hand swept across her thigh and up to her waist where he began to maneuver her shorts off.

She broke their kiss. "What are you doing?" She tried to mask her concern.

"We talked enough," he panted before kissing her again. "I want to make love to my woman."

With as much zeal as she could muster, she tried to return the strength of his passion, but she knew where things were heading and she felt dirty.

She moved her head playfully. "Let's take this to the shower, baby."

Sleepy slid her shorts off and now he was working on removing his clothes. "I can't wait."

He wanted her desperately. It had been months since he felt her warmth and his love wouldn't let him hold out another minute. He grabbed her breast and began massaging her nipples through her tank top before he started sliding down the length of her body. He wanted to orally reintroduce himself to his pleasure palace, but she jerked her body upright. Diego spent all night and part of the morning relentlessly coming inside of her. There was no way she would let him taste another man's nut.

"No!" she said alarmingly. Acacia saw worry lines crease on his forehead at her refusal for chow chow. She shook her head as she thought of a way to rebound from her distressing reaction that wouldn't make him curious to pry for answers. "No, baby. I need to feel you inside me now." She reached for his hammer as she snaked her body with unbridled desire to reiterate her fraudulent lust and longing.

It's the lesser of two evils, she thought.

That ascended the frown he briefly wore into an uncontrollable grin. He raised up and removed his shirt and t-shirt in one motion before he found his comfortable lay in between Acacia's trembling legs.

Sleepy rubbed the head of his swollen dick up and down her *out of commission* cooch, massaging what he had mistaken as her juices which instead was his brother's cum.

The abundance of moisture made him lose his cool, "Damn, Ma, you're so wet."

Acacia died a little on the inside when the words left his mouth.

As he pushed himself inside, she cringed and winced a little from the discomfort. Diego had beaten her vaginal walls to a pulp and the feel of anything behind him felt like abuse. He felt her jump underneath his thrust and assumed she needed a different tempo.

"I'll go slow," he groaned.

"Mmm hmmm," Acacia moaned as tears slid out of the corners of her eyes. She didn't need him to go slow, she needed him to stop, but she couldn't do that. She would look suspicious. She was supposed to want him just as badly as he wanted her. And truth was, she did. However, she felt wrong. Just minutes before he opened the door on her, his brother was so deep in her guts she thought they were one body. It was impossible for her to enjoy Sleepy when she already had her fill and refills of Diego.

Acacia was almost as stiff as a board except for the occasional rotation of her hips to throw him off the trail of suspicion. But her mind was elsewhere. She couldn't believe that she had become what she loathed. A liar and a cheater.

***

Samiyah had been parked outside of Elias' house sitting in her car for the last hour listening to the soul of Sarah Vaughn's *Wanting More* hum through her Bose system. Her mood was melancholy and she didn't see that changing anytime soon.

The light on her phone was blinking as a reminder of her missed messages. She checked her texts. She had seen Minnie's message from earlier. She planned on calling her tomorrow. She scrolled down to the unopened ones.

Acacia 3:09PM: I'm fucked up right now. You'll never believe this shit. Call me.

Acacia 3:31PM: It's sorta fuckin important. Call me!

Elias 4:18PM: Where you at?

I don't have time, Acacia. You can be so extra, Samiyah thought. She did however respond to Elias.

Samiyah 4:44PM: Outside.

Samiyah rested her head on the headrest and closed her eyes. She was trying to drown out the discouraging voice that told her she wasn't shit for hurting two undeserving men.

When Elias got the response from Samiyah, he opened his door to see her out front like she said. He closed the door back leaving it unlocked for her.

Daytime turned into night. Eli looked at his watch and noticed it was nine o'clock. Hours had passed and it was time she came inside. He walked up to her car and pulled at the handle, but her door was locked. He tapped on the window. Samiyah was asleep, but the rap on the glass woke her. She raised her head off of the steering wheel slowly, disoriented. She unlocked the door and he opened it.

"Let me get you inside, ya heard me." Eli reached for her and she poured herself into his arms unable to support herself.

Once she was fully out of the car, he swooped her into his arms and her arms instinctively wrapped around his neck with her face cradling against his chest. He walked her into the house and gently laid her on the sofa while he zipped back outside to get her keys and purse out of the car. He hit the alarm to her vehicle and locked up his house once inside.

"Thank you," Samiyah spoke drowsily.

"That ain't shit," he waved off. "You hungry?"

"Uhn uhn," she shook her head. "No appetite."

"You need to eat something. Don't let your situation fuck you all the way up, ya heard me. Nah, I'ma lay up there and whip up some tacos. Go take you a bath and relax yourself while I cook this gourmet meal."

Samiyah smiled his way, "If it wasn't for you, my day would be complete shit."

"We been rockin' for too long for me not to have your back," Elias said.

He headed into the kitchen to whip up dinner, and Samiyah headed into the bathroom to run a hot bath.

She searched his cabinet for Epson salt, Calgon, or something to add to her water. She didn't find anything. "Eli," she called out, but he couldn't hear her. She walked into the kitchen where he stood over the stove preparing dinner. "Eli, do you have any bubble bath, bath salts, something to put in the water?"

He extended his hand in an introductory manner. "The name is Eli, not Elise," he spoke sarcastically. "Of course I don't have no shit like that, but I do got some Dawn dishwashing liquid, ya heard me. Works just the same," he offered.

"You are so *projeckerish*," she snooted.

"St. Bernard projects, Jumonville St. all day," he boasted.

She shook her head. "I'm good on that."

"A'ight then." He returned his attention to his browning meat.

"Ssss," Samiyah moaned at the heat against her skin as she submerged herself into the crystal clear water. She sat timidly still until her body acclimated to the temperature, then she slouched down comfortably.

Moments into her soak, Elias walked in. "Eat this." He handed her a slice of plain toast.

"Why?" She questioned.

He lifted the drink in his other hand. "I made you an Amaretto and Pineapple. Figured you needed a lil' something to knock the edge off."

"You ain't never lied." She took the glass and sipped it immediately. "Umm," she savored its flavor.

"I, Chef Homeboy, is 'bout to finish wrapping up dinner. You good?"

"I've got nothing and no one. What you think?" she spoke her truth, sarcastically.

"You *got* me and I was referring to this moment," he clarified.

"I knew what you were talking about. I was being pissy. My bad. But I do need you to bring me my garbage bag full of clothes out the car?" Eli shook his head *yes*. "Thank you." She took another swig of her drink.

"You straight," Elias confirmed before he walked out.

"Oh, Eli," Samiyah called before he fully disappeared.

He stuck his head back in the door, "Yo."

"For the record, if I don't got nobody on my side, *no one*," she stressed, "I know I got you."

"Til my casket drops," he vowed.

Chapter 8
The next day...

After a few hours of shut eye, Samiyah awoke feeling drained as if she'd hadn't slept a wink. She sat up and looked around Eli's guest room. It felt awkward and although she'd crashed there a time or two in the past, that was different. Before, she was able to leave and return to her own king sized bed or that of her lover in which case she had neither now.

Those grave thoughts punctured her heart and brought about a fresh batch of hot tears that spilled down the familiar trail over her cheeks. But she had to convince herself to stop weeping because her eyes were terribly throbbing from already haven cried overtime.

She used the backs of her hand to wipe away the wetness and reached for her phone. Samiyah hoped for a text, a missed call with a voicemail attached from either Gerran or Cedric, but no one had reached out. Justified as they were, she felt abandoned, nonetheless.

It was still dark outside because the sun hadn't clocked in for its morning shift. It was unambiguously too early to disturb Eli, but she didn't want to be alone. Samiyah contemplated laying back down, but her idle mind was driving her stir crazy. She just hoped he'd understand.

She peeled herself from out of the bed, pulled her V-neck t-shirt down over her boy shorts as she exited her new dwelling space. She descended down the stairs and walked through his dining room and into the hallway that led to his master suite in the front of his house.

Samiyah peeked inside of his cracked door before she quietly pushed it all the way open. He was spread-eagled across the bed and his naked body was entangled in the sheets. She walked over to the side of the bed where his arm was dangling off and tapped him gently.

"Eli," he didn't respond. "Eli," she nudged him again."

He stirred in his bed, flipping over onto his back. "Huh? What?" He stammered.

She shook her head. "Never mind. Go back to bed," she spoke half-heartedly. Samiyah twirled around to retreat back to her room when she felt a tug at her wrist.

Coffee

"What's the matter? You can't sleep?" His voice was gruff.

She shook her head. "No, I can't."

Eli propped up on his elbows as he wiped sleep from his eyes. He glanced at the time. It was 6:03AM. *Shit*, he thought. He had stayed up consoling her until three o'clock in the morning, but he didn't go to sleep until an hour afterwards. His mind was flooded with unwanted thoughts of his own. "You need to talk?" He offered.

She shook her head *yes*. "You know whoever said *It'll be all over in the morning*, lied." Her bottom lip began to quiver and tears fell shortly after, on cue. "I'm sorry. I'm just having the hardest time and you're all I have," she sniffled.

"I'm all you need." He lifted the covers, inviting her to climb in. "Let me hold you."

***

G'Corey stood over Minnie, double checking to see if she was deep in a sleep. After he listened to her snore for twenty seconds, he determined it was safe to sneak out of the house and handle his business. *This is the last time I'll creep out on you. I promise*, he silently vowed.

He headed for the front door quietly, pausing whenever he heard the creaking sound from the floorboard under his foot too loudly. Once he stealthily locked the door, he got in his car and cranked the ignition. He whipped out his secondary phone and sent a quick text.

6:05AM: Let's make this quick. Meet me at the spot.

He snapped his flip phone shut not waiting on the response before he pulled off. She had what he needed and he couldn't wait to get it. Pressing his foot down harder on the gas pedal, he headed her way in a hurry.

***

Elias held Samiyah from behind in the spoon position as she nestled her body snuggly against his, trying to find comfort as she lay. She closed her eyes with the intent to get the rest she so desperately needed, but after fifteen minutes she realized sleep and a peace of mind were

68

going to evade her. In an aggravated fit, Samiyah began crying again waking Eli out of his doze.

He instinctually pulled her in closer to him, wrapping his arm around her waist. "Yah, let it out." He placed a reassuring kiss on her shoulder. "I won't go to sleep unless you do."

Hearing Eli tell her to let go felt like he gave her permission to be completely vulnerable. So, with no holds barred, she wailed even harder. The more her body jerked from the force of the cries pouring from her soul was the more her ass jumped on his sleeping giant. Eli felt his soulja waking up, preparing to report for duty but that wasn't for them.

He pulled away from her. "No, don't." She pushed back into the nook of his curve. "Don't let me go," she whined.

Eli attempted to divert his attention onto something that would piss him off, so he could ignore that the feel of his best friend's bodacious body rubbing up against his was turning him the fuck on. His train of thought went back to La'Tasha and how she bruised his ego by disrespecting his playa. That may have been water on a duck's back to another, but a man like himself needed redemption for that stunt she pulled. No one was to ever place him on the short end of the stick.

The harder he tried to cage the Leo in him, the harder his beast became. "Samiyah, if I don't get out this here bed," he blew out hard as his eyes rolled to the back of his head, "I might not be able to contain myself, ya heard me," he warned.

Samiyah rolled over to face him. "I don't wanna be alone, though." She looked into his eyes as she dried her own. She pulled in closer to him, locking her arm underneath his and anchoring his shoulder.

His dick did relentless jumping jacks on her thighs. "Samiyah, I'm not strong enough for this. You not the only one feeling some type of way."

Her lips parted and Eli could feel the sporadic pattern of her breathing brush against his bare torso. Samiyah placed small kisses on his hairless chest. "I just wanna feel loved right now," she whimpered.

Unable to resist the temptation any longer, he rolled her over onto her back. "I can do that." He situated himself on top of her and while between the folds of her legs, looked her squarely in the eye and wasted no time before he leaned in to kiss her passionately.

Samiyah promptly grabbed the sides of his face, returning the strength of his kiss as she closed her eyes to further drown in his ecstasy. Her hands began to travel down the course of his toned body as he grinded his pelvis against her purring kitty.

He broke their kiss. "You sure you want this?" Eli had to ask. Lord knew he didn't want her to change her mind, but he had to be certain before they went to the point of no return. Had she been anybody else, half naked and in his bed, they would have known what it was. However, once it was all said and done, Samiyah was good people, *his* good people and he couldn't play her like that.

"Don't you?" She asked with longing in her voice.

Elias didn't need to hear another word. It was about to go down!

He slid his tongue back into her mouth and took her breath away. He then trailed that same tantalizing candy licker along the course down her neck to her erect nipples. As he attentively nursed on each of her breasts, he began fondling her clit through her soaked underwear. That made her back arch as she moaned out in pleasure.

"Mmmm," she gyrated her hips and threw her head back.

Suddenly, Elias paused long enough to sit back on his knees as he pulled her panties off. Samiyah switched on top of the sheets as the anticipation brewed. Once they were off, he threw them on the floor and mounted her again. He pressed his body against hers as he inserted one finger—two fingers into her ooh la la.

"Damn, Yah." He took notice of how warm and wet her wonder was. He removed his fingers and brought it to his nose and inhaled her fresh showers. "Fuck!" he called out moments before they lip locked again.

Samiyah winded her hips to match the intense movement of his pelvis. Lights. Camera. Action! The moment had come. He unwrapped her arms from around his back and pinned them alongside her head. Body to body, his inflexible muscle knocked at her opening, demanding to enter her paradise. And with the slight maneuver of his lower half, his snake found its way in her garden.

The slip of her slide helped to ease his thick and lengthy dick inside.

"He turned his head to the side. "Shit!" He groaned at the mean clamp of her snatch.

"Shit!" she called out seconds after him as her walls ached, accepting his girth.

Elias rubbed his hands down the stretch of her arms until their fingers interlocked. He pushed, pushed, pushed his way until every inch of him was submerged deep within between her slippery walls. She howled and gripped his hands tighter as the feel was un-fucking-believable. His timing was everything. He knew when to change pace, how far to go, when to tease and all of that happened as he either necked or kissed her lips.

Samiyah had fantasized a time or two about Elias and the work he'd put in, but nothing prepared her his Michael Phelps' stroke. Her stomach muscles contracted each time he loco-motioned in then out. "Ummm," her moans endorsed the physical pleasure he was giving.

"Ahhh." Eli felt his sack tighten, summoning him to release, but it would be a cold day in hell before he allowed himself to prematurely bust. He pulled out his creamy covered rod to force the nut that was at the tip to ease back down. He had to settle his racing thoughts, so he could last longer than ten minutes and aside from that he needed to strap up. He'd gotten so propelled into the moment, he dived straight in without a safety jacket.

Samiyah had climaxed already, but she had yet to achieve the big O. She fretfully questioned, "What's wrong?" She panted, pushing his body back down so he could reenter without waiting for his answer.

"Hold on." He took a quick breath.

Elias reached underneath his pillow where he kept condoms stashed for easy access and instants like this. He had never entered a woman without a jimmy before. He never trusted one enough to go there, but he did with Samiyah. He just had to know what her wet *wet* felt like swallowing him whole. But as good as it felt, he managed to tear the golden wrapper of the extra-large Magnum. He rolled the latex down the dimension of his shaft. Once it was on securely, he smoothed over her legs with his hands before he continued.

Samiyah enclosed his waist with her stallionesque legs. And within minutes, the tight space she allotted him to maneuver within her walls purposely made him hit that *eye twitching* place.

"Oooh, that's my spot." She was in full falsetto. She clasped her arms around him, gently digging her short nails into his back.

"Ah, shit! Ah, shit!" Elias echoed as her p-muscles strong armed his incredible hulk.

"I'm 'bout to cum. Oh, shit! I'm 'bout to—"

Elias covered her mouth with his hand. "Don't say that shit," he sexily growled. Those four words somehow triggered his urge to do the same. But it was too late, he already felt the rush that took him higher than any drug. When he realized he couldn't stop the blast threatening to rip, he roared like a lion, "Grrrrrr."

When the last drop dripped, he pulled out and removed the soiled prophylactic before collapsing on top of her. They couldn't believe they both went there, but in that moment they were glad they had. They gave each other what they needed. Eli fulfilled her need to belong to someone who loved her and Samiyah stroked his esteem.

A minute or two passed and he felt himself rising to the occasion again. She reached her hand past his waist to massage his aching member to its full glory. They were drunk in the moment and no words needed to be vocalized. Their desire spoke loudly enough. Elias grabbed another condom and round two was in session.

***

By the time G'Corey pulled up to his destination, Black was already leaning against the side of his tricked out whip, wearing a back sack, awaiting his arrival.

G'Corey jumped out of his ride and immediately headed in his boy's direction.

Black walked up to him, did a special handshake and ended it with a one arm chest bump.

"What's up, my dude?" Black greeted while he plucked the finished Black & Mild cigar into the air.

"Coolin'," G'Corey responded as he hustled up the steps to Tracie's house. He pulled out the keys he took from out of her pocket the night of the confrontation. His plan was coming together smoother than expected. After he removed his trap and money stash out of her house, he would have no further reasons to ever dart across her door seal. And although his actions were cold-hearted when he maliciously aborted her baby with the intolerant ass whipping he handed her, he knew that also solidified the severing of their ties.

When G'Corey found the right key to unlock the iron screen gate and door, he waved to Black to follow him inside.

They headed straight to the back of the house to retrieve the two bricks and $150,000 of his money from out of the safe located under the floors of her bedroom closet.

"You gon' fly straight once this here is handled between us?" Black asked as he pulled the fifty grand from his knapsack in exchange for the two kilos of coke G'Corey was coming off of.

"Yea. Fuck having ties to this operation. I'm just gonna hand you over this shit and be done. The game been good to me, but I got too much to lose, nah."

"I feel that." Black nodded his head at his decision to wash his hands.

G'Corey knelt down and jimmied the loose boards to expose his safe. He punched in the security code and the clicking sounds of the locks disengaging echoed. G'Corey opened the door fully only to discover a handwritten note in place of his cash and products. "What the fuck?"

"What's up?" Black stepped closer to G'Corey to see if the answer to his question was an obvious one.

G'Corey remained silent as his eyes swept over Tracie's death wish.

If you're reading this, it means you fucked up. Don't trip, though. All of your money and shit is in a safe place and you'll get your issue back. Just stop trying to duck me. We a family. Love always, Tracie plus one.

G'Corey balled the paper into a knot and let out a guttural roar. "I can't believe this shit!" he barked.

Coffee

Chapter 9

It was tradition that each New Years' Eve the three ladies got together for lunch. They went over past ups and downs and shared visions of what they wanted the New Year to bring with it.

Acacia was the first to arrive at Razoo on Bourbon St. in the New Orleans French Quarter area. Moments later, her waiter approached her table and asked what she'll have to drink.

"I'll have the Bacardi Hurricane," she ordered scrutinizing the menu. He nodded his head and as he spun around to leave she called out for him. "Excuse me, sir." He turned toward her. "Make that two," she held up two fingers. She took the liberty to order a second one when she spotted Samiyah slow strolling inside.

Samiyah couldn't sit her purse down before Acacia hit her over the head with questions.

"Umm, nice to know you're alive. Why hadn't I heard from you in two days?" She rolled her neck. "Are we beefing? I text and called boo-coo times. I needed to talk. I had shit goin' on."

Samiyah took her seat and placed a brick wall up using her hand. "I got shit goin' on, too. You're not the only one. Damn!"

Acacia couldn't see the ball of emotions in Samiyah's eyes for the sunglasses she wore, but she could see the twist of her lips and hear the *no play* in her voice. So, she pressed her own chill button. "My bad, blame my anxieties. Are you alright?" She touched Samiyah's forearm.

Samiyah bowed her head slightly and shook it from side to side. "No."

Just then the waiter walked up with both of the 32oz alcoholic beverages. "Thank you." Acacia hurried him off. "Do you want to wait 'til Minnie gets here or do you want to talk about it now?"

"I slept with Eli," Samiyah said flatly. She needed to blurt it out before she kept it bottled inside.

"You did what—huh?" Acacia was taken aback. The news shocked her. "How did that happen? When? Why?" She stumbled over her words, spitting them out so fast. "Eli?"

"Calm down. He was what I needed given all the jacked up shit that has happened to me," Samiyah clarified.

"I'm here," Minnie chimed as she approached the preoccupied ladies. She leaned over to kiss Samiyah on the cheek and did the same with Acacia before taking her seat. "What did I miss?" she asked elatedly. She looked to both of her friends who were silent until Samiyah spoke up.

"Nothing really," Samiyah spoke casually. "I was just telling Acacia about the expensive front row tickets to the new Saenger Theatre play entitled *You're fucked!* Staring Samiyah, Samiyah, and oh, Samiyah," she spoke sarcastically.

"I knew something was wrong when I didn't hear from you." Minnie grabbed her hand. "What happened?"

"I don't want to make this all about me. I'll give y'all the short version, okay. And ask one question only. I haven't processed all of this," Samiyah reasoned.

"Okay, Minnie shook her head.

"Yea, okay." Acacia did the same.

"The morning after the storm my apartment burned down. I lost everything." Minnie covered her mouth and gasped and her eyes watered. Acacia was just as surprised. "I was with Boyfriend #2 when Boyfriend #1 caught me red-handed. After they fought, both of them left me as they should have, I guess. But Elias came when I called. I'm staying with him 'til I get on my feet, and we had sex." Minnie's mouth hit the floor. "You can breathe, Minnie." Samiyah shook her out of her trance.

Minnie stood up to hug Samiyah from behind as she remained seated. "Wow! Umm, is there anything I can do? You need money for bills?" She had a ton of questions to ask, especially the love square she created, but she felt her financial stability was most important. She could ask about the men another time.

"Yea, what do you need? Probably clothes, huh? I'm sure I have some new things you can fit. Plus, I have some rainy day money I can give you," Acacia added.

"No, thank you. I have a couple thousand in my bank account. Besides, I'm not gonna impose on y'all's pockets."

The waiter walked back to the table. "Do you ladies know what you'll be eating?"

"Ah, ummm, sure," Minnie addressed him. She ordered their usual dishes, although she felt no one would have much of an appetite.

Acacia leaned closer to Samiyah and held a side bar conversation as Minnie read off their usual orders.

"Did Elias take advantage of your situation?" Acacia had to ask.

"Never that. I think I took advantage of him." She lifted the shades slightly upward, so she could dab at the tears threatening to escape.

"What about—"

Samiyah suspended her pointer finger in the air. "Uhn. Uhn. One question, remember?" Acacia sat back into her seat leaving well enough alone, for now. The waiter retreated, leaving the ladies to themselves. "So, I know based on both of y'all texts there is something we can talk about other me and my so called life. Minnie? Acacia? Who wants to go first?"

The girls looked to one another. "Well, I'll go," Minnie decided. "Samiyah knows this already, but Acacia I'm six weeks pregnant."

Acacia damn near jumped out of her seat in excitement. "Awww, I'm so happy for you. I hope it's a girl so you can name her," she paused for added drama, "Acacia!"

"Ah, no," Minnie declined.

"What about my middle name, Carmelita?" Acacia propositioned.

"Umm, we're going with biblical names, boy or girl." Minnie rubbed one side of Acacia's pouty cheek. "And look at this amazing ring my husband bought me?" She modeled her hand. Both girls nodded their approval at how gorgeous the platinum set was. "Now, on to the not so good news." She proceeded to tell them about the stranger at her door and how she wasn't able to confront her.

"Oh, hell no!" Acacia was the first to respond. "You sure it wasn't Kawanna?"

"She isn't the red herring," Samiyah assumed. "She's too scary for that."

"*And*," Minnie interjected, "she's my friend." Both Acacia and Samiyah smirked at her statement. "I'm just as puzzled as you guys, but I wrecked my brains about it and I came up with nothing."

"Tsss, damn finding the key," Acacia noted. "If I was you, I would have climbed out my window to check the bitch."

"But you ain't her and she ain't you," Samiyah said to Acacia. "Speaking of you, what about you? What do you want to share with us since you were on the verge of dying through your unclear text messages?"

"Good news about Sleepy, I hope." Minnie casted her vote.

"Yes, but I did a lot more than talk to him. We're back together."

"That's what's up," Samiyah acknowledged.

"Awww," Minnie cooed.

"Don't go breaking out the champagne. I almost got busted in bed with his brother." Samiyah and Minnie was dumbfounded to silence. "My situation has a bit of a shock value, I see."

"You?" Samiyah questioned in disbelief. "Were you seeking revenge or something?"

"I didn't even know it wasn't Sleepy because they're identical twins. Plus, I never thought in a million years he would show up at my door. Y'all, I was so drunk, and he looked just like Papi."

"I don't wanna get too personal, but didn't you—oh, never mind." Minnie swallowed her words.

"Hell, I'll ask. Couldn't you sexually tell you were sleeping with another man?" Samiyah voiced the question Minnie was too bashful to ask.

"Now that I think about it. Yes. But in the moment, I thought Sleepy was just really happy to be home. And I mean *really* happy."

"Sex was that good?" Samiyah inquired.

"God, yes! But I'm disgusted. Not only did I enjoy it, but I didn't tell Sleepy the truth when he begged me for it."

"Why didn't you? I would have," Minnie surmised.

"And again I say, *she* ain't you and *you* ain't her," Samiyah repeated, but this time to Minnie.

"We all *know* you would have confessed until Jesus returned, Saint Minnie. *I* didn't have the heart to hurt him." She shook her head at herself. "Oh, but that's not it."

"There's more? Minnie asked disbelievingly.

"Uh huh. Sleepy is going to ask that Diego stay in town, so they can reestablish their brotherly bond. Some bullshit about him dying has Papi all shook up."

"That was callous, Acacia," Minnie reproached.

"No, this is effed up. He needs to return to New York and stay there, indefinitely."

"Oh, what a tangled web we weave." Samiyah quoted Sir Walter Scott just as the waiter stopped to check on them.

"Is everything okay?" he asked.

"Yea, but I'll be needing a *to go* box." Samiyah then looked at their untouched food at the table. "Make that three boxes. Also two refills of this Bacardi drink and an Arnold Palmer for the mommy to be."

He smiled and left once more.

"Well, you know the way you bring your new year in is the way you will spend the remainder of that year?" Minnie announced.

"Who told you that?" Acacia distrustfully asked.

"Everyone knows that." Samiyah agreed with Minnie. She mentally reviewed all of their conversations. "Damn, I hope that doesn't mean drama for us." She reached into her clutch and pulled out her cell phone. She knew it was pointless to text Gerran again, but had to try something to reverse the shit course things were taking.

Samiyah: 2:38PM: I really hope you reply back. I need to talk to you and I have things at your house that would mean the world to me if I can get them. I have not a pot to piss in or a window to throw it out of. Literally! And I truly have nothing without you. Please say I can come by.

Acacia casted her eyes downward and sighed. "If that be true, this can't be good."

Minnie observed their grim faces and thought more of the statement. "We're going to be fine. It's just silly superstition, that's all."

"Let us hope," Samiyah said woefully, clutching her phone for a response that never came.

The girls spent the remainder of their afternoon purging with the optimism that whatever bad juju was upon them didn't follow into the next day. The New Year.

***

Eli was lying in bed with his arms folded behind his head and one leg on top of the other, shaking. It was his way to calm his nerves whenever he found himself thinking too much.

The rump in the sheets with Samiyah had him fucked up. It wasn't that he regretted the hellafied sex on repeat the other morning. He just wasn't sure the L would have went down had they both been in different states of mind.

Sex with Janesssa did little to derail his thoughts off of La'Tasha and sex with Samiyah reinforced how good it felt to sleep with someone who was just like him. But as dynamic as the explosion between him and his best friend was, they knew it couldn't happen again. They would only be using each other, and they were more than a matter of convenience.

However, Eli was faced with an unfamiliar dilemma. He found himself keeping up with the number of days it had been since he last spoke to La'Tasha. *Four of them.* Elias ping ponged back and forth about calling her first just to go smooth off, but something always stopped it from happening.

Must be a sign, he thought. *Leave that skank be. She ain't shit no—*

His phone vibrated alongside him, taking him off of his soap box. The caller ID displayed *her* name.

You finally decide to call you lil' mu'fucka you, he said to himself before answering.

"Oh, nah you can talk since you don't got a dick in ya mouth, huh?" He sarcastically laughed.

"Uhn uhn," she said sweetly. "I been through with that. You sound salty, though. Was wittle ole you missing lil' ole me?" She made light of his apparent aggravation.

"Man, get your mind, right." He blew her off.

"It sounds like you want me and you don't know how to say it, so I will. My place or yours?"

"You think it's that easy? Like yo ass don't need to address that bullshit stunt you pulled."

"Damn, Eli. I thought we had a simple understanding. We don't sweat each other, what we do, or how we do it." She hesitated for a moment before she asked a clarifying question. "Mind telling me where those signals got crossed?"

"Trust me, ain't shit fucked up, ya heard me. That was just some foul shit you did, having another thuggah there when you knew I was coming."

"I don't like waiting *or* having to explain what's already understood. We have no rights to feel anything about anything. But would it help if I told you I rather it was you that night?" La'Tasha's voice was cotton candy sweet.

"Hell no!" Eli damn near yelled.

"I didn't figure it would," she said dispassionately. "Well, what's up with me and you?" She moved right along. "My girls are doing their thing tonight and I—well, I wanna do you. So, tell me, my place or yours?"

What Elias liked about her ass were the same things he couldn't stand. He thought more of the situation and accepted that he couldn't be upset at her gangsta. She did exactly what he did. How could he be mad at that?

"Bring that ass here and don't be on that bullshit."

"I never am," she explained. "Oh, yea. I want to see some explosive fireworks for midnight, so be naked when I get there."

Coffee

Chapter 10
New Year's Day...

Samiyah woke up to the sound of her text message alert sounding off. It had been more than eighteen hours, but Gerran finally responded.

8:46AM: Come by. Your things are packed.

A lump formed in her throat when she saw his heartless words read across the screen.

8:47AM: I will be there within the hour.

Samiyah hopped out of bed and into the shower. In no time, she was dressed and headed out of Eli's door.

As she turned onto Tennessee St., she felt her foot release off of the gas slightly. Subconsciously, she wasn't in a rush to stand before the firing squad. But like she'd done with Cedric, she had to face him too.

She pulled into his driveway behind his Impala. She sat in her car contemplating what she would say in her own defense before she knocked on his door.

Hey, Gerran. How have you been? Nah, don't ask that shit, stupid. Fucked up in the head is how he's been. Alright. Don't casually speak, just ask if y'all can talk. Shit! Do I apologize off the bat? No. Save that for last. This is nerve wrecking. Just freestyle from your heart, Yah.

Realizing that no introduction seemed fitting, Samiyah decided that she'd just wing it. She opened the screen door on the side of his house, rang his doorbell and waited for his other Timb to drop.

***

G'Corey walked inside of his home with an assorted bouquet of roses and a dozen of doughnuts from Tastee's on Esplanade Ave. Her favorite anytime of the day snack.

"Happy New Years, bay-bae." G'Corey kissed Minnie. He made certain not to walk inside empty handed.

"Happy New Years, honey." She smelled the flowers and blushed before taking the glazed delights out of his hands. "Where is your breakfast?"

"You gonna eat all that? By yourself?" He chuckled.

"Watch me." She challenged, taking a bite into one.

"Handle your business, ya heard me." G'Corey left Minnie in their bedroom and took a seat in the living room.

He turned on ESPN as a deterrent. Minnie couldn't stand *Sports Center* and stayed away from it which was perfect. He needed time to think over his next steps in relation to Tracie and he didn't need to be distracted.

G'Corey had assumed she was checked in at Mercy Hospital being it was the closet facility to accommodate her and he was correct. Verifying she was a patient there was the extent of information the nursing staff would give him. But he needed to know when she would be discharged.

Fuck! He mouthed.

He had been lurking around the campus for the last two days, but either he was gonna shit or get off the pot. So, he actually contemplated whether he should visit her, but he wasn't sure if Tracie would cause a scene. The mere fact that One Time hadn't come knocking on his door with questions pertaining to his involvement on her assault told him she had kept quiet. But there were no guarantees she wouldn't take a different course knowing he would be at her mercy.

G'Corey determined Tracie was a cancer and he would have to eliminate her altogether if he didn't want her infecting other areas of his life. His new plan of action was simple. The crazy bitch had to *die!*

***

Aside from the door opening, the first thing Samiyah noticed was the mid-sized box that Gerran held in his hands.

What type of shit is this? she thought.

She instantly became infuriated because he was clearly demonstrating that all he intended on doing was silently giving her things to her, as if his hands were completely clean in all of this.

"This is how we do it?" Samiyah questioned, not reaching for her belongings.

"You want your shit or not?" Gerran rudely asked, pushing the box into her chest.

"I want to talk first." She pushed past him and into his house.

Gerran unwillingly gave way as she stood behind him waiting on him to turn around. He placed the box on the kitchen counter.

"What's there to talk about?" Gerran inquired uninterestedly. "You wanna tell me how it was a mistake and you were just lonely for me, but because I was so fuckin' busy taking care of your impatient ass you had to find someone to slide in your pussy to keep it warm?" His lips curled tightly.

So much for taking the delicate approach, she thought.

"That was unnecessary and scathingly disrespectful," Samiyah scolded.

"Say what?" His brow furrowed. "What else you expect from me? Sympathy? Understanding?" Each word came out like something nasty on his tongue.

Undeterred, Samiyah said, "A little of either wouldn't harm the situation." She took a calming breath then continued. "Listen, I was dead ass wrong for having another man. But truth is you isolated me from you. Everything revolved around your business. I didn't even come second, I was *last* in most cases."

"So, it's my fault? Is that what you're saying?" Gerran's nostrils flared to the size of quarters.

"I'm not casting votes for who's right or who's wrong. I'm just—"

"Well, someone gotta be the blame," he justified. "And I don't think because I dedicated my life to making yours better qualifies me as the fuckin' reason you weren't able to keep ya thongs on."

"Let me explain," she begged. Samiyah began expressing her remorse for the role she played in vandalizing their love, then she went on to express how Cedric even happened.

As she spoke, flashes of Samiyah's boyfriend sexing her came to Gerran's mind. He saw him part her legs effortlessly and climb between them. He imagined their kisses were intense and while in the throws of passion, she would call out her lover's name.

Gerran became so overheated with fury he literally began sweating. His palms got wet and he found it difficult to breathe.

He curtly cut her off. "I wasn't good enough for you or something?" Gerran questioned angrily.

"Yes. You—"

"Liar! How? When you found it fitting to tramp your ass out to someone who wasn't me?"

Gerran was taking shots, but she declined verbal retaliation. Samiyah just pouted and mildly bounced in irritation. "I can't make you understand because you don't want to understand."

He closed the gap in between them. "Make me." He gripped Samiyah by the arms. Tears threatened to betray his generally unemotional behavior.

Samiyah saw the conflict of love and war in his eyes and there wasn't a thing she could do except touch the side of his face tenderly.

"I'm so sorry." She dropped her voice to a whisper. He lowered his head onto hers and fought back the urge to release the stinging pains in his heart through his cries. "I wish I could take it all back," Samiyah unrealistically hoped.

"But you can't!" Gerran switched emotions again, backing away from her. "You gave up six years *for what?*" His voice cracked. "I ain't never loved no woman but you," Gerran growled indignantly before angry tears slid from his eyes.

"I know," she cried, walking toward him. She grabbed the sides of his usually shaven face and wiped her thumbs underneath his eyes to dry the wetness. "I'm sorry." She tried to give him eye contact, but he refused. "I'm sorry, Gerran. I'm so goddamn sorry," she spoke unevenly through her own cries.

Her voice was soothing and her touch was comforting. It was just what he needed to calm the volcanic emotions threatening to emerge from his chest.

He forcefully clutched her face and narrowed his eyes. "How could you?"

She shook her head, fretfully. "I'm sorry."

"What the fuck, man?" His chest heaved from his shortness of breath.

"I'm sorry," she repeated.

"I fuckin' loved you!"

"I still love you," she reminded.

Gerran looked intently at her when she said those four words and he wanted to believe her. They'd been through too much for it not to be true. Then without approval from his head, he followed his heart and kissed her powerfully.

He tongued her like she was his first meal in days. He trembled to devour her. He had no idea how much he yearned for her 'til that moment.

Gerran yanked her tights and panties down in one swift motion. Samiyah stepped out of them fully as she quickly removed her sweater. They gave each other a penetrating gaze before they hungrily resumed another lip lock.

The surges of their desires gave them octopus' hands. They were all over each other. His hard body pressed against her soft made his eyes roll and his dick became the stiffest it had ever been.

In the middle of his kitchen, he picked Samiyah up underneath her arms and her legs coiled around his waist. He eagerly untied the drawstring from around his waistband so he could pull himself out and push himself into her.

His inflexible muscle stood at full attention and with little guidance it found its way into Samiyah.

"Aaaahhh," she moaned as he penetrated.

Gerran bounced her easily on his shaft that was already saturated with the silk of her cream. He buried his head into the pillows of her breast as he held her tightly around her back with one hand, cupping her ass with the other.

While in the midst of losing himself, he started hearing unwanted voices.

Dawg, this pussy for everybody. Ask her man. You may be playing in the snatch, but she cuming off of that thuggah, he thought.

Gerran was trying to drown out the clash of voices and mental imageries that popped in his mind of her betrayal. But the sound was too loud and the vision was too clear.

"Ha. Ha. Ha." Samiyah exhaled with every pump inside of her passion fruit.

She felt so good, but the wetter and hotter her *ooh wee* became was the madder Gerran became along with it.

"Aaarghh." He bucked her on his stallion so fast he threatened to lose his balance. Gerran was trying to fuck the haunting statements in his head out, but he couldn't.

Samiyah was breathless, attempting to keep up with his accelerated thrusts. "I'm coming, baby. I'm coming." Her vaginal muscles involuntarily clinched him as her body embraced the climatic wave of pleasure.

Gerran walked her over to the wall, pressing Samiyah's back against it. In an almost sexually possessed zone, he started pumping hard, then harder.

"Baby, that hurts." Samiyah tried to brace herself from his now ruthless pounding, but he was in a trance. "Gerran," she called out once more.

He clamped his eyes shut tightly as more heated tears streamed downward. He was incapable of blocking them out. However, with a few more shoves, Gerran released his floodgate and came heavily inside of her.

He groaned in pleasured agony as his knees buckled beneath him. Samiyah kissed his forehead and wrapped her arms around his neck as she allowed her feet to touch the linoleum beneath her.

Gerran looked at her then closed his eyes, shaking his head right before he opened them again. He thought he could erase the pain, but no amount of love making, sexing, or straight fucking would delete her dreadful deed, and staring into her face force-fed him that reality. It tasted too bitter to swallow, so he spat it out.

"Get dressed. Take the box. Leave," he instructed, heartlessly.

She looked at him sideways. "Baby, why would you make love to me and then do me like this?" She was confused by what had just happened. But so was he.

"'Cause I still love you, but all in all it's not enough to overlook what you've done." Gerran pulled up his boxer briefs and jogging pants and leaned against the wall. "You should go—for good."

"Really? Just like that? Her voice quaked.

He dropped his head. "Yea," he said heartbroken, himself.

Samiyah grabbed a few paper towels and wiped the waterfall of Gerran's seed from between her thighs and put her panties and leggings back on. She looked pitifully at him because he refused to see his contribution to the demise of them.

Reality was a son of a bitch and Gerran was the mother fucker. She couldn't believe he couldn't use an ounce of rationale. It was clear to her that everything was *her* fault.

His verdict was obviously final and the silence became eerily uncomfortable, so Samiyah headed for the door with her box.

He still had his head hung low with his fist balled into tight knots.

Samiyah placed one foot outside of the door, then called his name to get his attention.

"Gerran," he looked up. "You may not have pulled the trigger, but you damn sure put the gun in my hands. Have a good fuckin' life."

On that note, Samiyah left feeling more dejected than before she arrived.

Coffee

Chapter 11

"**M**s. James, we will be releasing you today. However, before your discharge papers are signed, your doctor requires you to speak to our counselor, Ms. Brock, for your exit review. Are you up for that?" The nurse asked of Kawanna.

"Sure," she responded as she casted her eyes off to the side.

Kawanna had been hospitalized at DePaul Hospital since Christmas Day when her cousin, Delight, had found her sprawled across her bed from a pill overdose infused with high levels of alcohol consumption.

Although she had nothing to go home to, having already stayed a week had her beyond ready to leave. She was exhausted from attending mandatory group therapy sessions three times a day. She was sick of taking the required dosage of medication because it made her feel mental and she didn't feel she needed it. Plus, she was over being relegated to a restricted area for limited recreation. Kawanna couldn't wait to taste freedom.

The nurse signed off on her chart and walked toward the door. "Happy New Years, Ms. James," she smiled before existing.

It is a new year. I wonder why God saw fit for me to be in it, Kawanna thought lowly of her worth.

She got out of her bed and went into the bathroom, perching her hands on both sides of the sink, she stared intently at her reflection.

"What the hell is wrong with you, Kawanna James? You're a fuckin' embarrassment. You know that? Loving a thuggah who clearly doesn't love you. Are you serious? You're a damn joke. No wonder why he played you. You're a fucking—joke!"

Kawanna took very critical shots at herself and had begun crying because she didn't like the woman she'd become, but she didn't know no other way to be.

Minutes later, she heard a rap at her door before she heard the click of the locks opening.

"Ms. James?" The counselor called out, cautiously stepping inside of her room.

"In the bathroom, one moment." Kawanna ran cool water from the faucet, splashing some onto her face. She stepped out and saw a very short statured woman standing near her bed. "You're the counselor I'm scheduled to see?"

She walked over toward Kawanna with an extended hand. "I am," she spoke with a warm and professional tone. "Have a seat," she offered.

Kawanna sat across from her at the small round table located near her window.

"I reviewed your chart and conferred with your medical staff, but I would like to delve a little further beyond the diagnosis and prognosis they have listed in your folder. Is that alright?" she asked.

Kawanna shook her head *yes*.

"Good and if I go any place that makes you uncomfortable, please feel free to stop me."

Kawanna nodded her understanding.

"Well, it's documented that you attempted suicide. What triggered you to take action on your life?"

"I wanted *sleep* not *suicide*. I guess I went too far trying to achieve it," Kawanna explained.

"Very well. What sparked your decision to use both Vodka and Unisom to find sleep?" She refashioned her question.

"Wait. What I say goes into a permanent file or something?" Kawanna was cautious.

"No. Not with the hospital it doesn't. It's for my records within my office in the event you would like to see me outside of here. All the doctor need from me is my evaluation of our friendly meeting."

"Oh," Kawanna sat back into her chair, folding her arms across her chest. "Everything I say is private, between me and you, right?"

"Absolutely," she smiled.

Kawanna sighed deeply. "Where do I begin?"

"Wherever you like. I'm here to listen."

***

"Happy New Years, Bonita."

"Feliz año nuevo, Papi." Acacia sat up in their bed, stretching her arms.

Sleepy sat up alongside her and kissed her shoulder. "I'm happy to be back. I really missed you," he confessed.

"I wish you would have come home sooner." She tucked her chin into her collar bone and lowered her eyes.

"I'm here now, Ma. And as long as you keep your promise to me, I will keep my promise to you," Sleepy reminded.

She interlocked her fingers with his and kissed his knuckles. "It's a new year. I will give you a new me, a better me."

"And I vow to give you all of me, forever."

Acacia thought more about what they'd discuss the night before. Everything brought a smile to her face with the exception of Diego.

Sleepy felt duty-bound to let the past be the past in lieu of his brother's uncertain future. And aside from that, he felt it would do his mother, Ava, good knowing her only living boys were working things out.

"I don't want to sour the mood, but don't you think asking your brother to stay with us is a hasty decision?"

"No. I don't. I mean I do have my concerns, but I may not have another five years to bury the hatchet with him. Some things are more important than holding a grudge, Ma. You do understand, right?"

Once upon a time, Acacia was all for their reconciliation especially since neither Janel nor Diego confirmed they had slept with one another, but she also understood how he couldn't get past the suspicion.

But today was a different story. Problem was, she couldn't tell him the real reason it was a bad idea to allow Diabolical Diego back into his life.

"I do. I guess I don't want you thinking something will ever happen between him and I like you suspected of them." Acacia tried to plant a seed of doubt against Diego without looking guilty herself.

"Two reason why that won't happen. One, you are devoted to me. Two, he will work with me on the yard in our office as a seasonal employee until he goes back to the Bronx. He'll only be home when I am."

"Has he agreed to this?" She uneasily inquired.

"Nah, I'm running everything by you first."

Acacia knew any hesitation on her part would lead Sleepy to believe she had a deeper reason to deny Diego's extended visit and she didn't want to warrant the twenty-one questions, so she opted to go along to get along.

"He's your family. How could I say no?"

Sleepy laid back onto the bed with his arms folded behind his head. He stared up at the ceiling as if God could be found in the eggshell paint.

"You know, if I didn't try to make amends with him, I'd never be able to forgive myself? A small part of me feels like I don't owe him nothing, but then again I can't have my stubbornness condemn my soul."

"How long are you looking for him to stay with us?" Acacia hoped that a week or two at max would be his answer.

"Not sure. Weeks. Months, maybe. I don't know. All I do know is I can't let the Angel of Death come for him without having some peace with my blood." He pulled Acacia downward to lay on his chest and kissed the top of her curly head of hair. "Whether I like it or not, he's a part of me and that means I have to do this."

Acacia remained silent. She didn't know what to expect, and she wasn't eager to find out.

***

Minutes elapsed and Kawanna hadn't uttered a word. However, her counselor was patient and she had no intentions on bullying her into talking.

Finally, Kawanna opened her mouth to speak.

"G'Corey." She cleared her throat and pronounced his name clearer. "G'Corey. He's the reason I'm here. That makes me stupid, huh? To be in a psychiatric hospital because of a man."

"Not at all. It makes you human," she comforted.

That eased the tension Kawanna was feeling having to talk to a stranger whom she assumed was ready to judge her with her critical pen and pad.

"Well, I'll tell you how we began, so you'll understand how I'm here," Kawanna suggested.

The counselor nodded her head and Kawanna spilled her heart.

"I met G'Corey two weeks after a really bad break-up from a relationship that lasted three years. I knew it was too soon to even talk to another man, silly me. But he was persistent that night and I needed to feel wanted. We flirted back and forth and before I left the pool hall, he asked for my number. I didn't think he would use it, actually. So, I was most surprised when he called me no sooner than I got home."

"Hello?" Kawanna answered and then looked at the strange number one more time before she placed it back to her ear. She heard the volume of the radio go up, but the caller still hadn't said anything. "Hellooo," she repeated.

Dark and lovely/No one above thee/Ooh, girl, you really got it going on/I wanna spank you/I wanna thank you/ You're the reason why I sing this song.

A smiled creased upon her lips when she heard G'Corey's raspy voice sing along with Lo-Key's I Got a Thang 4 Ya song from the early nineties.

"I can't stop thinking 'bout you, ya heard me," G'Corey stated after he finished his brief serenade.

Kawanna giggled into the phone. "I didn't take you for the sappy type, but it's cute when a thuggah can show more than one side."

"I'm different, ya dig? You never know what you'll get fuckin' around with me."

"I see," she cooed. "Ummm, I'm not complaining, but shouldn't you be having fun with ya boys?"

"I should, but I rather be having fun with you. Let me come over to your place."

Kawanna visualized some pretty freaky things happening if she allowed him to come by. She imagined that his package was just as thick as his build and that made her kit kat melt. "I don't know if that's a good idea." Kawanna crossed her legs which didn't stop her clit's heartbeat from thumping.

"You don't know if it will be a bad idea, either," G'Corey rebounded. He chuckled, "I'm good people and I ain't tryna do nothing you don't want done. I just wanna talk to you some mo'. Face to face, not this over the phone shit."

Kawanna wanted to shout hell yes, but she stalled to make it seem as if she had to consider the answer. "Alright, my address is..."

When they disconnected the line, Kawanna scrambled around her apartment, tidying up a bit. She lit some incense and turned on a shower. After her quick wash, she threw on some lounge clothes that was sexy and easy to come off just in case it went there.

Thirty minutes later, he was knocking on her door. She finger combed through her twenty-two inch extensions and spot checked her breath before she answered the door, casually.

"Hey," she nervously spoke.

G'Corey wore a stone face, stepped inside and kissed her almost immediately. Kawanna couldn't resist him, so she didn't try. She gave into him that night. Over and over again.

Three months later, Kawanna wanted to know how he labeled their involvement. When G'Corey confirmed she was his girl, she lit up because it would make telling him she was pregnant easier. And she would finally be able to share her relationship with her best friend, Minnie.

She wanted to tell G'Corey over an intimate dinner that weekend, but he told her he had plans he couldn't break.

"No worries. A girlfriend of mine asked that I come to her event on Saturday. We can hook up for breakfast the next day. Cool?"

"That works, boo." G'Corey talked to her for a few more minutes and then hung up the phone.

Saturday evening had come and Kawanna and her cousin, Delight, arrived at the New Orleans Ernest N. Morial Convention Center. Minnie was receiving an award for her academic achievements from Dillard University.

The ballroom was filled to capacity. It took half an hour to find the guest of honor and when she did she couldn't help but notice who her plus one was.

Kawanna grabbed her stomach and hunched over slightly.

"What's wrong?" Delight asked when she felt a tug at her arm, stopping her from walking.

Kawanna started gasping for air. "G'Corey is here and he is with—Minnie?" She was bewildered because her boyfriend and baby's father blew her off just to accompany her friend? They looked so cozy together, side by side.

How do they know one another? She questioned.

Delight spotted him holding Minnie around the waist, kissing the side of her face and delightfully laughing with the people standing alongside them. It was obvious they were a couple.

"Don't cause a scene. Let's just go. You can talk to him in private," Delight advised.

"How could he?" She cried into her hands. Her cousin escorted her out of the building without Minnie nor G'Corey knowing.

The next morning when G'Corey arrived, Kawanna was on ten.

"When were you going to tell me you were seeing someone else?"

"Huh?" G'Corey was stunned.

"Those plans you couldn't break was the same ones I was at. I saw you with her," she gritted.

"Saw me with who?" G'Corey planned on denying it.

"Minnie!" She screamed. "You're fucking my best friend?"

"I'm not fucking her!" G'Corey defended. That much was true. He had been dating Minnie for two months and she believed in waiting.

How the fuck I landed two friends? G'Corey asked himself.

"Does she know about us?"

"Of course not. She ain't that type of girl."

"How could you cheat on me? You told me I was your girl!" She shrilled.

"You had me wrong, then. You my girl. You just not my girlfriend."

"Huh?" Kawanna looked at him baffled. "But—but what about the baby? I'm pregnant."

G'Corey began waving his hands side to side, rapidly. "You can't have it. I don't want no more kids."

G'Corey?" She wailed at his insensitivity.

"Why you buggin' out. I thought you told me you a ride or die chick?"

"Really?" She questioned the man who stood before her.

"Ah, yea." He grabbed Kawanna around the shoulders. "Look, no one starts off at the top. You gotta work your way up. Play your position and you'll get what you want in due time. But right nah, she got shotgun."

She blew her top. "Get off of me," Kawanna demanded, jerking herself out of his hold.

G'Corey advanced her, placing his hand at the crotch of her shorts. She tried to remove it, but his latch was too strong. He pressed her against the wall and with much resistance managed to slide two fingers into her moist vagina.

"She don't want me to get off," he referred to the wetness that glazed his fingers.

"It doesn't matter what she wants," she panted. "Get out!" she cried.

G'Corey unzipped his jeans and allowed them to fall to his feet. He pulled his Johnson out through the slit of his boxers. Kawanna tried objecting, but his magic stick had a way of making her go against herself for him.

He inserted himself inside of her and walked her over to the sofa where he continued to work her into submission. By the time he pulled out of her peach, he gave her clear instructions.

"Schedule an abortion ASAP and our business is our business."

"There you have it. Somehow she became the wife and I became one of many on the side. But at that point, I was already in love with him, so I dealt with it." Kawanna began to shamefully cry. "I quietly rode for him like he asked for well over two years and I have nothing to show for it. And sometimes a woman gets tired of going through shit."

It was concluded that she wasn't a threat to herself. She just had a bad reaction to loving the wrong man.

Ms. Brock offered upon her release that she continue weekly sessions with her at her office.

Kawanna knew she needed help, so she agreed.

Chapter 12

Minnie was nineteen hours into the New Year and still hadn't spoken to two of her best friends. Lately, Kawanna had been M.I.A., so although it was weird not to receive a call from her, she sort of expected it. They would have a sit down at some point to discuss the direction their friendship had turned. But as for Samiyah, she knew she was going through it and to not hear from her worried her gravely.

"Baby," Minnie got G'Corey's attention. He looked her way. "I need to pass over by Eli's house and check on Samiyah. She hadn't returned my text or called back and something tells me she needs me."

G'Corey looked at the time. It was seven o'clock. "How long will you be?"

She hunched her shoulders. "I don't know. It just depends on how the night goes, but I will call and keep you posted." She kissed him on the lips as she grabbed her purse and keys.

G'Corey walked her outside and saw her into the car. "Text me when you make it there," he reminded.

She nodded her head, started her engine and pulled off. He waved bye before he rushed back inside.

The window of opportunity opened, so it was time he climbed through it. Visitation stopped at eight pm. G'Corey was still leery about showing up at the hospital. He wasn't sure if she would ring the alarm upon seeing him, considering the Texas size mud hole he stomped off in her ass. However, he needed to get the location of his luchini and return her ass to sender.

Fuck it! he thought.

He had a quick stop to make at Walgreens and then he was on his way to handle business once and for all.

***

Oh, baby, I'm just human/ Don't you know I have faults like anyone?/ Sometimes I find myself alone regretting/Some little foolish thing, some simple thing that I've done/But I'm just a soul whose intentions are good/Oh, Lord, please don't let me be misunderstood.

Eli stood in the doorway of Samiyah's room listening to her sing the late Nina Simone. Anytime she felt blues'd by anything, the soultress settled her mind.

He tapped his knuckles on the door to alert her of his presence. "How you feeling, Whoa?"

"Melancholy." She gave a one word reply.

He walked over to the CD player and pressed stop. Elias reached for her hands and stood her to her feet. "You been quiet since you got back from Gerran's, but ya boy not gon' let you sulk and kill the good vibes in this castle," he kidded. "Let's grab a drink somewhere and you can air all this shit out."

"Nah, I ain't up for it." She shook her head. "There ain't a drink strong enough to help me cope with this."

"A'ight, then. Well, come out of this room. It's depressing the hell out of you." He led her by the hand and into the front room. He sat on the sofa and pulled her down next to him. "Run it," he stated.

Samiyah took a deep breath and sighed. "Gerran—"

Ding Dong, the doorbell chimed, pausing Samiyah.

"You expecting somebody?" Eli inquired, raising up to answer.

Samiyah shook her head *no*.

He thought for a brief moment it was La'Tasha returning for some more of that comeback, but it wasn't. It was Minnie he identified through the peep hole. He opened the door.

"Happy New Year's, Elias. Is Samiyah home?" she asked.

"Happy New Year's." He gave her the customary church hug and welcomed her inside.

"Sorry to drop in like this," Minnie apologized.

"You family. It's all gravy," he reminded.

"Happy New Year's, Yah Yah." Minnie extended her arms out to Samiyah to embrace her in a loving hug.

Samiyah stood up to greet her, lowered her chin onto Minnie's shoulder and closed her eyes as they rocked.

Elias sat back down on his leather couch. When the ladies broke their hug, Samiyah sat right back under him inside the coil of his arm. Minnie reached into her purse and grabbed her cell, sitting alongside her.

"Let me text G'Corey to let him know I made it over here." Minnie sent her message. She then redirected her attention on her girlfriend once she sat her phone on the coffee table. She observed how at peace she appeared burrowed into Eli. If she didn't know any better, she would have assumed they were a genuine couple.

"I'm sorry I didn't call you or text to say I was okay. I tend to retreat inwardly when I'm in pain. Selfish, but that's my way," Samiyah acknowledged.

"I know this about you and because I know you'll drown before you reach for help, I had to come by to love on you. You're my sista." Minnie became sentimental.

Too much estrogen was floating in the room and it made Eli queasy. To offset the mushiness, he broke out in a beat box and belted the famous question Whoodini posed in 1984. "Friends! How many of us have them?"

That put a smile on Samiyah's face and even harvested an all-out laugh when Minnie rapped Ecstasy's verse accompanied by The Whop.

"Fuck it!" Eli shouted before retreating to grab his eighties collection. He put on an UTFO record and bust some old school dances of his own.

Minnie grabbed Samiyah's hand and coerced her to move to the grooves, too.

The New Year didn't come romantically packaged the way Samiyah had hoped, but with friends like the ones she had, she would be able to weather the lows of life.

***

G'Corey had some get well balloons in one hand, flowers in his other and a syringe in his back pocket when he approached the nurse's station.

He premeditated his exact steps. Firstly, he would give her the peace offerings he brought. Apologize for his sporadic behavior and beg for forgiveness. Secondly, he would convince her that she was still his soldier and if she wanted to prove her loyalty toward him, she would have to tell him where his trap was. Finally, whether she cooperated or not, he'd kill her in her hospital bed by injecting the empty needle into her vein causing an air embolism that would quickly lead to a heart attack or stroke.

"How may I help you, sir?" The nurse asked.

G'Corey spoke in his most astute voice, "Yes. I'm here to see Tracie Terry." He cracked a fraudulent smile.

She looked at her watch. There was still half an hour remaining for visitation. "Sign and print your name here," she pointed.

Wynter stepped toward G'Corey. "Excuse me, sir. You don't need to do that. Ms. Terry was discharged earlier today."

"Huh? The other lady just told me to—"

"I apologize for that. She wasn't aware," Wynter corrected.

"What time did she leave?" He asked a pointless question.

"I'm not at liberty to say."

His face turned sour. "Of course not." He felt extremely salty. G'Corey let the balloons float to the ceiling and left the flowers on the partition. He wore a scowl so dirty, Wynter instantly felt intimidated. G'Corey turned around and marched out.

He reached for his second line and dialed Tracie's number. It went straight to voicemail. He called her again. Voicemail.

"*Fuck!*"

G'Corey headed to her house.

He made it to Shrewsberry in ten minutes. From where he stood, it didn't appear she was home. No lights looked to be on. G'Corey rummaged through his pockets for her key and once he found it, he unlocked it and rushed inside.

"Tracie?" He called out. "Tracie?" He walked through the darkness of her shotgun home. When he determined she wasn't there, he sat down on the couch in the living room feeling defeated. It felt to him that she was on her Eliot Ness shit or she was simply one lucky S.O.B.

G'Corey was on fire because he kept drawing a blank when he tried to ponder on her whereabouts. He didn't have time to continue the cat and mouse shenanigans, but it seemed like that was the game he had to play. He rose to his feet and began pacing the floor, yelling out explicative in the process.

Half an hour elapsed and still there was no Tracie. His patience ran anorexic thin and the pressure he was feeling was so intense, he had to somehow alleviate the steam. Instinctively, he ran up on a wall and punched a hole into the sheetrock.

He drew his hand back, shaking the stinging pain that coursed through his fist. "Shit!"

He stepped outside and onto the porch. He looked down the street both ways, impatiently. "Where the fuck yo ass at?" He grumbled.

***

Before they knew it, it was nearing eleven o'clock.

"Holy mackerel. I didn't know I was here this long." Minnie noticed the time. "I need to get home before my husband begins to worry about me."

"I'm surprised he hasn't blown your phone up," Samiyah stated.

"Me too," Minnie agreed. "Let me call him and let him know I am on my way." She pressed speed dial number two on her phone and the send button. He didn't answer. "Humph. No answer." She tried again and it was the same nothing result.

She sent a message.

10:43PM: Baby I called twice. On my way home.

"I hate to see you leave. Give me a hug before you go," Samiyah pouted. Minnie was a pleasant distraction from her otherwise jacked up day.

"Come here, big baby," Minnie joshed. "You know I'm a phone call away." They hugged before Samiyah saw Minnie to her car.

"Love you, friend. Thanks for cheering me up."

"You're welcome. Talk to you later." Minnie pulled off and headed home.

Samiyah walked back inside. Locked the door and sought out Elias. He was in his room, sitting on his bed shirtless with a pair of below the knee basketball shorts on.

"I thought you were going to your infamous Roll Out party with Jacobi." Samiyah sat on the bed next to him.

"I thought so, too." He paused and then laid back on his bed with his feet still planted on the floor. "But they got some shit that's more important than fat pussies to fall into."

"In your world? They do? Like what?" Samiyah questioned.

"You," he answered. "I ain't gon' leave you alone like this."

"Awww, you don't have to babysit me. I am gonna feel some type of way for a long time to come. Besides, you love your *in with the new, out with the old* orgies."

He pulled Samiyah by the arm, bringing her closer to him. She lay on the side of him, resting her head on his chest. "Touché. But I know my options, so let a thuggah *love* you." He tickled her at her side and she damn near jumped out of her skin trying to get away from his frisky hands.

"Alright—alright," she laughed.

They settled back into a comfortable lay. "I love you, yea. Thanks for choosing me over those randoms."

"It ain't nothing," he minimized.

"It's major to me. It's been raining in my life like a muthafucka." She became teary eyed. "But you been my umbrella. Thanks for that."

"Fa'sho."

"You know if you showed this side of you to another woman, she would be head over heels in love."

Elias didn't respond. He just cradled her in one arm and talked about non relationship matters until they both fell asleep.

***

Minnie pulled up to her house and noticed that G'Corey's car wasn't there. She reached for her phone again to call him. He answered on the third ring.

"I'm pulling up right now," he mentioned the moment he picked up. Before he got out, he locked his second phone in the glove compartment where he always kept it. It was actually the safest spot he could think of. Minnie never rummaged through his things and she rarely was in his car.

G'Corey cut his lights off as he parked. He hopped out with a bag from Winn Dixie. He was smart enough to pick up some things from the store to use as an alibi.

He walked up to her car door and opened it. G'Corey kissed her on the lips. "Your friend a'ight?"

"She will be in time. But where did you go?" She jumped right into questioning him.

He lifted the bag. "The store. I picked up some Sparkling Cider for you and some Henny for me. I figured we still had some time to celebrate the start of a new year."

She smiled and headed for the front door. "That's cool, but why didn't you answer my calls?"

"I was in the store, my phone was in the car and I didn't think to check it."

"Oh," she accepted. They walked inside. "Let me get the glasses for our toast."

"Do that." He tapped her lightly on her behind. She giggled and trotted off into the kitchen.

G'Corey rubbed his tired eyes with his thumb and middle finger. He had yet another unsuccessful attempt at trying to get his own shit from Tracie. And each day his dilemma went unresolved, he was convinced that fucking around with bitches were nothing but trouble. He couldn't wait to be done with every last stinking one of them heifers and just be about his wife.

Coffee

Chapter 13

The next day, Sleepy headed out to the hotel on Bullard Ave. where Diego had been staying for the last couple of days. They had talked twice before, but this would be their first time seeing one another since Diego left his house.

Diego was standing in the parking lot of the Comfort Suites waiting on his arrival.

"What's really good, yo?" Diego dapped Sleepy through the window of the driver's side before tossing his luggage in the bed of his F250 then getting in on the passenger's side.

Looking at Diego was like staring at his own reflection. They resembled each other down to the letter. The only way people were able to tell them apart was based on their names tatted on their chest amongst the other distinct and plentiful tattoos, but even then, unless they were shirtless a person couldn't identify who was who.

However, their likenesses stopped at their physical appearance. Internally, they were two different people. Sleepy was a humble dude who worked for everything. If he couldn't afford it, he didn't need it. Diego, on the other hand, had a sense of entitlement upon him which made him feel like somehow everyone, especially his brother, owed him something.

"I'm glad you decided to give us a chance, yo. I've missed you, son." Diego smiled as wide as a Cheshire Cat.

"Me too," Sleepy spoke apathetically.

"It doesn't sound like it." Diego observed his tone and body language.

"Am I jumping for joy? No. But it's the right thing to do. I may not like you, but I still love you," Sleepy admitted honestly.

"Wow! That's fucked up."

"It's real, though. Shit don't just revert to the good ole days just because you want it to. That's why I suggested you stay awhile so we can work on changing that."

Diego repeatedly stroked his low trimmed beard while looking out of the window." I hear you," he said dispassionately.

Diego continued to stare at the passing vehicles while glancing over at Sleepy disdainfully. If anyone had a reason to be upset, it was him but he planned on playing nice—for now.

***

Tracie was resting in the bed of her auntie's spare room, thinking about all of the uncalled-for advice she received from some of the nurses, doctors, police, and even the dietician during her hospitalization.

Nurse Wynter was the main one advocating for Tracie's safety and giving her preachy guidance as if she needed it. However, one thing she said resonated above all.

"Whatever you do. Please don't go home for a while. If he strikes again but doesn't kill you, he will kill your baby."

Tracie wasn't sure G'Corey would go that far, but she wasn't ready to test him. Not at the expense of her unborn, at least.

However, walking away wouldn't be easy because she was able to swallow the abuse, all she knew was disappointment, abandonment, and heartache. She was trained that life was a *dog eat dog* world. The physical and mental abuse she suffered from her parents before she ran away at fourteen hardened her, and by the time G'Corey came along, she was already numb to the pain.

But her growing baby was going to love her without conditions. He wouldn't despise her like Tracie's father had because she wasn't the son he wanted nor would her baby mistreat her like Tracie's mother had because she resented having children so soon in her youth. Her baby, instead, would love her, no questions asked. After all, all she ever wanted was to be loved.

So, the thought of losing her child made her decide to take Wynter up on her instruction and recuperate without threat of another altercation. It was a no-brainer since she was just as in love with the baby inside of her as she was his father.

However, Tracie still refused to abandon her ideas of the perfect family she knew she could have with G'Corey. She just couldn't allow their misunderstandings to result in her miscarrying. So for now, she would remain in Baton Rouge until she was able to execute a fail proof plan to have her happily ever afters.

***

Elias was in the kitchen preparing to down the remaining orange juice straight from the container when he heard a knock at his front door.

"Huh?" He checked his watch and saw it was creeping up on eleven o'clock in the morning. He looked through the peep hole and saw his homeboy, Jacobi, bouncing on his tip toes and holding a rectangular box.

Elias opened the door, then gave him the five hand slap dap followed by a chest bump. "What up, boy?"

"Too much," he responded, stepping inside from the stiff chill the forty degree weather brought. Jacobi placed the box on the coffee table, removed his throwback Saints starter jacket, skully, and gloves. "Goddamn, it's colder than a muthafucka out der." He blew into his hands to warm them.

"Hell yea it is," Eli agreed. "But this bipolar ass weather could have tomorrow feel like ninety something degrees around this bitch." He then directed his eyes to the box. "What all you got in there?"

"Funny you ask," Jacobi grinned. "I bought you some doughnuts since you a ole Krispy Kreme ass thuggah."

"Fuck you, dawg." Elias laughed as he plopped down on the sofa.

"*Ha. Ha. Ha.* You done got all sweet on a thuggah, for real." Jacobi continued to rib him as he bit into a bear claw.

"I didn't do shit." Eli grabbed the jelly filled one.

"Oh, that much I know is true." He referred to Eli's no show at their annual freak fest held every year at the W Hotel last night. "Nah, what was your bullshit reason for not coming?" He cupped his hand around his ear in the shape of a C, waiting on an answer.

Jacobi was a full-time comedian. Everything was a joke even if he himself was the butt of it. So, before Elias responded he already knew what was going to follow.

"My dawg going through it and I wasn't going to leave her alone."

Jacobi animatedly sprung to his feet, stuck his chest out, and placed his hands on his waist. "Here I come to save the *day*!" He sung the opening of the Mighty Mouse cartoon.

Eli threw his Nike slipper at him. "Man, you play too much."

"A'ight. A'ight," he chuckled. "But on some real shit, what's been up with you, dawg? I can feel you on being there for Samiyah, but what's the deal with La'Tasha? Dark N Lovely got your nose wide the fuck open."

"It ain't like that."

"Like the hell it isn't," Jacobi corrected. "I've watched you pine over lil' mama for months but shit got even realer once you tapped that ass. You changed the game up and got soft on ya boy, but what's funny as hell is you don't see it. Look, I just wanna know—who's taming who?" He threw his hands up as if to surrender.

"Anyone ever told you *you* talk too much?" Eli shook his head. "I don't lap behind nobody. La'Tasha ain't nothing but a cut buddy."

"You sho? 'Cause you've dissed me a few times on the strength of her. Makes me wonder if she's wifey the way you been acting."

"I ain't gon' front. I like her, but I can't commit to a long distance carrier, let alone a long term relationship. All we do is fuck. Straight up."

Jacobi rose to his feet and began putting on his gear. "If you say so, gummy bear." He smiled widely, showcasing his slugs at the top and bottom of his mouth that shined against his velvety dark skin.

They threw a solid dap and embraced each other with an one arm G hug before Jacobi hustled down his porch steps and jogged to quickly get inside of his Firebird to escape the hawk that chillingly blew across his face.

Elias sat back down on the loveseat after locking his door and thought about what he held back from their conversation concerning La'Tasha.

They were truly just a fuck thing, but the thought of having something exclusive had tiptoed in his mind a time or four.

La'Tasha wasn't the jealous or nagging type. She loved football and beers. Lil' mama was an educated thugged out misses. Books *and* street smart. She wasn't difficult to figure out, either. Her words weren't ambiguous, she meant what she said. But the coup de grâce was La'Tasha's freaky side, her bedroom theatrics were on point. Overall, she was the homie in heels.

After he went down his mental checklist of why she was the shit, he frowned.

Had I really changed? Eli thought. *Hmmm.*

The number of women that had rotated off and on his dick had decreased recently, but he never made the connection to La'Tasha until now. Eli began to wonder if there was any truth to what Cobi spoke of.

Nah, not E, he reasoned.

He reached for his phone to browse through the fuckable candidates he didn't mind breaking off. To keep his playa status current, he needed to get a few more up to date stamps in his *ass*port.

Elias refused to accept that he had a love jones.

Coffee

Chapter 14

A week and a half had passed and Diego was feeling quite comfortable in the Santana/De La Rosa home although it made Acacia uneasy. He hadn't said much of anything to her because she had been underneath Sleepy like a titty baby. That made him smile, of course, because he knew the harder she strove to avoid him was the stronger her desire was to be with him. Diego didn't apply himself at much, but women he exceeded in. He could write an entire book on how to snatch one.

Acacia was in the kitchen making breakfast for herself and Sleepy as she usually would. Diego stood by the entry of the doorway and watched her plate delicious smelling Pineapple Quesito, a Puerto Rican breakfast pastry. She was humming softly until she turned around and spotted Diego.

She was able to identify him immediately because his energy was so much different from her man's.

"What the hell you staring at?" She smacked her lips.

Diego leaned backwards to see if Sleepy was walking down the hallway before he responded. "You were much nicer the first day we met." He taunted her.

"Piss off," she whispered between pursed lips.

He walked into the kitchen and grabbed a plate, biting into the powered puff pastry before she could prevent him.

"That was for Sleepy's? She hissed.

"Its mines now, just like everything standing before me will be." He boldly declared.

She was about to pop off at the mouth, but she heard Sleepy call her name before stepping into the kitchen.

"Good morning, Papi." Acacia changed her attitude and stood on her toes to greet him with a colorful tongue kiss.

When they pulled away, their lips made a smacking sound. "Good morning to you, too," he smiled. "What's up, Diego?" He threw his head back.

"It's murking season." He lifted the second Quesito to his mouth. "Ma can throw down."

He smirked at the compliment as he observed one remaining dish. "Acacia, you ate already?"

If she told Sleepy no, he would decline his breakfast so she could eat. She didn't want him doing that, so she told him she had. "Si, Papi. This is yours. Have a seat." She escorted him to his chair while shooting laser beams at his brother.

Diego looked her up then down hungrily before standing up from the table. "I'll leave you two be." He pounded Sleepy. Thanks for breakfast, Ma."

Once Diego was in his room, he closed the door and stretched out on the bed. Living with Sleepy again brought him back to their room mating days in their old hood in S. Bronx on E. Tremont Ave.

They shared a seventh floor cramped one bedroom tenement for a year after his release from juvie at eighteen. At sixteen, Diego was sentenced to a two year bid at Spofford Juvenile Center out in Hunts Point. He had gotten hemmed up with a gun charge during a robbery gone wrong. He was a stick-up kid and his motto was: *If I can't make it, I'ma take it.*

Sleepy saw fit for Diego to live with him since staying with their parents and other four siblings weren't an option. Although Sleepy confused himself with being Diego's father at times, there were instances where they were best friends.

They had this crushing game ritual they played on shorties that gave them rhythm called WWF, *World Wide Fucking.* Some boricaus knew they were being tagged by both brothers and some had no clue. Diego vibrantly recalled one hook up gone wrong.

Diego was posted up when he saw something he liked walk past. It was the typical summer's day of horny teenaged boys. It was his crew of five fellas, Sleepy included, chasing skirts.

Diego stood six foot one, had short, cold black curly hair, a baby face and a killer smile. That day he wore his usual baggy, blue jeans, a long white tee, a Knicks' snapback, and a pair of Air Forces.

He was always the more outspoken one of the brothers, so he was considered the fisherman. He hooked them, but both he and Sleepy ate off of the same plate.

Why not? They shared everything from the womb, they'd joke.

Diego shot his game at one girl he saw passing. "What's really good?" He tilted his head back.

He reached out to touch her hand, but she pulled away. "Don't touch me! She snooted.

Diego turned his lips at her. "You ugly anyway. Fuck outta here." He waved her off and the fellas chuckled.

Sleepy dapped off everybody. "I'm out. I gotta go to work."

The fellas peaced him out and continued their conversations and joking until Diego spotted someone else of interest.

It was a crush he knew from his high school at LaGuardia Performing Arts. They shared a couple of classes, but the only thing concrete he knew about her was her name, Isa.

He walked away from his boys and followed her into a small bodega on the strip of Fordham Rd. "Aye yo, Lemme holla atchu." She kept walking toward the cooler. "Slow up." Diego pepped up his step, then stood alongside her once he caught up. "You didn't hear me calling you back there?" He pointed behind him, smiling.

"I heard you calling for shorty, but you know my name so you couldn't have been talking to me," she sassed.

No one made him nervous, except her. Something about her made him want to go turtle and hide in his shell. She made him blush without trying and he smiled a smile that made him look and feel goofy.

Isa was out of his league anyway. Chances were she'd never go for a guy like him, so he abandoned his pursuit and turned around silently.

She called out for him, "If you start over, we can see what happen." She tilted her head and smiled once he faced her.

Diego smiled too. He got her number that day and unlike any of the other females he called in the past, he was actually digging her.

Three months had passed and Diego and Isa talked every day and whenever possible they saw each other, all without having had sex. That surprised him because he was never into knowing a girl outside of the bed. However, things were different with Isa and he liked her for more than a hit and run.

Coffee

One morning Isa decided to make a surprise visit to his apartment. She never been inside before, but she knew where he stayed because he showed her from outside of the building.

She knocked on the door and anticipated telling Diego she was ready to be his girlfriend and that morning was the perfect time to show him how much.

Diego was knocked out on the sofa with the covers over his head and didn't hear the rap at the door. Sleepy pulled himself out of bed and answered the door half awoke.

"Good morning, Diego." Isa held her hands in front of her to stop the jitters.

Sleepy wiped his eyes and smiled at the slender cutie. He had never seen her before, but it was apparent she was looking to crush. The only girls who ever came to see either of them knew about the Bone Room. WWF!

"Are you going to let me in?" Her innocence floated on top of her words.

He looked over his shoulder, Diego hadn't stirred once. "Ah, sure. Come on in."

"Who's that?" she whispered, pointing at Diego.

"My brother. Don't worry about him," Sleepy told her as he escorted her into the room.

Sleepy cut on the light switch and closed the door once she was inside.

"You're such a guy," she teased. She looked around at the posters on the wall of Biggie, Pun, and Fat Joe to name a few rap artists. The stacks of tapes lined against the side of the wall alongside the cassette player and the mountain of shoe boxes of all of their sneakers.

Sleepy sat on the edge of the bed, staring at her. Something about him seemed off just a little, but she considered it had everything to do with waking him out of his sleep.

"I came over to tell you something," she said softly.

"You not gonna say it from over there are you?" He reached out for her hand and pulled her in between his opened legs. He held her around the waist as he looked up at her.

116

Feeling his basketball sized hands rest above her apple bottom, gripping her sides had intensified her urges to give into him as she planned.

Diego was rough around the edges, but she found him sincere. He clumsily tried his hand at being a gentleman when they were out in public, but his thuggish nature always shined through. Isa adored that he attempted to be different with her.

She was nervous. Isa imagined giving her virginity away to her husband, but she really liked Diego and she wanted to know what it would feel like to go all the way with him. He never pressed her about sex, but she knew he wouldn't wait around forever.

"I want to be yours," she said timidly.

"You are." Sleepy played along.

Isa smiled brightly. "No." She shoved her finger gently into his shoulder. "I mean like this." She placed his hand over her B cup sized breasts.

She swallowed hard, but she wanted to make it official.

Sleepy rose to his feet and towered her five feet nothing frame. Holding her with one arm, he stretched out the other to turn off the light.

The room was pitch black even during morning hours due to the aluminum foil on the window and the dark curtain that draped it as well.

"Take your time," she reminded.

Diego would have known what she meant by that, but Sleepy didn't.

After thirty minutes of intense and sweaty sex from the girl he now knew he deflowered, he left out of the room. He told her he'd be back and for her to stay there for round two.

Isa pulled the covers over her completely naked body. "Okay, baby," she smiled, but he couldn't see it.

Sleepy walked over to Diego and shook him slightly. "Wake up! He moved him more forcefully. "Wake up, bro!"

Diego groaned as he shifted. Sleepy put a finger to his lips and whispered. "WWF."

"Word?" Diego smiled. "Who?"

"Funny shit. I don't even know her, but she asked for you when she came by an hour ago." Sleepy chuckled underneath his breath.

Diego swiftly pulled the covers off of him and swung his feet to the floor. Sleepy sat down to take his place on the sofa, so his brother could go in for the next shift.

"Diego. Your clothes," Sleepy spoke softly.

Sleepy was stark naked and if Diego was going to pull off the switch successfully, he needed to walk in the same way Sleepy had left out.

Diego paid him no mind. Sleepy hunched his shoulders and laid down under the covers. How Diego handled his tag was all on him.

Diego felt his stomach ball into a knot because the only girl Sleepy didn't know about was Isa. As he stood on the opposite side of the door where his answer awaited, he kissed his cross medallion chain that rested on his belly.

He pushed the door open and cut on the light switch. She popped her head up off of the pillow and sat up.

"Diego," her eyes lit up.

His eyes welled with tears. "Yea, shorty."

"Why are you dressed? Was I not good enough?" She felt insecure and pulled the covers up to her neck.

"Nah, you was perfect." He tried to disguise the hurt in his voice.

"Come here." She patted a spot on the bed. "You want to make love again? I promise I won't keep stopping you." She touched his bicep the moment he sat down beside her.

Diego was fuming on the inside. If steam could have projected itself out of his ears, they would have. Isa was the only thing that was pure in his fucked up life, but now she was soured by no fault of her own.

"Nah, you had enough for your first go around." He cracked a painful smile. "Get dressed and let me walk you home."

Isa wasn't sure if she did something wrong and she felt too embarrassed to ask. So, instead she made one small request. "Can you hold me for a little while?"

As she lay underneath the covers, Diego laid on top of them and held her from behind, stroking her arm. A few tears slipped from his eyes because he knew today would be their last time together.

She wasn't a hoe, but going inside of her behind Sleepy would have made him see her as one.

It wasn't every day that a knucklehead, like himself, could get a gem. A true sparkle. And for that reason, animosity festered in his spirit.

Sleepy should have known Isa wasn't one of the expendables. In Diego's mind, he felt it was intentional on his brother's part. He felt the grudge he already had against Sleepy strengthen.

On top of being the good son with the clean record, a bright future and a good heart. Sleepy also smashed his good girl.

"I'm not taking no more L's when it comes to him," Diego concluded.

Diego shook his head and felt blameless for any and everything he'd done in the past and for what he'll do in the future.

God seemed to have looked out for the good son, so it was obvious to him he had to get it how he lived.

Same plate, Sleep, he mischievously thought.

"What's yours is mine, big brother. Always had been and always will be," he reasoned out loud.

Coffee

Chapter 15

"**I** have an appointment to see Dr. Watkins for my two month prenatal check-up." Minnie smiled as she glanced at the appointment card tucked in the edge of her dresser's mirror. "I wish you was able to come with me."

G'Corey walked up behind her and wrapped his arms around her securely, placing his hands on his lil' one. He snuggled his head against hers and spoke into Minnie's ear. "What if I told you I can?"

She spun around to face him. "What do you mean?" Her voice had a surprised giggle in it.

"We talked about me finding something on land, so I don't have to keep leaving you to go on dem waters. I mean we stacked up hella cake and with lil' one coming. I need to be home with y'all, ya heard me."

Minnie burst out crying, cupping her face into her hands. "No—No."

"What's the matter, baby?" G'Corey frowned, unable to thoroughly read her reaction.

She wiped her face and cleared her throat. "No more lonely nights. I'll have my husband home. I'm crying because I'm happy, that's all."

He smiled generously as he kissed her appreciatively before he kneeled down, raised her shirt and kissed her exposed skin. G'Corey gently rested his head against her stomach.

Suddenly the hormonal bug jumped off of Minnie and clung onto him.

"Outside of my other kids, you mean the world to me," he spoke to his bud. "You make me wanna be a better daddy. Man, I love you already."

"Awww," Minnie rubbed the back of his head. "You're gonna make me emotional again." She fanned her eyes with her free hand.

G'Corey rose to his feet. "Nah, I done missed out on a lot of my children's lives. I soured things with Tamera when our kids were young, getting caught up in the allure of the streets and lost out on a lot of shit." He looked down at her, directly in the eyes. "I'm not allowing *nothing* to block this opportunity, ya heard me?"

She reached up to hold his face. "*Nothing* is gonna stop you. I am your wife and this is your family."

"Say it again," he yearned for confirmation.

"Nothing is gonna stop you from having *this* family." Minnie pointed at her chest and then their baby.

Her eyes were reassuring and G'Corey always believed what she'd tell him. He rubbed out the mist forming in his eyes, kissed her forehead and then her lips before he stepped away. Minnie visually followed him into the living room.

G'Corey sat hunched over on the edge of the sofa with his elbows resting on his thighs and his hands bridged together, hanging his head as low as his spirits had suddenly dropped.

Having a deceptive heart in the face of a pure one felt like literal fifty pound weights on each shoulder.

G'Corey looked over to his wife, who pretended not to stare at him, and admired her. She was beautiful both in and out and now she was carrying something so beautiful.

How the fuck did I luck up? He asked of himself, repeatedly.

As hard as he tried, he never could answer the question.

G'Corey remained in deep thought. He was turning thirty at the end of the month, but he still did shit like he was fifteen. He shook his head.

I'm a grown ass man, he told himself. *I have eleven year old twins and another baby one on the way. A six-figure joint bank account that says I'm the muthafuckin' man even without the dope shit. And I got someone who married my black ass and will love me 'til death do us part.*

His days of living a double life were over. The sham of working offshore was done as of today. The random freaks he flipped from time to time were as good as over. It had been weeks since he last had seen or spoken to Kawanna, she was chaptered as well. The only thing that troubled him and endangered the new leaf he was turning over was Tracie.

He still hadn't been able to locate her and he got pissed all over again every time he thought about it. He was almost willing to charge his money and product to the game, but her breathing would always present a future problem even if she temporarily chilled.

122

After fucking around with that bird for over a decade, I should've known she was more stress than she was worth! He griped.

Minnie couldn't ignore the grumbling he was doing under his breath, so she walked into the front room and sat beside him. She placed a comforting hand on his thigh. He stared at her short manicured nails before he looked to the side at her.

"Baby, what's the matter?" The lull of Minnie's angelic voice forced his eyes to close and his lips to curl into a smile.

"How can anything be wrong having you with me?" he said with all sincerity.

She kissed him on his temple. "You just look like something heavy is on your mind. Are you having second thoughts about your sudden decision not to return to work?"

"Nah, I just wanna do right by y'all. I've fucked up so much. Excuse my tongue, ya heard me. But effin' up is what I know and on some real talk, I'm afraid I can mess this up too."

"Has the road been smooth all of the time? No. But I think you've gone too far by saying you are an *F* up because you're not. You are a loving and caring man. My man," she smiled with her eyes. "A little rough around the edges, but you always mean well. And for the record, you aren't going to mess anything up, so stop talking like that, please." Minnie chastised him sweetly.

He gave her a triple peck kiss on the lips. "You got dat," he agreed.

G'Corey had been doing things to surprise her into amazing moods lately, so she felt it was only fitting to do the same for her guy. She had been contemplating this for a while and it couldn't have fell on a more perfect day.

Minnie got up and opened the front door, she wanted to check the temperature outside. It was a warm and sunny day. A clear contradiction to the winter season.

She rubbed her hands together. "Baby, get dressed. I wanna take *you* somewhere."

"Take me where?" G'Corey raised one of his thick eyebrows.

"I can't say. You'll just have to wait and see," she giggled. "Chop! Chop!" She doubled clapped, ushering him off of the sofa.

G'Corey grinned with excitement. Men loved to be surprised by their ladies just as much as women expected it. He smoothly snapped his fingers to the Prince beat in his head and then began moving to the groove of it.

"I don't care where we go/I don't care what we do/ I don't care pretty baby/Just take me with you."

G'Corey couldn't have sounded worse as he animatedly sung off key, but his mood seemed to change almost instantly and that was all that mattered to Minnie. However, by the time she was finished with him, whatever was truly on his mind would be blown out.

***

The mid-morning sun shined through the open vertical shutters that aligned each side of Elias' front door, enabling the natural light to shine its golden hue brightly into the house effortlessly.

Samiyah made it a point, even as strenuous as it was, to sit in the living room every day, so she wouldn't become conditioned to the depressing ritual of staying in bed.

She sat on the sofa Indian style with her journal on her lap. Samiyah needed to release and often time she found writing therapeutic. And today was one of those times she had to make her pen cry because she was literally tired of doing it. She flipped open her book to the first blank page and began flowing.

Entry Date: January 10th

Although I've been pushed to the point of no return.

I never thought I would have to play the Usher role and let it burn.

Love Knows No Boundaries? That's a lie. I found them and I crossed them.

I cheated on Gerran, my first love, and I lost him.

When we first started dating, he always told me: Nothing will tear us apart.

Just have my back and keep it real and most importantly *Don't Fu#k with My Heart!*

I should have listened, but my *Bonds of Deception* ran deep. Hell, I thought I was *Boss'N Up*.

Both Cedric and Gerran gave me everything from money to shopping sprees, any kind of luxury. I was the black Ivanka Trump.

Juggling two men, though? What the hell was I thinking of?

Now they feel I'm poison and off limits like *A Dangerous Love*.

One day to the next, I went from *Sleeping in Heaven, Waking in Hell*.

Watching two men I love war over me like I was territory stolen from *The King Cartel*.

Cedric was cold-hearted, but what did I expect?

But at least leaving him, I still had some kind of respect.

But Gerran's a different story. His hateful goodbye ripped through my soul and tore me from limb to limb.

I may have no clue what hell looks like, but I now know *The Devil Wears Timbs*.

Despite it all, there's not a day that goes by that I don't miss you.

I beat myself up because I shouldn't have dissed you.

And as long as we're apart, I don't think this pain will stop.

Because as long as I breathe, I do believe, I'll love you, Gerran, *Til My Casket Drops!*

A teardrop fell onto the page of her journal and stained the end of her entry like it was her signature. She closed her book and held it against her chest snuggly.

Elias walked in the living room and saw Samiyah looking like a sad song. "Say, bruh, I'ma need you to snap out of this here funk you in."

She looked up to him with doe eyes. "Tell me how," she countered.

"You gon' get yo ass up. Wash *that* ass and get dressed. We gon' head across the river to Oakwood Center and I'ma buy you some fresh gear 'cause tonight," he slapped his hands together and rubbed them, "we goin' to The Top Notch."

"I don't wanna go out," she opposed.

"But you need to, so go on upstairs and handle dat."

"Eliiii." She carried his name longer than required.

He didn't reply. He simply looked at her with a stone face that said, *but you heard me!*

Samiyah pooched out her lips in protest. One part of her was game to go so she wouldn't be trapped inside her own head, but an even bigger side of her wanted to listen to Keith Sweat's *Come Back* on repeat and mope.

She knew she was misreading his stare, but it seemed his eyes housed pity for her and she didn't want nobody's pity. She let out a reluctant sigh.

"Alright." She huffed, unfolded her legs and stood up to retreat to her room.

Deep down Samiyah was sort of glad Eli bullied her into getting out with him. She didn't actually want to be left alone, although alone was the easiest thing she could do.

Elias smiled as she disappeared. He was gonna get her right and tight, tonight.

Chapter 16

"**W**e're here," Minnie sang the moment they arrived at their destination in Gretna.

He looked out into the parking lot, clueless. "I wanna be surprised, ya heard me, but I don't know what for." He smiled nervously.

"It'll dawn on you in a second." Minnie stared at the kid-like expression that coated his face as he tried to recall the significance of where they were. "Matter of fact, wait here," she instructed.

G'Corey sat in the car as he watched Minnie walk inside of Gambino's Bakery on Lapalco Blvd. It still didn't register until five minutes later when he saw her walk out holding a pastry box with both of her hands.

He rushed out of the car and opened the door fully, so she could walk through. Then he covered his mouth and burst out laughing. He realized why she brought him there.

"Ohhh," he called out. "This is the same day and place I met you." He took the box from her hands and kissed her excitedly.

Once they separated lips, Minnie opened the lid of the box for G'Corey to read what was written on the caramel doberge cake she ordered weeks in advance. It read: *I have something sweeter than this!*

"Word?" G'Corey raised a suspicious eyebrow as he placed the cake in the backseat and then sat up front.

"Word!" she confirmed, mimicking him.

Minnie then reached into the middle console in the vehicle and pulled out a gift wrapped rectangular box. She handed it to G'Corey.

Based on the shape and weight of the box, he knew what the content was and that placed a smile on his face. He tore off the paper and saw the *Kenneth Cole* insignia across the top of the case.

Minnie sat anxious for his response as he opened and examined his special gift. It was a brown, stainless steel, causal link strap watch and he loved it.

"This thang nice," he admired. "Oooh, it's bad, bae. Thank you. Give me a kiss."

She did as her man requested, tasting the spearmint candy that dissolved on his tongue.

He took off his current wrist wear to then sport his new piece, but Minnie stopped him. "Look on the back of it, first."

He turned it over and saw it was inscribed. It read: *It's about time we met.*

January 10th to most was just an ordinary day, but for him it was the day he met an angel. *How did I get so consumed that I forgot today?* G'Corey pulled her closer to him to kiss her for her touching words, but the tight space limited his movement. "Bump this!" He got out of the car and lightly jogged to her side, opened her door and pulled her out. He began tonguing her more passionately than he did on their wedding day.

He then hugged her tightly around the neck, taking hard breaths because he had gotten choked up. Minnie squeezed him around the waist just as closely. She was happy she didn't keep walking that day when a thuggish looking guy held the door open and asked her *her* name.

They pulled apart, but not without kissing again. When they broke their connection, Minnie told him that she wasn't through.

G'Corey bounced on his toes. "Damn! I gotta get you home," he spoke impatiently. His soulja began saluting from his jeans, making it painfully obvious that he was aroused.

She blushed then waved her finger from side to side. "Uhn, *uhn,* not yet. I'm not done."

G'Corey shifted himself through his pocket. "Well, let's hurry up then 'cause I got something I wanna start when you finished."

She laughed at her man as he rushed to get back into the car. She followed suit, started the engine and headed to the next spot.

***

It had been almost two weeks since Kawanna was released from the hospital and today was the first day Delight would see her since she had brought her home.

Kawanna made her promise that she would save her questions, speeches, and reprimands for another time. And although it was hard for her cousin to bite her tongue, she did.

Days had gone by and Delight was tired of Kawanna weaseling off of the phone because she didn't want to have the real deal Holyfield conversation.

But today was the day Kawanna would have to face the piper and have a sit down with her and talk woman to woman. The suicidal stunt she pulled purposely or accidently had to be addressed. Now!

Delight knocked on the door as a complimentary alert to let Kawanna know someone was at her door before she took the liberty to use the key she kept to let herself in.

"Kawanna," Delight called.

"In here," Kawanna said, rolling her eyes in annoyance.

It wasn't that she wasn't happy to see or hear from Delight, she was just tired of explaining her actions to people because she didn't understand them herself.

Delight bent down to hug and kiss her baby cousin on the jaw before she sat across from her. "How have you been, Miss Lady?" She greeted her warmly.

"I've been okay," she said mildly.

Delight noticed the book alongside her. "What are you reading?"

Kawanna looked down at it. "Oh, it's just a self-help book my therapist recommended.

"Oh, really? How far have you gotten and is it helping any?" Delight was pleasantly surprised because the closest Kawanna had ever gotten to reading grouped words were off of a menu.

"This is actually my third book and yeah they're helping. I mean it's still hard and I cry a lot, but I've managed to fight the urge to call G'Corey so far."

"That's so good." Delight rejoiced in her small revelation. "I've always told you your price tag was higher than what he paid for you."

"Sad, but you know I never knew what that meant? I took it to mean I should have been juicing his pockets or something, but you know I'm not money hungry. So, the message went over me." She swiped her hand over her head.

"You know it never sat well with me, all of the sideline things you did against your friend, but I knew it was your life to live and to learn from. But I'm very happy you're waking up now because you're *better* than the role you've played all this time."

"You think so?" Kawanna looked to her with a desperation to hear something positive.

Delight stood to her feet, walked over to the sofa where she sat, and kneeled before her. She opened her arms and Kawanna fell into them. "I know so."

Kawanna wrapped her broken wings around her cousin and cried like she never had before.

***

"We have arrived," Minnie announced, pulling into a parking space in City Park located in Mid City minutes away from their home.

She got out of the car and headed to the back of her vehicle.

"What you doing back there, woman?" G'Corey stuck his head out of the window before he stepped out.

"Unpacking the trunk." Minnie pulled out the blankets and a wicker basket.

"Step aside. I got dis." He removed the mini chest and other miscellaneous items.

"Initially, I was going to have a living room picnic with you, but since the day permitted and I didn't just want us to be cooped inside, I decided to bring it outdoors."

"I ain't never done no picnic before."

"I love them. When I was small, me and my mama would have *you and me* time, as she called it, right here in this park. We would feed the ducks, ride the train and the pony." Minnie was embraced with nostalgia. "Good times I tell you. Good times," she reminisced.

He enjoyed seeing Minnie's dark brown eyes glow with child-like adventure. Her innocence is what made her special from any woman he'd ever met. It was also the major reason he didn't know how to treat her right. But he had every intention on learning—*today*.

Once G'Corey got a grip on what all he was carrying, he faced her. "Where you wanna take this?"

"I can carry more than this cake and blanket." She tried to reach for something out of his hands.

He backed away slightly." You already carryin' my lil' one, you good."

She blushed.

There she goes again with that smile, he thought.

She waved her hand. "Follow me, then. There's this secluded spot, not too far away, underneath the moss tree that is cozy *and* shaded."

The spot Minnie stopped at was not too far from one of several ponds the humongous park offered. The contorted tree was still plentiful with leaves as moss dangled from multiple branches creating a curtain effect.

Minnie stretched out the blanket and removed her shoes. G'Corey helped her down into a seated position although she didn't need the assistance. She began pulling the food she had prepped the night before out of the basket.

There were turkey, ham and cheese sandwiches cut in the shape of triangles, fried chicken drummettes, deviled eggs, and jambalaya with D & D smoke sausage. And she topped it off with a pint of his favorite drink, Hennessey.

"If I don't got the best *mutha umm umm* wife on the planet," G'Corey boasted to no one. "Bae, when did you do all this?" He stuffed a delectable egg inside of his mouth.

"While you were sleeping. You know you don't hear didley when you knock out."

"Right, right!" He agreed as he then removed his Jays.

Minnie grabbed a paper plate from out of the bag. "You're ready to eat?"

"Nah, not yet." He placed his head on her lap, laying on his back looking up at her. "I wanna rap to you."

She stroked his hair that was in dire need of a cut. "What's on your mind?"

He double coiled his finger. "Come here."

She leaned down some, "Hmmm?"

"More."

Once she came closer to his face, he stuck out his tongue and flicked it across her lips. Minnie smiled, then kissed him. The kiss became so engaging that G'Corey got up from her lap and sat on the side of her and melted her face with his hot kisses.

He pulled away. "Let me stop before I wake this sleeping giant and have to get you home early, cutting this evening short," he warned.

Allowing him to travel inside of her love didn't sound like a bad idea, but she wanted to proceed with their date. "You're right. Let me pour you a glass and we toast," she changed the direction of the sail.

They held their drinks in the air, his signature brown and her sparkling cider.

"To us and a couple of forevers," Minnie pledged.

"Forever, ever, ever," G'Corey chimed in.

They clinked their glasses and partook of their liquid devotion.

***

Later that afternoon, Sleepy knocked on Diego's door and invited him to a game of one on one. Acacia had dozed off on the sofa while they were watching Armageddon, so he took the necessary time to bond with him.

Half hour into the friendly competition, both men were drenched in sweat and talking noise about each other's skills.

Diego shot a three pointer in the driveway of Sleepy's home. "I'm ill with this rock." He boasted as he shot another jumper.

"You're nice with it." Sleepy gave him credit.

"When was the last time we played hoops?" Diego dribbled the ball in and out between his legs that he opened and closed like scissors.

"We had to be fifteen or so," Sleepy thought back.

"We used to hit up Tremont Park every weekend. Every dude in the hood had NBA dreams on the court." Diego rotated the ball around his waist in a circle.

"What's ya man's name who used to be super cold and nobody could check him?" Sleepy tried to recall the young star.

"Isiko? Isiko Cooks?"

"Yea, that's him. He ever went on to play for the Knicks like he always bragged about doing?"

"Nah, streets got 'em. Son got blasted and that changed all of that. No one heard or seen from him until years after the shooting. But when he reappeared, those cats who bust at him, vanished. Isiko put down the rock and picked up the ratchet. It was murder she wrote for a long time fucking around with him. But after he handled blood business, he opened up a few youth centers out in Brooklyn. He said it was his way of atoning and helping others not walk down the path he traveled."

"Damn," Sleepy shook his head.

The fellas caught up on more stories and even laughed like there was never a five year gap in their relationship.

Suddenly, Sleepy decided to drastically change the topic. His health had been a subject Diego had been avoiding on the few occasions he brought it up. "When you gon' see about your kidneys?" Sleepy questioned.

Diego stopped bouncing the ball. He held it in place with his foot and then sat on top of it. "I can't see myself goin' to dialysis three times a week, yo."

"What? You just gon' get sicker or worse, die?" Sleepy balled up his face in curious wonder.

"I don't think about it. I mean the docs told me they were deteriorating in all, but I've been feeling better. Look, it fucks me up to focus on that shit." Diego became uneasy and started shifting his eyes. "You wanna finish getting dunked on or what?" Diego stood to his feet and commenced to playing the game.

Sleepy thought to tell him what was best, but then he decided against it. Diego always had an issue with Sleepy thinking he had to be a fill in dad whenever Angel Sr. wasn't around.

Sleepy tabled the talk for another day, but he had plans on revisiting the conversation.

Sleepy snatched the ball from Diego in mid jump. "D up." He allowed his tongue to hang from his mouth before he spun around and took it to the hole.

They dapped then chest bumped.

"That was a good one," Diego acknowledged. He iffed in one direction but then went another. Sleepy followed closely behind him, but Diego slammed it in the middle. "In yo face!" He clowned.

The game went on for another hour before they called it quits and headed inside. It had been a long time since Sleepy felt good about hanging with his brother, but today was indeed a new day.

Chapter 17

It was nearing six o'clock. The temperature dropped down into the high seventies. It was perfect cuddle weather and that was what Minnie and G'Corey did as they took in their celestial views. The skies were a three color hue mix of blues, pinks, and reds. It created the sexiest back drop to their evening.

The park was already scarce, and the later it became the less activity went on around them. It almost felt as if the world belonged to only them.

"Tell me something that you've never shared with anyone before," Minnie asked of him.

G'Corey sat silently, probing his mind for something he never disclosed. "I used to want to be in New Edition back in the G."

"Really?" Minnie chuckled.

"Hell yea!" He motioned his hands and arms in a N.E. dance kind of fashion to *If It Isn't Love* to show his skills.

Minnie threw her head back laughing at how comfortable he was being himself at any time.

"Okay. Okay." She caught her breath. "Now tell me something deeper than that."

"Something deep? Like how deep?"

"Bottom of the ocean, deep." She stared at the side of his face as he looked straight ahead into the horizon.

Seconds turned to minutes, then Minnie saw uncomfortable lines crease in his forehead as his eyes tightened. She wasn't sure what he was conjuring in thought, but she almost wish she wouldn't have asked him to go there.

G'Corey draped his arms around his knees that were bent into his chest and let out a hard sigh. He looked to her at his side and then forward again. "I have an older brother."

Minnie's eyes widened. It wasn't because he just mentioned having another sibling for the first time. It was the way his voice shook when he said it. She wanted to ask why this was her first time hearing it, or why no one else said anything about it but all that came out of her mouth was the word *okay.*

She reached for his hand to interlock her fingers with his. It was her soundless way of showing support for whatever pain centered around his brother that he never uncovered— until now.

He squeezed her hand firmly and continued, "His name was Ryan."

Was? Minnie inwardly questioned. But he didn't leave her curious for too long.

"His life was stole right in front of me." He shook his head as he visually recalled the day. "That bullet should have been for me because my dawg was everything I wasn't. He would have been somebody great. That thuggah was smarter than a muthafucka too." He cracked a brief smile. "He wouldn't have just been a doctor or some shit, he would have owned a hospital."

Minnie was hesitant to ask, but she did anyway. "What exactly happened to Ryan?"

"My ole fake ass daddy wanted to get a pardon for being a piece of shit father to Ryan and bought him these cold blooded Animal Print Bally shoes for graduation. The day he decided to wear dem bitches was the day some thuggahs put a gun to head to rob him for 'em."

He looked off to the opposite side and attempted to suck back the inevitable flood gates. "Seventeen years old with a bright future and just like that, he was gone."

"I'm so sorry, baby." Minnie gasped, then rubbed his arm consolingly.

G'Corey continued, "I was thirteen when he died and that's when the leash came off. I couldn't be contained. I was straight wildin'. Shit didn't matter after that day for many years to follow. People. Me. Nothing. The only reason I even finished school, ya heard me, was for him. He loved school for some reason and I loved him."

There was silence, minus the choking sounds he made while preventing himself from balling. Then out of the blue, he blurted. "Man, I miss my dawg." G'Corey jabbed into the air before he covered his face and broke out into a full fledge cry which in turn started a chain reaction.

His eyes may have misted a time or two, but she never saw a tear before. Now they were free falling rapidly. That twisted her heart into a knot.

Minnie got on her knees and held him sideways, cradling his head into her chest and rocking him. "I wasn't intending to bring you to a painful place, baby."

He said nothing, but he nodded his head in understanding.

Minnie was perplexed. If her girlfriends were hurting, she knew what would make them feel better. But there she was with her other half and she was clueless.

She wiped his face with the sleeve of her sweater dress and begged him to stop crying. She now positioned herself in front of him and cupped his face, forcing him to look her squarely in the eyes. "It's okay, baby." She kissed his trembling, wet lips. "It's okay."

Minnie placed a hand on his chest to feel the speed of his heart. It was racing and she felt like it was all her fault. She needed to calm him and the first thought to come to her mind was an indecent one.

Darkness began to cover them like a blanket, but she could still see him as he could her. She pushed him backwards, so he could lean onto his elbows and straightened out his legs as she began unbuckling his belt.

"What are you—" G'Corey reached out to block her hand.

Minnie looked around the distance of the park and saw no one who could visibly detect what she was about to do for her man. She moved his hand away. "Shhh. Let me love you." A tear fell from her eye.

She rose to her feet and stepped out of her panties, dropping them to the ground. G'Corey looked up at her perched on his forearms. He was about to sit up, but his body was too stiff to move just like his baby maker.

Minnie shelved her fears and concentrated on being his love drug to numb the pain he was in. She had just the antidote and it was found in the warmth of her love canal.

She pulled down his jeans and boxers to mid-thigh level. She knelt down beside him, blew into her hands and rubbed them together to create a heated friction. Then she grabbed ahold of his pole and began gliding her hands up and then down.

"Sssss," G'Corey hissed at the touch of her clutch. With the last of the evening's light, she saw his painful expression transform to erotic pleasure.

Minnie straddled above him and slowly descended onto his fat pussy pleaser.

"Oooo," her mouth curled into the sound she was making as she sucked him into the softest place on earth.

G'Corey ran his hands along the outside of her thighs up to her plump ass and held firmly as he assisted her in her up and down motion.

Each time her juicy lower lips kissed the base of his dick, his eyes tightened and he gritted his teeth. Then Minnie did a slow tease going up his pole, stopping at the sensitive tip of his dick to contract her P muscles on the head before going down in an explosion.

"*Shit!*" G'Corey sharply yelled before turning her over, placing her gently onto her back.

His dick pulsated so strongly that his boner threatened to break out of its skin. He had to simmer the ache by easing it back into her snapple.

When their bodies reunited, they both moaned out in unison. His growl was deep and hers was high. The sounds of his pelvis slapping against her thighs blended in with the splashing crashes of water, from the nearby pond, being spouted into the air then cascading downward.

The exotic feel of Minnie's slip and slide made G'Corey pump deeper with more speed. He dropped down to bury his mouth into her neck to muffle the vulgarity on the tip of his tongue.

Minnie arched her back when he persistently knocked at her G-spot, "Aaahhhh. Oooohhh." She took a few hard breaths in between. "Baby, I'm 'bout to cum."

"Cum for me, baby." He urged her to release as he felt his climatic wave coming forth.

He thrust himself inside of her energetically as she creamed, soaking the blanket and earth beneath her.

The tremble of her legs confirmed he was finally able to relieve himself.

"Aah! Aahh! Aaahhhh!" G'Corey grunted as he pumped all of his life force inside of her.

He stroked a few more times as his beast retreated on its own. He pecked her lips twice before getting up. "Let's get out of here, baby." He stood to his feet, then assisted her up.

She pulled down her dress. She couldn't believe she really did that. It was almost like she had an outer body experience, but she didn't regret it. Not after seeing the look of satisfaction on his face. It was priceless.

"What got into you?" G'Corey grinned as he gathered their things.

"You did," she answered with a womanly wow.

"I see ya. I definitely see ya."

The short ride home was a quiet one, but there was no tension between them, only an undeniable connection.

When they pulled in front of their door, Minnie parked then turned to face him. "I want to say this one time and I will never bring it up unless you do. Your brother shouldn't be tucked away inside the vaults of your mind and heart. And since he means so much to you, let's honor him. Boy *or* girl, we should name our baby Ryan Daniels."

She didn't wait for a response. She faintly smiled, stepped out of the car and motioned toward the front door.

G'Corey tilted his head and gave the *huh and what* look. Then he felt his eyelids rapidly bat a couple of times. It had to be her pregnancy that made him feel super linked to his softer side because he wanted to shed a tear for her gesture. He knew how dead set she was on giving their child a biblical name.

He got out of the car and stood behind her on the steps. "I thought you wanted a name with meaning," he stated.

She twirled to face him. "That name has an abundance of meaning."

He managed to bridge those tears back and smile. "I think my dawg would like that, ya heard me."

She smiled and nodded her head, placing the key inside of the lock. He tugged at her arm to get her to turn around again.

"Minnie, you know you can never leave me, right?"

"Lucky for you, I'm not."

Coffee

Chapter 18

Samiyah didn't feel as beautiful as she truly was, glancing at herself in the mirror.

She wasn't much of the *shop to you drop* diva on her retail excursion with Eli earlier, but she did manage to pick out the hot number and accessories she was wearing for tonight's shindig.

She wore a form fitting red pencil skirt that stopped right below the knees and pronounced her sexy gun slinging hips. Her chenille off the shoulder black sweater was complimented by a pair of five inch leopard skin pumps.

She pinned her locs in a messy up-do that feathered to the front along with a pair of gold chandelier style earrings that brushed across the shores of her shoulders.

Samiyah wasn't big on make-up, so her process to enhance her slanted eyes only required mascara and the red matte Mac lipstick that accentuated her plump, pouty lips.

Elias tapped on the open door of her room before stepping in. "That's the hot girl I've come to know and love." He stood behind her and playfully jiggled her booty, showing the utmost respect for its splendor. "You won't have no problem getting a replacement tonight, ya heard me."

"I need a break from men for a while, so I don't need a replacement. Right now, I'm just trying to get through a night without crying over my have nots."

"Get back on the horse when you ready, ya dig. I'm just letting you know you can gain a few stalkers with that 'fit on." Eli stood in the mirror and brushed his waves forward. "How ya boy looking?"

She eyed him from head to toe. "Everything about you is on point."

Elias wore a V-neck Polo sweater and a pair of Levis that rested on top of his high top Polo boots. His jewelry game was simple. He sported three carat diamond studs earrings in both ears, a Cartier watch, and a gold and diamond bezzled bracelet that shined like the high noon sun on his wrist.

Elias was ready to get out and enjoy himself even if Samiyah wasn't. He had to pick up the tempo in his personal life because he found himself wanting to give La'Tasha time she didn't have much of, but tonight he was going to get him a new line-up to supplement those late nights or early mornings when she wasn't free to panty drop.

He lifted his sleeve above his watch and saw it was nearing eleven. "Let's be out."

"Let's," she repeated as she followed him out of the house.

Thirty minutes later, they arrived on Decatur St. at the Top Notch. Elias killed the engine, turned on the overhead light and faced Samiyah.

"Here's the deal. Tonight is strictly 'bout letting go so if you walk in there feeling like you look, then you gon' have a good ass time. I want you to enjoy yourself, for real. Moping over them thuggahs ain't gon' bring neither one of 'em back, ya heard me."

Samiyah nodded her head. "You right."

"Can I get a smile up out cha?" Elias lips parted slightly, showing his straight white teeth.

Samiyah leaned over to give him a kiss. It felt so natural to do. His eyes closed the moment her soft lips pressed against his. One peck, but it was packed with so much love and appreciation. She sat back into her seat, but not before she wiped off what little lipstick she left behind. Then she smiled.

"Even if I don't smile on the outside, I always smile with my heart for you."

Elias bobbed his head up and down. "That's what's up." He clicked the light switch off, jumped out of his truck and opened Samiyah's door. "You ready to tear this muthafucka up, Queen B?"

She grabbed his hand and stepped out. "I'm ready for whatever."

They approached the usual wrap around line, but Elias never had to wait in them.

"What up, my dude?" Eli dapped the bouncer before he and Samiyah passed through to security and entered the club.

"It's Ole School Saturday here at Top Notch. We gon' jam to eighties hip hop, but N.O. style, ya heard me. With dat Trigga Man and Brown beat added to these tracks, we gon' *rat ta tat*, ya dig. Let's gooooo!" The deejay announced as he threw on Salt and Pepa's *Push It.*

The notorious intro of the song came on and a shy smile creased Samiyah's lips. This was her joint, but who didn't like the dynamic duo? The beat took ahold of Eli and he nodded his head as if to say, *yeaaaa*.

He grabbed both of her hands and backed up on to the dance floor as he lip synced Hurby Lov Bug's part.

"Now wait a minute y'all/This dance ain't for everybody/Only the sexy people/So all you fly mothers/Get on out there and dance/Dance I said!"

Samiyah began laughing at Eli's animated faces and moves, but her arm rose over her head almost instantly, then she dropped her hips and began bouncing to the beat just like him.

Every classic joint that ever came out in that decade spun on the ones and twos. Cherry, the club owner, hit her niche when she opened her rendition of night entertainment.

After an hour of dancing, Eli stepped away from Samiyah to mack a honey dip on the second level of the club. Samiyah had gotten into her own zone, so she was fine by herself on the dance floor.

No sooner than he stood on the loft style platform, he spotted another woman of interest down below entering through the doors with her posse of divas. He walked right past the beautiful Hershey coated sista he had his eye on and headed toward the other fine chocolate in designer heels.

It took him a few minutes to reach her from where he was. She had her back facing him as he approached from behind. Elias slid his hands around her waist and pulled her into him, naturally pressing her ass against his dick.

La'Tasha smiled without turning around the moment she identified it was Elias based on the scent of his signature Ralph Lauren cologne.

He lowered his head next to her ear. "You the sexiest muthafucka in here, ya heard me."

She blushed before she turned around. She tiptoed to reach around his neck and hug him, kissing him at the neckline.

"Can the sexiest muthafucka in here be in your bed tonight?"

"You already know," he answered.

"Come find me when you're ready to leave."

He cupped her ass, then slapped it. "No doubt."

La'Tasha kissed him on the lips and they parted ways—for now.

"We gon' slow up the pace for all the lovers in the building." The emcee switched the upbeat record to a slow jam.

That was Samiyah's cue to exit the floor. As she excused herself through the crowd, a brother grabbed her by the hand and asked her to dance with him. She smiled and considered taking him up on his offer until she heard the song selection.

I never met a person quite like you/Someone that makes me feel loved/I wanna be the one that you are thinking of/The one that brightens your day.

Samiyah's mood plummeted at the switch of the track, she snatched her hand away and rushed off through the club in search of the restroom. She was on the verge of tears at the memories that came crashing to her mind.

When her and Gerran first started dating, she had sung the same song bouncing off of each wall in the building now in dedication to him several years ago at St. Mary's talent show. Her version of Anquette's *I Will Always Be There for You* won her first place for the contest and in his heart.

Not truly paying attention to where she was going, she physically bumped into Cherry.

"I'm sorry," Samiyah said, stepping off to the side to continue her stride to the ladies' room.

"Samiyah?" Cherry grabbed her by the arm when she noticed it was her who almost knocked her down.

Samiyah didn't respond. Instead, she hurriedly wiped her face to camouflage her pain. Instinctually and out of concern, Cherry took Samiyah by the wrist and walked her over to her VIP section. They walked past one of Cherry's four bodyguards before stepping up into her reserved spot that overlooked the entire club.

"What's the matter, Maw?" Cherry sat her down on the plush, velvet, circular style lounge sofa.

Samiyah bowed her head and shook it side to side, covering her face with the hand Cherry wasn't holding. "I don't know you like that to bomb you with my issues. I won't do you that." Samiyah declined telling her *her* problems.

"Well, I told you any friend of Eli's is an automatic friend of mine, but no pressure." Cherry rubbed Samiyah's back in a circular motion. She looked straight ahead into her club, but spoke to Samiyah as she did. "You gotta let that stress go."

"I don't know how." Samiyah sniffled as the song came to an end.

"I'll show you. Have a drink with me." She waved Anastasia, the VIP's waitress, over to her section.

"Boss Lady," Anastasia nodded her way.

Cherry smiled, "Prepare a virgin Black Mamba.

The waitress smiled. She knew every woman who'd ordered that needed help walking to their cars once they were through because he was the biggest drink they'd served. Fourteen inches of chocolate deliciousness to be exact. "Right away, Boss Lady."

Samiyah assumed the order she placed wasn't from one of her three bars, but instead the special list. "Wait!" She shot her hand up to get Anastasia to come back, then she scooted closer to Cherry to speak discreetly in her ear. "I can't afford that nor am I in the mood for a strong drink."

Cherry looked at her slowly and methodically. Maybe that particular one was going to be too hard of a pick-me-up, but she knew she needed something to knock the edge off. "Very well, Samiyah." Cherry signaled Anastasia to bend down toward her mouth. "Change that to a Head Banger Cherry Twist."

A wicked grin formed on Anastasia's face, revealing the adorable gap in between her upper teeth. "Right away, Boss!" She trotted off.

"I told you I—" Samiyah started.

"Don't worry about cost. It's on the house and don't even fix your lips to say you don't need this because the tension on your face says otherwise."

One of Cherry's workers approached her with a concern. She double patted Samiyah on the thigh. "Wait here for Anastasia. She'll be back to get you. Relax, okay?"

Samiyah nodded her head and then sat back. Moments later a different waitress came delivering a cocktail.

"I didn't order this." Samiyah waved her hands, declining the beverage.

"Cherry had me send this over. It's a sweet Bourbon Sunrise. It will sneak up on you, so be careful not to guzzle it." She handed her the tall, slender glass.

Samiyah smiled and accepted it, removing the umbrella before taking a sip. "Ummm, not bad." She took another swig. "Not bad at all."

Elias spotted Samiyah and walked over to her. As he was about to step inside, a thuggah too booted up for his taste extended his palm into Eli's chest. "Off limits, homie."

Elias pushed his meaty hand off of him. "Don't touch me, dawg." He looked at the short, body builder looking man upside his bald head.

Samiyah quickly stepped over to the entrance and told the man she heard Cherry refer to as Rock that Elias was okay to let in.

Rock remained unfazed at Eli's glare and removed the rope to let him in.

"*Thuggah!*" Elias said one last time as he stood on the side of him before walking past him.

Once inside, Elias' testosterone cooled down and his stomach took center stage as he noticed the buffet set up along the wall. He grabbed a plate and helped himself. With a sky high feast before him, he sat next to Samiyah. "Who you know in VIP?"

"It's who *you* know," she replied. "This is Cherry's personal VIP. She was sweet enough to let me chill here when I went through a lil' swing."

"Yea, she good peoples."

"Speaking of good peoples, she comped me a drink."

"See what happens when you listen to Elias?" He referred to himself in third person. "What kind of drink you getting?"

"I don't recall and at this point I ain't trippin'." She drank the remainder of her Bourbon. "Humph, this was really good." She examined the empty glass.

Eli was scooping a spoon of red beans into his mouth when suddenly he lost his appetite. EU's *Da Butt* was bumping and of all the women there, he spotted La'Tasha cutting up on the dance floor. She was fully bent over rotating her derriere all on some thuggah's dick.

Samiyah read his expression and even tried to follow his eyes, but it was impossible to see what he was looking at.

"Eli what's the matter?"

He shook his head *no* to answer *nothing*, but he kept his eyes glued on the problem. He reached into his pocket and removed his truck keys from his house keys and placed them in her hand, opened his wallet and counted off ten twenties and gave her that as well.

"Look, enjoy your drink, ya heard me. When you finished doing you, take my truck and head home."

"What about you?"

"I'ma be straight. Hit me on the hip if you need me." He kissed her cheek and exited the room.

Seconds later, Anastasia came for Samiyah. "This way. Your drink is ready."

Coffee

Chapter 19

Anastasia led Samiyah down the familiar hall and into a side room with simple instructions.

"Remove all of your clothes. Lay face down on the massage table, underneath this sheet," she patted. "Also, I prepared the same drink you had earlier in case you didn't want any of the chilled bottle of red wine."

"Thank you." Samiyah stood in the middle of the dimly lit room.

"One more thing. Is there a particular style of music you would like playing in the background?"

"Uhh, R&B would be fine, I suppose." She hunched her shoulders.

Anastasia turned the XM radio to her requested station and set the volume at a comfortable and relaxing setting.

"Your party will be in to join you in fifteen minutes. Enjoy," she smiled and left out.

Samiyah spun around the room and was amazed. The most attractive and eye catching piece was a ceiling high wall mounted slate waterfall in the middle of the room with cascading running water that gathered in a well at the bottom of it. The sound was tranquil.

The walls were painted a calming beige color with an accent wall of taupe and every piece of furniture was cream colored with the exception of the dark woodwork that punched masculinity into the room.

Samiyah walked over to the table where her Bourbon Sunrise sat and smoothly downed it. She was already feeling nice from the first one, but this one was guaranteed to have her floating.

After putting the empty glass down, she slowly stepped out of her clothes to the rhythm of the song playing softly in the background.

As she pulled her sweater over her head, she dropped it to the floor and kept her hands in the air, swaying to the sultry sound of Ron Isley serenading her.

Hey girl, what's your fantasy?/I'll take you there to that ecstasy/ Ooh girl, you blow my mind, I'll always be your freak/Let's make sweet love between the sheets.

Samiyah closed her eyes and zoned out. She sensually unzipped the back of her skirt as if she was putting on a performance while shimmying out of it. The alcohol was definitely taking her to another level.

Her suitor stood watching from the crack in the door, opting not to come in as Samiyah's strip tease was a turn on.

The song ended and another began. It was R. Kelly's *Down Low*.

Samiyah pulled back the sheet and lay underneath them. She placed her head into the doughnut shaped hole on the table. There was an inscription on the floor and it read: *When on the wave, ride.*

Humph, Samiyah thought as she pondered the saying.

She then heard her door open and shut. Seconds later, she felt the light trace of fingers glide from her leg, over her booty, and up her back. Finally, a voice accompanied the touch.

"Are you relaxed?"

Samiyah's eyes drew inward because she recognized the voice. "Cherry?" She raised her head and looked over her shoulder.

Cherry stood dressed in provocative bedroom attire. Her hair that she normally kept in a messy bun with her Chinese bangs was hanging down, flowing past her shoulders. She looked so inviting. So feline. So soft. So not Samiyah's cup of tea.

"What are you doing here?" Samiyah questioned half turned over.

Cherry smiled and raised the warming lotion in her hand. "I'm giving you a tantric massage."

"A what?"

"Listen, it's a stimulating massage that you'll appreciate. Trust me. *And* this won't go anywhere *you* won't allow it to. So, turn over and enjoy the ride." Cherry guided her back into the face down position.

Samiyah resisted Cherry's gentle nudge moments before she digressed and went along with the flow.

What the hell, Samiyah thought. Maybe it was the alcohol lowering her inhibition but then another thought entered her mind. *What's the harm in a massage?*

***

Elias stood at the bar, watching La'Tasha from a distance. Kid 'n Play's *Gittin' Funky* was bumping through the speakers and she was bumping on yet another dude.

He wanted to look away and do what he set out to do. Meet new honeys and reshelf his line up, but he was a moth drawn to La'Tasha's flame.

He wasn't sure why he was getting mad, but he was.

"Hey, cutie. You wanna dance?" A woman of his type stood in front of him.

Elias looked down his nose at the brick house with a baby doll face and sneered. "You see me dancing?"

"Tsss." She threw up the brick wall and excused herself.

Elias watched her walk away. He knew he'd regret dismissing her fine ass come morning, but at that moment he was too hot under the collar behind one broad to get all bent out of shape behind another.

He cut his eyes at La'Tasha and finished off the rest of his Crown, slammed it down and made a beeline in her direction.

The way Eli shifted through the crowd one would have sworn he'd caught his wife fucking on the dance floor, but he wasn't a husband or a boyfriend for that matter. He was just a jealous lover in denial.

La'Tasha was bent over with her hands on her knees bouncing her ass on the man who was gyrating against her shake.

Eli walked up on her and pulled her up by the arm. "You looking like a whole hoe out c'here," he chastised.

"What?" She looked down at his hand gripping her arm and then up to him.

Elias let go of his hold. "We're leaving."

"Lil' mama, what's up with dat?" The guy La'Tasha was dancing with asked, referring to Elias policing her.

She shook her head and hunched her shoulders. "I don't know, but I'm 'bout to see." La'Tasha left the young man where he stood, looking foolish as she followed Elias outside of the club. "What the hell was your problem in there?"

"I don't have a problem. I'm ready to go," Elias made known.

"Why are you tripping? Did I Bogart you when you were grinding on those women in there?" She pointed to the club.

"What you ate for breakfast?"

La'Tasha was caught off guard. "Huh? What does *that* have to do with *this*?"

"We both just asked irrelevant ass questions," he snapped.

La'Tasha squinted her eyes as if she could get a clearer picture of the man standing before her. "Eli? Are you jealous?" She laughed a Def Comedy Jam laugh and pointed her finger at him. He didn't say anything. She got her kicks off of him, then her laughter died down to a small chuckle. "Awww, there's enough of me to go around."

"Yea. Yea. Where did you park?" He ignored her antics.

"Hold on," she giggled beneath her breath. "Let me send a text to my girls."

She sent a group message to the three friends she met up with at Top Notch.

1:33AM: I'm out. Elias needs me to fuck him to sleep. I'll holla.

"Let's go, big baby," she teased.

"I got yo big baby, alright." He grabbed her around the neck and walked with her to her car.

I ain't no Tony Danza, but I'ma show her who's the boss, Elias smirked.

***

Cherry stood at the end of the bed. She squirted the kiwi flavored warming lotion into her hand and massaged it into her palms. She pulled back the sheet and exposed the lower half of Samiyah's body from the top of her thighs on down. She lifted her foot off of the table and began giving her a penetrating massage.

"Oooh," Samiyah whispered beneath her breath. She was caught off guard by the immediate sensation.

Cherry was delicate with her touches as she moved to the other foot, up her calves and then onto the backs of her thighs. Her head tilted as she bit down on her lip, running her hands over Samiyah's silky legs felt like heaven to the touch.

"I'm about to uncover your top, exposing your back and ass. Are you with me?"

Samiyah lifted her arm to a level position and gave her a thumbs up.

Cherry then pulled the sheet from off of her upper body and covered her, legs down. Her eyes bulged as she saw Samiyah's shapely buttocks beg her teeth to sink into them.

She squeezed an ample amount of the fruity tasting lotion onto her body and began working Samiyah into an enchanted place. Cherry felt Samiyah's reservations of having a woman touch her melt further off into the distance. Her light moans and relaxed muscles were a dead giveaway.

When Cherry was done kneading the kinks from her back she leaned down by Samiyah's head, pressing her breast onto her back as her lips grazed her ear. Her words were soothing, "Turn over."

Samiyah was slightly embarrassed to flip over because she was afraid her hardened nipples would show how much she had been enjoying Cherry's feminine caresses.

"Don't be shy. It's only a massage," Cherry reminded.

Samiyah hesitantly rotated onto her back but with her arms folded around her chest to shield her nipple erection. Cherry briefly sized her naked appeal up then down before she peeled her arms off of her and placed them at her sides. She smiled when saw her ripe melons.

Cherry gently brushed her fingertips over Samiyah's eyes to close them. "Relax," she whispered.

Cherry formed prayer hands between her chest plate and spread them over her breast and up to her neck and back over her Double Ds.

Samiyah sucked in her breath and rolled her neck slightly each time Cherry's soft hands applied the right amount of pressure over her bosoms.

Tell me what I gotta do to please you/Baby anything you say I'll do.

Cherry had sung along with Joe as she trailed her hands over Samiyah's tensed stomach right before she smoothed her thighs apart, placing her warm mouth on Samiyah's surprisingly wet pussy.

"Ahaaa," Samiyah sucked in her breath while her body jerked at the sensation. With disbelief to what was happening, her hands shot downward to push Cherry up and off of her, but the eye rolling tongue kiss against her lower lips demanded that she didn't.

Cherry slid her hands underneath Samiyah's ass and cupped it as she buried her face in her hidden treasure, sensually sucking and tongue fucking her spot.

"Ummm. Ooooh. Aaahhh." Samiyah embarrassingly covered her mouth to silence her moans. She couldn't believe she was enjoying it as much as she was. She also found it odd that each time she told Cherry *stop*, the word *don't* preceded it.

Cherry's swept her fingers over Samiyah's swollen clit as she flickered the tip of her tongue at the base of her pearl. The more she worked her middle was the more nectar that began seeping from the folds of Samiyah's petals.

An intense build form the pressure Cherry was applying to Samiyah's cherry caused her legs to vibrate violently while every muscle in her abdomen began contracting rapidly.

"Oh, shit!" She grabbed Cherry's head and held her in place. "Right there. Right there. Right there!" She cheered her on as Cherry did magnificent things with her mouth.

Cherry then inserted her fingers inside of her heated cavern, eager to locate the spongy tissue within so she could send her overboard.

"Ummm," Cherry hummed as she continued to dine on her peach.

With a little more pressing and pushing, Cherry found what she was looking for and Samiyah's eyes grew big when she did.

Samiyah's mouth formed the perfect O. "Ooohhhh! Oooohhhh! She whined. I'm about to—"

"Cum in my mouth," Cherry mumbled.

Samiyah was bucking her hips faster, arching her back off of the table as she gave into an orgasmic tidal wave so strongly she felt her heart damn near burst out of her chest.

"I'm cum—" The strength of the orgasm cut her words short.

But now it was Cherry's turn to keep Samiyah gripped in place. She locked her arms around Samiyah's thighs to prevent her from running. Samiyah came but she wanted her to make it rain, so Cherry honed in on that sensitive spot which made Samiyah go wild.

"Stop! Stop!" Samiyah began chanting unable to bear the tortured pleasure, but Cherry refused her request.

Cherry was determined to make Samiyah's pussy shoot cum into the air the same way fireworks exploded in the sky. She needed to write *Cherry* on her kitten.

With a persistent tongue, Cherry's mission to please was fulfilled. One final calculated stroke turned Samiyah's fountain on.

"Oh, shit! Oh, shit! Ooooohhh!" Samiyah trembled as she came waterfalls. The height of her squirt was a sight for sore eyes.

"Let that shit go, baby." Cherry massaged her inner thighs as she watched Samiyah's super soaker wet the bed, the floor, and more.

As Samiyah's release began to die down, it occurred to her that it was a woman who brought her to ecstasy and she became flushed with humiliation.

"I gotta go." Samiyah stood on wobbly legs and gathered her clothes, covering herself as best as she could in the process. She had no intentions on cuddling, having pillow talk, or returning the favor.

Cherry chuckled as she watched Samiyah clumsily move about. "There's an encore if you wish to stick around."

"Uhn uhn," Samiyah shook her head all the while putting on her shoes. She had to leave, pronto. She placed her hand on the door knob so she could quickly exit the den of Sodom and Gomorrah when she heard her name.

"Samiyah," Cherry made eye contact with her once she reluctantly looked back. "Taste you later."

"No you won't," Samiyah snapped as she rushed out into the hall, closing the door behind her.

"Yes I will," Cherry heard her confidence break the silence in the room.

***

Two hours and two condoms later, Elias was wiping the sweat off of his brow.

"*Fuck!* I love your ass." Elias blurted the words faster than he took the time to think about them.

La'Tasha looked over her shoulder. "You don't love me. You just love my doggy style," she jested.

"I said *ass*. Not *you*!" He recovered quickly.

"Whatever, thuggah," she said as she peeled herself from under him. "Look, I'm about to hop in this shower. But if you can get it up, I'll put it down. You 'bout it?"

Elias didn't want to seem too eager to jump back inside of her good *good* because it would make his earlier slip of the tongue seem legit, but who was he fooling? "I'm 'bout it, 'bout it!" He sprung out of the bed and followed her into the bathroom where he was gonna tear that ass up one last time for the road.

Chapter 20

By the time La'Tasha brought Elias home, it was 4 a.m. He stepped into his dark bedroom, cut the light on and found Samiyah laying in his bed faced up and wide awoke.

Elias stepped out of his boots and pulled his sweater over his head, leaving on his jeans and wife beater. He plopped onto the mattress, laying directly beside her with his hands bridged across his stomach. They both stared at the ceiling silently for a few minutes until Eli spoke up. "I'm fucked up, ya heard me."

"Me too."

"You first."

Samiyah held her breath unsure if she was really ready to release her sinful shame. She shifted her eyes like rolling marbles in search of the answer, but decided to blurt it out, cut and dry. "I let Cherry eat my cherry."

Eli didn't hesitate to follow up with his woe. "I told La'Tasha I love her."

Samiyah bolted up to a seated position and looked at him strangely.

He stared back at her. "What?" He opened his hands quickly as if to catch something. "Why you looking at me? Did I look at you?" Elias questioned, pointing out his non judgment reaction to her *girl on girl* action.

Samiyah took note and calmed down, laying back beside him. "Sorry," she apologized. "But do you *love* her? I mean you love sex. You love to stay fly, but I never heard you put love and any woman's name together."

"I know, right? But I think it was the liquor infused with good pussy confusing my sensibility. I ain't never loved deez hoes." Elias shook his head. He was tripped out that he, Macaroni Tony, would ever slip and say such bastard words to a woman he's was sexing.

"What did she say?"

"A fuckin' Snoop Dog verse. Ha! *Bitch* think she a rapper nah?" He scoffed.

"From everything you've told me about her, it looks like she is to you what you are to her. Maybe if you showed her something different, she would too," Samiyah assumed.

She knew his feelings were bruised whether he would admit that or not.

He swatted his hand in the air as if to dismiss what Samiyah stated. "Back to you. Don' think I didn't catch what you said about ole girl. How that sexy shit happen?"

"I'll let you know when I know," she quipped.

"Did you at least like it?"

"Ah, yea," she answered his question hurriedly before he could finish asking it. "I've had my share of good licks on my peaches & cream, but no thuggah came close to what I felt tonight. I mean I thought Anacoda's nasty lick was the best, but even he didn't hold a candle to her," she recapped.

"Took you a lil' trip on the wild side, huh bruh? Doesn't seem like you in Kansas anymore, Dorothy."

"Hush ya mouth." She poked a finger into his side.

He laughed a little and scooted away from her slightly out of reflex. "You loved that shit, girl. Real talk. You going back, huh?"

"Like *thee* hell. I got caught up in the rapture once." She held up one finger. "But there will be no second time."

"Whatever, lesbian," Elias kidded as he shielded himself from Samiyah's play punches. "Chill. Chill," he surrendered. "I already know what time of day it was. It's just life and—"

"Shit happens." They both chorused.

"It sho'll does," he yawned. "I'm tired as hell."

In a domino effect, Samiyah yawned as well. "Me too."

"Say no more." Elias double clapped his hands and the lights went off. He rolled Samiyah onto her side, spooned her and they both fell asleep.

***

Later that Sunday evening.

Sleepy and Acacia walked inside exhausted from their five mile run around the neighborhood.

"What up, bro?" Sleepy addressed Diego after he caught a second wind the moment he spotted him sitting on the couch in the living room. Diego rose to his feet and pounded Sleepy off. "Ain't shit. Just watching this marathon of Tales from the Darkside."

"Oh, shit!" He dapped Diego off again, this time leaning into his chest. "Remember we used to sneak and watch it while Mommy and Papi were asleep every Saturday night?"

Diego covered his chuckle. "Hell yea, son. And we used to be scared out our damn minds, sleeping with the lights on and shit."

"Man," Sleepy smiled. "You couldn't tell me that wasn't real life."

"Me either," Diego agreed as he sat back down.

"Baby, I'm 'bout to hit this tub up." Sleepy kissed Acacia on the lips.

"Okay, I'll go start dinner. "Acacia began walking out of the front room.

"What you cooking, Ma?" Diego rubbed on his eight pack.

Hidden beneath the shield of her fraudulent smile was contempt. She turned to face him, "Mofongos."

"Ummm. I can't wait to grub on that."

Acacia twisted her lip, touching Sleepy around the waist before she disappeared into the kitchen.

"I'll join you in a couple to check out a few of those episodes." He pointed at Diego.

Diego threw his head back in recognition of Sleepy's plan to bond as they had been doing the moment he officially became a houseguest.

When Sleepy retreated out of the room, Diego muted the television and listened for the sound of the bathroom door closing from his bedroom before he bolted off of the couch and jetted into the kitchen.

Over the two weeks he'd been there, he pretty much knew he had a twenty to twenty-five minute window to make his move. Acacia had been successfully avoiding him, but her game of dodge ball ended tonight.

Diego looked at his watch. It was 6:43PM. He heard the bath water shut off and his clock was officially ticking.

Acacia stood at the counter deveining the shrimps she was using for their meal when she felt Diego grab her around the waist, firmly pressing her into his groove of his package.

She tried to spin around, but he had her locked in his hold.

"Diego!" She curtly called out his name right above a whisper. "What the hell are you doing? Get off of me!"

"I can't." He moved one of his hands up her breast and rested it around the curve of her neck, still maintaining his hold.

She clutched the knife more firmly and growled. "I will stab you until you do."

"You won't," he spoke assuredly as he brought his hand back over her breast.

She tried to jerk out of the compromising position she was in, warning him again. "Stop it! I mean it."

"Say you want me and I will fuck you so good. Right here and right now."

"I don't want you," she openly admitted.

"Yea? Then why your nipples hard?" He then rushed his hands down her tensed stomach and into her spandex and cupped his hand over her pussy. She jumped at his intrusion. "And why is pussy wet?" He spun her around. She leaned her upper body away from him as far as she could. "I'm not fucking around with you, Acacia. I'm just gonna fuck you, straight up." He glared into her eyes.

"Don't make me," she threatened, raising the knife above her head. Her anxieties kicked in and she began breathing hard.

Diego wasn't buying her wolf ticket. He went forward with his plan. He grabbed her wrist and pinched her nerve under the squeeze of his fingers, forcing her hand to drop the kitchen utensil to the floor and then he kissed her forcefully.

She wiggled and squirmed and tried to get out of the pinned position she was in, but eventually her fight turned into submission. She could no longer ward off her desire to have him.

When Diego felt her restrained assaults turn into fanatical touches, he violently turned her around. He snatched her pants down below her knees, unzipped himself, and pulled his dick through the slit of his boxers.

Anticipation to feel him once more took ahold of her good sense not to go there especially with Sleepy being under the same roof. But there was a fire set ablaze inside of her that couldn't be put out until she gave into him.

She shifted the food haplessly into the sink, clearing space for her to lean frontward. Diego pushed her forward and pulled her ass out toward him.

"Sssss," she moaned softly as he spread her French vanilla cheeks apart and drove himself inside of her Spanish fly.

He threw his head back and bite his bottom lip to suppress the carnal urge to roar from the feel of his slippery slope pummeling her insides.

Diego looked at his watch at it was 7:00PM. Sleepy would be coming out of the bathroom at any minute, but because he didn't cum he was afraid he would have to keep going until he did.

Acacia started whining from the magnificent feel of his rough bucking and the looming fear of being caught even added to the intensity, but she had to end their tryst. "Diego, stop."

"Shut up!" He ordered, grabbing her tighter so he could grind in her further. The smacking sound from his skin slapping her skin was getting progressively louder the more her snatch began contracting around the head of his dick. "Ohhhh," he groaned.

"Stop it!" She began fighting him off and out of her, but that only strengthened the beast in him which ultimately turned her on more.

"Oh, shit!" She jerked at the sound she heard off in the distance. That sudden movement on her part and Diego's constant pumps caused her to fiercely cum. She covered her mouth as tears streamed down her cheeks. "Mmmmmmm. Mmmmmmm," she whimpered.

"Aaahhhh," Diego bust his sexual assault weapon the moment she came, loosening his hold around her.

She composed herself a little and pushed him off of her, knocking his weakened body backwards. She pulled her pants up quickly, disregarding the stream of cum rolling down her leg. "You son of a bitch!" she angrily whispered.

"What's going on in here?" Sleepy demanded to know the moment he stepped in the kitchen.

Acacia looked at him as if she'd seen a ghost. "Ah. Umm. Ah," she stumbled over her words.

"I scared her by accident." Diego stepped in to save her.

"Yea." She bent down to pick up the knife. "He startled me."

Sleepy confusingly twisted his face and then began taking deep inhales. "What's that smell?"

Diego remained calm and waited to see how Acacia would answer.

"Huh? Smell what? I don't smell nothing," she answered like a guilty person.

Unexpectedly, Sleepy's look of pisstivity turned into an all-out laugh. "That's my point. I don't smell my food, woman. You should have been done by now."

Acacia laughed a nervous laugh. "Oh, Papi. I sat down for a minute to work out a sudden cramp in my calf."

"Word? Need me to rub it out?" Sleepy walked toward her with the intent to kneel down and massage her leg.

She backed away. "I'm okay now. Y'all boys go watch your shows and I'll have this done in no time." She shooed him away playfully.

"Are you sure?" Sleepy questioned, stopping in mid track.

She shook her head *yes*.

"A'ight. Let's leave, man." He waved Diego to follow him, then he paused. "Did you get what you came in here for?"

He smiled. "Oh, yea. I sure did," he spoke enthusiastically before following Sleepy into the living room.

The moment they disappeared she hunched over the empty side of the sink, turning on the cool water to splash over her face.

Fuck is wrong with me? She questioned.

Later on...

It was around 2 a.m. that morning when Diego could no longer ignore the ammonia smell in his nostril or strong taste in the back of his throat. He glanced over and saw Sleepy knocked out next to him on the sofa. The house was dark, but the television was still on providing enough light to guide him through the living room and into the kitchen.

Diego stood to his feet and instantly felt dizzy. He wobbled with his first step and found that he couldn't take the other. Suddenly, he had an uncontrollable urge to vomit. He attempted to take another step, but was unable.

"Sleep—" he called out his brother's name before he collapsed on the floor.

The sound of the thud pulled Sleepy from his slumber and when he sat up, he saw his brother laid out before him.

"Acacia!" Sleepy yelled as he rushed over to Diego and slapped him lightly on the cheek. There was no response. "Acacia!" He screamed frantically.

"What?" She called out from their bedroom.

"Acacia, come here quick!"

Hearing the urgency in his voice, she stumbled out of bed and down the hallway. She turned on the light as she entered the living room and saw Sleepy hunched over Diego. She immediately rushed over and dropped to her knees beside him. "Baby, what's wrong?"

"I don't know," he answered fearfully. "Diego? Bro? Wake up! Call 9-1-1. Hurry up!" Sleepy lifted his eyelids and saw white marbles stare back at him.

Acacia clumsily scurried to her feet and fretfully dialed the emergency line. She spoke impatiently to the dispatcher as she gave all of the required information. She hung up the phone. "They're on their way."

Sleepy nodded his head, not looking at her as he stayed focused on Diego.

Acacia couldn't keep still, she kept walking back and forth to where Diego lay lifeless and then away from the horrible image. On her walk back, she blurted, "Turn him on his side!" She pointed.

"Huh?" He looked back at her and then back to Diego. "Oh, shit!" Sleepy flipped him over and the bile he was choking on started seeping out of the side of his mouth.

Acacia began crying. She didn't understand what was going on and although only minutes had elapsed, it felt as if the EMTs were taking too long.

She opened the front door and ran down the steps to look down her street for those flashing red and white lights. Acacia was so amped she didn't register how cold the ground beneath her bare feet were. She just stood there bouncing in anticipation waiting to hear the ambulance draw near.

Minutes later, they arrived. One came out carrying her equipment and the other removed the gurney from the back of the wagon.

"In here," Acacia hysterically directed, leading the way.

The paramedic asked that Sleepy step back as she checked for Diego's pulse. He backed up and stood out of the way as asked. Acacia fell into him and wrapped her arms around her man and silently watched on until the lady belted to the other technician, causing massive alarm to both Sleepy and Acacia.

"He's coding!"

Chapter 21
One month later…

It took everything in Samiyah to keep her insides from coming out while she was making a Valentine's Day breakfast for Elias.

She sliced his favorite fresh fruit consisting of strawberries, canta-loupes, honey dew melons, and kiwis. She toasted two slices of Bunny bread and spread honey butter on top of it. But preparing his loaded omelet made her cheeks balloon like a blowfish.

"Oh, God!" She hid her nose underneath her shirt although that did little to mask the scent.

She'd never been a fan of eggs, but Eli loved them and if she had to run the risk of having an upset tummy, then so be it.

She plated his dish beautifully and sat it on top of a bed tray. Poured him a glass of cranberry juice and carefully carried everything into his bedroom where he was still in bed under the covers.

"Wake up, sleepy head," she chorused, walking toward his side.

He threw the comforter back and looked over his shoulder before he sat up fully. "Whoa nah. Breakfast in bed? For moi?" He smiled generously.

Samiyah mirrored his smile until it turned into a grimace. She quickened her steps toward him and placed the tray in his hands before she bolted into his bathroom, closing the door behind herself.

Elias heard the toilet seat slam against its porcelain back moments before he heard the revolting sound of her throwing up.

"Bluh! Bluh!" She released what little dinner she had from last night.

A minute later, he heard the toilet flush and the flow of running water from the sink. She stepped out and leaned against the wall in his bedroom.

"Give me a second to return. Enjoy your breakfast, okay?"

He looked down at his food and then back to her and faintly smiled. "I'll try," he said below his breath.

Samiyah headed upstairs and showered. Fifteen minutes later, she reentered his room.

"You feelin' better?"

"Umm hmmm," she climbed in bed next to him. "Did you enjoy your meal?"

"Yea. Despite the orchestra of fucked up noises coming from your mouth, I managed. It was on point."

She shook her head. "You make me sick," she giggled.

"I would thank you with a kiss, but I know what your lips been through."

"Boy, stop playing with me. I brushed my teeth and washed my face."

"But those lips, though." He pointed at them.

"Whatever. Give me my payment for slaving over the stove." She stretched her neck upward to receive a reluctant peck from him.

"So, you nervous about today?" Elias massaged her hip in a circular motion as she lay in the crook of his arm.

"Yes indeed. Just thinking about it keeps my stomach in knots."

"Need me to go with you for moral support or some shit?"

She shook her head *no*. "I'll be alright."

He hugged her closer to him and kissed her on top of her head. "Well, to pick your mood up a bit, you know I got something for you, right?"

She perked up. "You do?"

"Oh, yea. Look in dat top drawer on the side of you."

She rolled over and opened the drawer to the nightstand and retrieved a long gift wrapped box with a card attached underneath the purple bow.

"Open the gift first."

She did just that. Inside was a gold charm bracelet with a single two inch dragonfly dangling from it. "Awww, this is beautiful." She placed it around her wrist and turned toward him so he could clasp it on her. She turned her arm back and forth to appreciate the beauty of it. "Thank you."

"Happy Valentine's Day," he responded.

Her lips began to tremble and her eyes formed a watery gloss over them.

"Uhn uhn," he waved his finger. "No crying."

"No crying," she agreed. She wiped her eyes. "What made you choose this piece? What does a dragonfly symbolize?"

"The card explains it best." e reached it to her.

It read: *As a creature of the wind, the dragonfly represents change. Its iridescent wings are incredibly sensitive to the slightest breeze, and so we are reminded to heed where the proverbial wind blows—lest we run into stormy weather.*

"This is deep." She considered the irony between its representation and the choices she'd been making over the last year and more importantly recent months. She knew her reckless behavior had to come to an end. It had already cost her too much.

"I be on my zen shit sometimes," he joked. "But real shit. The jewelry designer suggested this piece when I told her what I wanted most for your life."

"And what do you want for my life?"

He thought seriously before he answered. "No more rain."

***

G'Corey had lost his battle to the flu that morning. That nasty bug had him fatigued with chills, body aches, a sore throat, the whole nine.

They had plans to go to the Lovers Only concert held at the Lake Front Arena with powerhouse performances from R&B's legends, but there was no way they'd make it. G'Corey was barely coherent.

My poor baby, she thought. Minnie gently patted a cool towel across his forehead to wipe off the accumulated sweat on his brow.

He was so groggy from all of the medicine he had taken. It broke her heart to see him in such discomfort. After she turned the air conditioning unit to a lower temperature so he wouldn't complain of it being too hot, she grabbed her keys so she could head out to the store.

She needed to make him a pot of her homemade chicken soup and get the ingredients to make a hot toddy concoction. That should have him walking at the least.

Minnie poked her head out of the front door and saw her neighbor had her tightly cramped between his and her husband's car. There was no way she could get out.

She blew out hard and slapped her hand against her thigh. "Gee-zusss." It annoyed her to no end when he compacted her car like a sardines in a can. Instead of knocking on his door or waking up G'Corey to have him move his car up, she simply grabbed his keys as well. Then Minnie rushed out of the door. Although he was in a heavily medicated in a comatose state of sleep, she still wanted to be back before he woke up.

***

Several weeks had passed and Sleepy was still in gut wrenching pain. There were nights when he couldn't sleep and doing anything for himself was harder than before. He had no clue losing a part of himself would be so traumatic.

"Acacia," he whined for her.

She rushed out of the kitchen with the glass of water he just requested of her a minute ago. Entering the bedroom, she walked over to his bedside. "Yes, Papi." She sat the drink down and then she assisted him to a seated position. "What do you need?" She tenderly asked.

"I need things to feel normal again. I've been having these anxieties and these good for nothing sedatives ain't doing shit." He raised his voice higher than usual.

"I know." She ran her fingers through the coils of his curls. "But things will get better in due time. Until it does, you know I am here for you and I will never leave."

He kissed her hand, leaving his lips pressed on them for an extended period of time. "I just been having the hardest time coping, but you make things easier. I love you so much, baby."

"I love you, too." She, in turn, kissed his hand. Then she proceeded to console him. "None of us know why God does what He do, but there is a reason. Just know Diego is resting now. And you, you will be alright. Okay?"

He wiped the single tear that dropped from his eye and nodded his head. She eased him under the covers and kissed him on the temple.

"I will be back to check on you later, my love." Acacia cut off the light and closed their bedroom door.

Acacia leaned against the door and exhaled sharply. She was exhausted. Although she had reduced her hours at work to accommodate being at home with Sleepy, his demands were like a full time job and then some, but she truly understood.

She came off of the door, cracked her neck from one side to the next and headed into the kitchen. It was still morning hours, but she needed to get a head start preparing his lunch and dinner for later because there was no telling when she would be pulled away from her house duties to be Sleepy's consoler.

***

Samiyah stared blankly at the building she sat parked in front of on Haynes Blvd. She was too nauseous to move. Every time she attempted to place one foot outside of her car, she felt another vomitus tantrum come upon her. She was too nervous to move forward with her plans, but she couldn't procrastinate any longer.

Frozen with fear, she regretted declining Elias' offer to hold her hand, at least to the front door. But it was too late to call him now because under her stupid persistence, she encouraged him to do something unforgettable for La'Tasha, so he was busy.

Now or never, she reminded herself.

She eased out of her car and her stomach churned. She closed the door and she felt a stronger rumble. She took one step and a dynamism so desperate to pour from an opening rose to her esophagus. The urge forced her to run to the side of the building. With both hands holding her locs behind her neck, she threw up.

Once she was done ripping her gastric lining, she wiped her mouth with the back of her hand.

"I can't do this," she tearfully admitted.

Samiyah had a change of heart. She was just going to have to explain to Elias that she lost her nerve to do it. He'd understand. He always did.

While reaching for her door handle, she saw a growing reflection in her tinted window that made her turn around abruptly.

"Gerran!" She sharply called his name.

"I saw you from out my window. What are you doing showing up at my studio?" He didn't look or sound too happy seeing her.

She rolled her tongue around in her mouth as if it could help it become untied. "Ummm. I wanted to—ummm," she took a mini inhale/exhale, "talk to you about something." Samiyah paused dramatically.

Gerran looked up at the sky, then down to the ground before looking back to her. "Talk to me about what?" He grew incredibly aggravated in such a short period of time.

She hesitated to speak, she was genuinely scared.

"What is it, Samiyah?" His voice thundered loudly, scaring a response out of her quickly.

"I'm pregnant!"

Chapter 22

"You're what?" Gerran's mouth dropped.

"Pregnant." She repeated herself without reluctance.

Gerran shook his head in disbelief. "Whoa. Whoa." He extended his arms and shook both hands rapidly. "You tryna say it's mine?"

Samiyah snapped her neck and looked at him sideways. "Yes! I am!"

He chuckled so heartedly she could see his Adam's apple elevator up and then down his throat. Then he stopped short of his laughter as if he couldn't find any more amusement in it. "Dude not claiming the baby, so you try your luck with me? Sad, Samiyah, just sad."

Angry tears began to slide down her face, then in a split second her annoyance turned physical. She lunged forward, aggressively pushing him in his chest with both hands. "Fuck you, Gerran!" She shoved him again. "Fuck you!" She roared. "I'm six weeks you cold-blooded bastard. Do the math!" She yelled.

Samiyah stormed the few feet over to her car and slammed the door shut once she was inside. Gerran walked over to the driver's side. Her news took him by storm, but he didn't expect her to suddenly leave because of his shock reaction to it. He waved his hand toward him. "Step out, Samiyah."

His voice was muffled, but she heard what he said. Had he not been so hateful, Samiyah would had been willing to stay, but instead she wiped her eyes, started her engine and peeled out of his driveway.

***

Minnie was one block away from her house, returning from the grocery store when she heard the police sirens behind her. She wasn't sure if the obnoxious sound was meant for her to pull over until she looked into her rearview mirror and saw the cruiser on her bumper.

She pulled over on the curb and the police officer did the same. With his lights flashing, he stepped out of his car and walked over to hers. Stopping first to check the tags on her vehicle before he motioned for her to roll down the window.

"How are you doing, ma'am?"

"I'm fine. Mind telling me why you're stopping me, officer?"

"You did a rolling stop at the four way on Moss and Dumaine St." He pointed behind himself. "I'm gonna need to see your license, insurance, and registration, please."

"Sure." She pulled out her ID and then looked into the console for the papers he requested. She assumed they would be there, but they weren't. She looked to the only other place it would be and discovered it was locked. She turned to the policeman. "I'm cutting off the engine to use my key to unlock the glove compartment, okay?"

He nodded his head and continued peering inside of the vehicle as she did so. Her eyes drew inward as she pulled out the information he needed. She handed it to him and watched him through the side mirror as he walked back to his car. As he ran her name, she refocused her attention to the phone she found amongst G'Corey's things.

It looked just like his phone, but she knew for a fact it wasn't because his was on the nightstand, charging. An eerie feeling grabbed at her gut. It was the same one she denied feeling several times in her past. *Intuition.*

The cellular began lighting up with an incoming call. She stared at the number, but didn't recognize it.

"Answer it!" Her gut shouted.

"No! Don't!" Her fear spoke louder.

The two inner voices went back and forth until the phone stopped ringing.

"Stupid! Her gut was furious.

"Don't listen to her," Fear comforted. *"Ignorance is bliss, remember? Aren't you happy with things the way they are? Don't ruin that."*

"Here you go, ma'am." The police officer startled her while handing her *her* things. While looking down, he continued, "I'm gonna have to write you a ticket *blah, blah, blah.*" His words trailed off into the land of babble. "Ma'am, are you okay?" He asked when he noticed the dry look of worry on her face. Minnie remained silent. He assumed it was the ticket that disturbed her. "This is not an admission of guilt. Sign her and you can be on your way."

She did as she was instructed.

"Have a nice day." The officer departed from her.

Minnie looked back to the silent phone light up again. It was the same number.

"*Don't do it, Minnie,*" Fear spoke.

Her gut didn't have to speak this time because it willed her to press the answer button.

"*Good girl.*" Her gut was satisfied.

Minnie's heart was racing. She wasn't sure why, but it was. The caller didn't say anything, but neither did she. A few seconds more of white noise transmitted between them until *she* said something.

"Hello? G'Corey?" She held the line waiting for him to respond. "You've been blowing me up and now that I'm ready to talk, you say nothing?" She waited a second more, then repeated his name again before she hung up.

Minnie closed the phone and it lite up again. Her nerves began crawling up her skin. She pondered on the familiar voice until it registered who the attitude on the other line belonged to.

"Tracie?"

Minnie was perplexed. Why would *she* be calling her husband? Why would *her* husband be calling her? Why was there another phone?

Her windpipe began to narrow, making it harder to breathe. However, her instincts told her she had to delve a little deeper.

As fear washed over her, she did just that. Minnie looked in the contacts, but there wasn't one single name stored. She then went to the text message icon. There were over one thousand messages between the in and outbox. Her heart stopped beating inside of her chest for a split second, but she continued.

Minnie's eyes grew out of her head and her mouth dropped as she read the first outgoing message.

"Oh, my God!"

***

You've reached Minnie Daniels and I'm unavailable to answer your call. Please leave me a message and I will call you back as soon as I can. Beep.

"Girl, I have called you boo-coo times. Where you at? Listen, call me when you get this, please."

Samiyah hung up the phone as she pulled up to her parents' home in Gentilly. She didn't see her father's car which was perfect. Although she was Daddy's little girl, she needed her mama.

She pulled out their house key and opened the door. "Maaaa," she called out.

Puffy, her mother's Persian cat, greeted her at the front door rubbing her white coat against her leg. Samiyah stooped down to pick her up. "Where's mama, Puff?"

"Right here," Ms. Mary appeared out of thin air. Samiyah placed Puffy down and walked into her mom's arms. "What's the matter, baby?"

She blew out a hard breath before she considered how she would tell her what was going on. "Have a seat with me, mama."

Mother and daughter walked into the living room and took a seat on her olive green microfiber sofa. Ms. Mary looked at her silently as she waited on Samiyah to speak.

"Ma, I'm pregnant."

Ms. Mary lips curved upward. "Are you happy or sad about that?"

"I don't know. On one hand I'm thrilled to be expecting again, but then on the other hand because of my situation I don't know if I should be excited about it. Plus, I told Gerran about the baby shortly before I came over here and he did everything but flat out call me a slut."

Ms. Mary rubbed Samiyah's thigh in a consoling circular motion. "He's denying fathering this baby?"

Samiyah's lips trembled too badly to open and respond, so she shook her head *yes*.

"Humph. I don't condone Gerran's rude behavior toward you, but he's still hurting from y'all breakup and considering the way things ended he probably feels suspicious."

"I hear you, Ma, but if you could have seen the way he looked at me." She shook her head. "I regret telling him anything."

Ms. Mary paused for a moment and then spoke again. "Don't get offended, baby. But how do you know this is *his* child?"

Without hesitation, Samiyah answered straight forward. "Cedric can't have children. He had a vasectomy two years ago." Samiyah looked into her mother's face and proceeded to answer the unasked question. "He had a one year old that died in a car accident. As a result, he became very depressed and even contemplated taking his own life. But with much time, he decided to just eliminate the possibility of ever feeling that level of pain again, thus he had the surgery."

"Oh," was her only response.

They sat in silence for a few minutes until Samiyah asked a rhetorical question. "Mama, what am I gonna do?" She poked out her lip and folded her arms against her chest.

"You're not alone," she reassured. "You know you are always welcome to come back home. Your father and I would love to have you here. Plus, we can help you raise this little bambino." She rubbed Samiyah's flat stomach.

"Ma, I don't know about—" Samiyah's text message alert sounded cutting her off in mid-sentence. "Hold on, Ma."

Elias: 3:41PM: How things go with ya boy?
Samiyah: 3:42PM: They didn't. He's a jerk!!
Elias: 3:45PM: You gon be straight?
Samiyah: 3:46PM: Got no choice.
Elias: 3:50PM: Don't stress shit. It's his loss.
Samiyah: 3:53PM: Ok and thanks. Love you.
Elias: 3:57PM: Love you too, ya dig.

Samiyah put her phone on the coffee table and resumed her statement. "I don't know about having this baby. I'm considering an abortion."

Coffee

Chapter 23

It took Minnie three hours, but she finally finished reading every single text message and viewed every scandalous picture and sexually explicit video he'd sent and received.

Either he was an idiot for keeping a trail or he felt I was the bigger fool, Minnie thought.

Dried tears stained her face as she sat parked in the same area where she was stopped by the police. She wanted to scream and start a riot, but she couldn't utter a sound. She felt numb.

Then her mind recollected every single person who'd forewarned her about G'Corey, and she heard them all chorus in unison, *I told you so!*

Minnie was beyond mortified. She clamped her eyes shut and shook her head side to side, but no matter how many times she stopped and opened them, she was still in the Twilight Zone.

She had no clue what to do, what to say, how to feel, but she knew she couldn't stay there isolated in his vehicle. But the level of anger she was feeling both paralyzed and scared the hell out of her.

Then Minnie snapped! She envisioned herself taking advantage of his weakened, sickly state and smothering him with the pillows she fluffed for his comfort right before she left. Perhaps, shoot him in his cheating dick with the .45 he kept locked away for protection and let him bleed out. Then another sinister thought came to her mind.

The Burning Bed, she thought of the movie based off of a true story of a battered woman's last resort. *I can set him on fire!*

The idea set well with her as she found the strength to turn the key in the ignition and drive to their house built on lies.

Minnie was happy her drive was short because her vision became crossed. She was that discombobulated. Seconds later, she pulled up in front of her door. She exited his vehicle barely closing its door.

Her hand trembled as she clutched the knob tightly to steady her intense body vibration. She managed to get the key inside of the groove after the third attempt. Once inside, she felt lightheaded and nauseous and the closer she came to their bedroom was the more her anxiety grew.

G'Corey remained asleep. Peacefully. Unaware that shit was about to get real. She looked at him contemptuously. She wanted to spit in his face and then slap the shit out of him before asking him a train of questions beginning with the words, *how could you?*

But she dared not to. Out of the two faces he wore, neither were going to be real.

Minnie's whole body shivered the longer she stared at him. He created a fool's paradise for her and she was none the wiser.

Was it all pretend? Why lie to me? What did I do to deserve all of this? Did you ever love me, G'Corey? She questioned.

Her angry inner voice answered. *You know that answer, Minnie. He couldn't have loved you because if he did, he wouldn't have fucked soooo many women including your best friend! And let's not forget about Tracie. The woman who begged him to come home to her and their unborn. Quit trying to reason this muthafucka's action and just handle your business. Take control of your life by taking his! Piece of shit don't deserve to breathe. Burning Bed. Burn that bed!*

Minnie unglued her feet and headed into the kitchen. There, they kept plenty lighter fluid for when the urge to grill was upon them. She grabbed both bottles and headed back into the bedroom where G'Corey lay undisturbed. She began dousing the entire bed with the liquid accelerant and suppressed her cries in the process.

After she emptied both containers, she fell against the wall and covered her mouth to muffle the wails of her wounded heart.

Don't second guess yourself, Minnie. You can do this. For every night he told you he was thinking of you, but really was sexing those countless cunts. Strike the match for that. He could have given you AIDS. He wasn't thinking 'bout us. Don't think about him. One toss and then walk out this bitch! Her angry inner voice was ruthless. She never heard from her until today, but she made plenty of sense.

Minnie came off of the wall and grabbed the box of kitchen matches that lay next to the candles on the nightstand.

Her body shook and her heart raced with the speed of an African Olympic track star. She was nervous but more pissed off. As sweat accumulated on her top lip, she struck the deadly match.

She may have been blinded by love before, but now she was blinded by rage.

***

Elias was slouched in his recliner in his bedroom watching an episode of What's Happening when he damn near jumped out of skin at the sound of the doorbell. It wasn't that he didn't expect company, his nerves just got the better of him because tonight was going to be unlike any other night.

He grabbed the remote and cut the television off. He stood to his feet, walked over to his dresser and leaned into the mirror. He onced over himself to ensure that he was looking extra debonair. Elias slapped his hands together and rubbed them slowly, signifying his own approval. *Damn, I never met a mirror I didn't like,* he smiled.

La'Tasha rang the doorbell again. He pepped up his step, spot checking things around the house as he picked up the stereo remote control and pressed play. Eli had the mix discs he picked up from the CD man in all five of the spindles to ensure nonstop mellow moods.

He swiped the flower arrangement off of the table. He was now set to answer the door and welcome La'Tasha into el casa de la Eli.

When Elias opened the door, he had the dozen of long stem roses held directly in front of him. La'Tasha smiled as she leaned forward to smell them.

Her brows went inward slightly. He never bought her flowers before, but she kindly accepted them with a smile. "They're beautiful."

He went in to kiss her, "So are you." He bobbed his head to further emphasize his appreciation. Wearing a red, turtleneck, form fitting mid-thigh dress with a pair of thigh high five inch boots, La'Tasha looked like red hot desire. "Come in," he escorted her inside.

La'Tasha noticed the transformation of his living room the moment she stepped inside. There were lit candles everywhere producing the sweetest tropical scents. It was truly a romantic sight to behold and considering it was Valentine's Day she expected nothing short of what she saw.

"Impressive," she commented, sitting her flowers on the table. Considering Eli's borderline misogynistic ways, she was pleased to see another side of him.

Eli poured her a glass of room temperature red wine and himself a shot of Crown. She stood in the middle of the living room swaying to Dru Hill's *So Special* when he handed her *her* drink. He wrapped an arm around her waist and she curled her arm around his. "Here's to a great evening." He raised his glass.

She clinked her glass against his. "Cheers." She sipped and savored the robust flavor of the Chilean Cabernet Sauvignon.

Still in his hold, he rocked her body to the symphony of melodies coming from his surround sound. La'Tasha swayed sensually to the beat. Eli rocked up almost instantly and she smiled a smile of satisfaction because of it.

Once the song concluded, he took her by the hand and led her into the dining room off of the living room where he had two places set for the candlelight dinner he prepared. She stopped at the seat reserved for her, but he in turn headed in the kitchen.

La'Tasha stopped him in his tracks. "Ummm, aren't you forgetting something?" She pointed to her chair.

"Fo'sho," he clapped his hands once and rushed over to her to pull out her seat. "Be right back," he said once he finished his gentlemen thing.

Eli was feeling pretty good about how the evening was going so far. Over the past few weeks, little by little, he was showing more interest in La'Tasha and he believed she was equally feeling him too. So, tonight he was going to cast his net and see what returned.

The dish he made was simple, but he wasn't sweating that. He was doing some Ohio Players' shit and it was bound to blow her mind. With an extra boost of confidence, he walked back to where La'Tasha sat looking radiant under the glow of the soft flame.

He served her *her* plate first. Once the good china touched his solid wood table, she covered her giggle with her hand.

"What?" He questioned seriously.

"I'm sorry. I'm sorry." She laughed harder. "This is something else," she pointed at dinner.

Eli had to laugh too. "Yea. I tried to be classy and make some spaghetti and meatballs, but I fucked it up. So, I cooked what I knew, ya heard me."

"You good. I don't cook at all, so you did one better than me." She threw one leg over the other, placed her napkin on her thigh and picked up his go to meal, el taco. La'Tasha took her fist bite still with a little chuckle in her system.

After they finished their meal, Eli took a page from Dave Hollister's *Take Care of Home* track and retreated into his bedroom, leaving her at the table for a moment

Moments later, he called for her to come to him. She delayed getting up as she processed where things were heading, but after he called her name a second time, she rose from her seat. As she turned down the hall leading to his room, she noticed a trail of roses directing her to him.

The petal path led all the way into a bubble bath filled with more flowers. The bathroom was a replica of the rest of the house. Candles galore were lit and the same wonderful fragrance potently filled the air. She stopped right at the bathroom door.

"Come here." Elias waved her in. He sat on the edge of the tub with his long sleeves rolled up over his elbows.

The short strut to make it over to him was sexy as hell and Elias licked his lips once she stood directly in front of him. La'Tasha rested a hand on his shoulder and he placed his hands on the dips of her coke bottle shape.

Without instruction, she unzipped her boots and stepped out of them. Eli rose to his feet and pulled her dress over her head, then removed her bra and panties. Her chocolate skin looked so damn divine.

He guided her into the tub, giving her a neck rolling sponge bath experience. After twenty minutes of aquatic pampering, he assisted her to her feet. Eli kneeled before her and towel dried her body, starting with her feet and working his way upward.

Elias knew La'Tasha was shedding her hard exterior under the heat of his attentive touches. So, he upped the ante. He kissed a pattern up her legs and over her thighs, coming close to her pearly gates but stopping short of it. He never ate pussy and as much as she wanted to feel his tongue, it wasn't in his foreseeable future.

He lifted La'Tasha up and held her under her tear drop as he carried her a few feet into his room, sitting her on his bed. She was ready for the business. It was evident from the arch in her back, the hardening of her nipples, and the intoxicating look on her face.

Elias wanted to go through with the rest of the wine and dine extravaganza, but her body was calling too strongly for him not to answer.

When she saw him tear out of his clothes hurriedly with the speed of a Tasmanian devil, she literally applauded. She couldn't wait to fuck, and he couldn't wait to love her down.

***

G'Corey woke up in a panic to an alarming smell of gasoline. Although he was still weak, he willed his body to sit up. When he looked around the room, his eyes settled on the gumbo sized pot of grits in the bed next to him with a handwritten note on loose leaf paper lying beside it.

There's more than one way to burn a man!

What the fuck? He questioned.

"Minnie!" He rose from beneath the soaked covers and stumbled through the house, using the wall as a crutch to guide his walk. "Minnie!" He called with more worry than the last time, but there was dead silence in the Daniels' home.

After thoroughly looking inside, he checked the back yard and the shed. No Minnie. He walked alongside the side of the house through the alley leading out to their street where he noticed her car was gone.

G'Corey was puzzled until it dawned on him what was happening. The gas was an attempt to take him out, but she obviously couldn't go through with it. The grits was the Al Green warning. And her disappearance was the nail in the coffin. His wife knew something, but how and how much?

G'Corey fought the urge to collapse where he stood and rushed back inside. He picked up his cell phone and dialed hers. After eleven straight unanswered calls, he threw on some sweats, a hoodie, and a pair of tennis.

"Fuck!" His echo carried throughout the empty house.

What do you know, Minnie? He became apprehensive.

G'Corey stuffed his phone and wallet into his pocket and headed to the tray where his keys lay, but he couldn't find them.

Shit! Where yo keys at?

Unable to find them, he immediately went for his spare keys in the sock drawer. He clutched them tightly and headed out. Once outside, he went to unlock his car door, but it was already opened. He looked both ways down his block before he cautiously got inside. There, he discovered his original set of keys still lodged in the ignition. He turned on the overhead light and saw the glove compartment door was left opened as well.

"Fuck!" He rummaged through the junk that clustered the tiny space and, trying to locate his second line. But it wasn't there. At that point he knew the jig was up. His wife knew everything!

Coffee

Chapter 24

It was 9:46 p.m. when Minnie checked into the Omni Royal Crescent on Gravier St. As she reached her room's door, the burden of the day unloaded on her shoulders. She leaned her forehead against the door and began crying as she slid her key card into the slot to enter.

Walking inside, she allowed the weight of the door to close itself as she made her way to the bed to have a seat.

Her phone had been ringing off the hook. Call after call, she knew it was G'Corey based on his assigned ringtone, *Ain't Nothing Like The Real Thing* by Marvin Gaye and Tammi Terell.

Humph. What a joke, she thought.

Minutes later, she heard Samiyah's ringtone. She answered.

"Hello," Minnie's voice was dry sounding.

"I'm here. What room are you in?" Samiyah rushed her words as she stood impatiently at the elevator.

"812."

"On my way." Samiyah hung up the phone. Moments later, she was peevishly knocking at the door. She was upset that Minnie carried the devastating news of G'Corey's mischievous deeds all day up until half an hour ago. There was no way she should have dealt with that alone.

With little energy, Minnie walked over to the door and pulled the lever downward causing it to open. No sooner than Samiyah saw her disheveled looking friend, she leaped inside and wrapped her arms around her.

Minnie began to talk but her words came out in mumbles as she choked on them. "Shhh, don't talk. Just cry and let it out," Samiyah held her tightly in a protective manner.

After minutes of silent consoling, Samiyah walked Minnie over to the sofa where they both took a seat. Minnie was still enwrapped in her arm as her tears continued to flow.

Samiyah rocked her the way a mother would, the way her mother just had when her cell phone rang. Still holding Minnie with one arm, she retrieved her phone out of her purse. "Oh, that's Acacia," she acknowledged. "I'll call her back."

"No. Answer it. That way I don't have to repeat myself," Minnie suggested.

"Okay." Samiyah pressed the talk button. "Hey, Acacia. I'm with Minnie and I have you on speaker. Some really bad shit happened today and Minnie is gonna talk about it," Samiyah said all in one breath before Acacia could speak.

Judging from Samiyah's tone, Acacia knew whatever bomb Minnie was going to drop had to be epic, so she responded with a simple, "Okay."

Minnie spoke for a very long time uninterrupted by either friend. After divulging her husband's nasty little secrets, she went on to confirm that their suspicions about Kawanna were true. Her blood boiled when she relived the earlier scene when she showed up unannounced at her house.

Minnie knocked on Kawanna's door for what seemed like forever. She didn't bother calling beforehand because she didn't want the venom in her heart revealing itself through her tone.

Minnie's fury was impregnated with hurt and devastation. What her husband did was inexcusable and she had every intention on dealing with him and hurting him the hardest, but she was her best friend and women were supposed to live by a sisterhood that no man can come between.

Eventually, Kawanna sprung up out of her bed when she registered the knocks at the door was real and not a part of her dream. She lazily looked through the peep hole. Minnie's head was bowed, but she recognized her no matter her position. Although she was surprised she was at her house, she was okay with it. She had been meaning to call her because she needed to explain the reasons she had been dodging her for the last two months.

Finally, Kawanna opened the door with warmth in her voice. "Hey, Minnie. Come on in—"

Whop!

Minnie punched her in the center of her face with a strong left jab, causing Kawanna to stagger backwards. Reflexes caused Kawanna to cover her broken, bloody nose.

"What the hell is wrong with you?" Kawanna blared from under the cup of her hand.

Minnie walked inside and closed the door behind her. "No!" Minnie shouted. "What's wrong with you? Sleeping with my husband. Have you lost your damn mind?"

Kawanna's eyes already teared up from the death blow Minnie delivered, but now they began to fall when she heard the cat was out of the bag. She hesitated to speak at first until Minnie charged her with a raised fist prepared to show her what two years of trained boxing could do an opponent.

"Alright," Kawanna waved her hands as she coward backwards into the living room. Minnie followed her further inside.

Kawanna was unaware of how much she knew, but it was already her plan to have a sit down with Minnie about the relationship that turned into an affair. Her continued counseling convicted her heart and she couldn't go on carrying the deceit. And although she wished she could have disclosed the sorted particulars under better terms, the outcome would still be ugly. So, Kawanna simply let it rip.

By the time Kawanna finished telling every single immoral detail, Minnie couldn't do anything except give way to her weak stomach and knees and plop down on the sofa she stood directly in front of.

Kawanna stood furthest away from Minnie. She needed comfortable distance between them just in case she decided to go psycho.

With bloodshot eyes, Minnie looked up. "Why didn't you tell me when you found out we were dating the same man?"

Kawanna didn't have an answer. She hunched her shoulders, childlike. "I don't know, Minnie." She wiped the tears from her face with the palms of her hands. "It was stupid of me and I wish I could take it all back, I swear. Please say you forgive me."

It all sounded like words to her. The same no weight carrying words G'Corey spoke day in and day out. Minnie stood to her feet and projected a cold glare toward the frenemy she now knew her to be. "Ask God for His forgiveness 'cause you won't get mine."

"And that was everything," Minnie concluded, throwing her head back as fresh tears streamed out of the corners of her eyes.

"I'll be a muthafucka," Samiyah grimaced. "G'Corey saw fit to play the game *that* raw? Been fucking Kawanna…"

"That bitch! Call her by *that* name." Acacia interjected to correct her.

Samiyah resumed, "…and countless other hoes but to top it off, Tracie's pregnant too?" She was so heated she had to stand directly by the air conditioning unit along the wall of the suite.

"Uhn. Uhn." Acacia took the floor. "You didn't want to go through with setting that ass on fire, I get that. But he needs to suffer. You should go home right now, make him think everything is sweet and cut his muthafuckin' dick off, then slap him with it."

Samiyah twisted her face as she heard Acacia speak sadistically.

Acacia continued, "All you have to do is soak a razor in vinegar for half an hour and he won't know you're slicing him up until it's over."

Minnie shook her head, giving no response.

Samiyah walked back over to her phone so Acacia could hear her question clearly. "Have you done that before?"

"No. I've never, but I swear I would," she affirmed.

Minnie chuckled sarcastically before her face went solemn. "I had no idea my 'together forevers' had an expiration date. This is so messed up." She stared into nothingness as she shook her head and gnawed at her nails, something she hadn't done in several years. "I don't have to inflict no physical harm on him, Acacia. He will get his. Karma will see to that!"

"Karma?" Acacia blurted the word like it tasted terrible. "Karma takes too long. I prefer my plan. It comes much sooner."

"Chill, Rambo. Damn! G'Corey isn't hittin' on shit right now, but that's still her husband. Have some type of compassion for what she going through. Shit is fresh," Samiyah spoke to the black widow spider in Acacia.

"Okay. Okay, I'm sorry, but just in case you change your mind. I have two cousins who can come in from out of town, fuck him up and be home in time for dinner. I'm just saying."

Samiyah shook her head. Finding Acacia's off switch was harder than diffusing a very sophisticated bomb at times.

Acacia pulled her ear away from the phone momentarily and then she returned. "Minnie, I hear Sleepy calling me. I gotta tend to him. I'll call you mañana?"

"That's fine," Minnie responded.

"I love you, girl. We will get through this, together." Acacia softened her tone.

"I love you, too." Minnie's voice crackled.

"Talk to you later, Acacia," Samiyah said before she terminated the call.

Minnie rubbed her temples, attempting to ease the looming headache. "I'm exhausted," she acknowledged.

"You should be. Come get in bed." Samiyah pulled back the covers.

Minnie didn't object. She dragged her worn out body over to the bed and climbed in. The blow to the heart and the baby she was carrying required that she rest.

Samiyah looked at the time. It was after one o'clock a.m. Gerran didn't bother calling her since she left him earlier that afternoon. *Go figure*, she thought. Samiyah kicked off her shoes and got under the covers with Minnie.

Minnie looked over her shoulder when she felt Samiyah get in. "You're staying with *me*?"

"Of course. I'm not leaving you alone."

Minnie reached for Samiyah's hand and gripped it tightly. Choked up on emotions she muttered, "Thank you."

"None needed. That's what friends are for," she reminded.

***

It was after three a.m. when G'Corey pulled up to his house and discovered his wife's usual parking space was still empty. He had combed the city for hours in search of any place she might be which were few considering her limited circle.

When G'Corey started his manhunt, his first stop was Kawanna's. There was no way Minnie could have known to search for a phone had that bitter broad not open her big ass mouth. But she wasn't at home when he arrived and that boggled him because she was always at the house.

G'Corey then went on to stalk outside of Minnie's parents' home hoping to see her pull up, but she never showed. He passed over by Acacia's. Nothing. Although G'Corey knew that Tracie hadn't been home in several weeks, desperation had him try her house too. It frustrated him to no end that he had no clue where Elias lived which would assuredly lead him to Samiyah's, Minnie's most likely choice. He was losing his mind because he had turned over every stone only to come up empty.

But then G'Corey had the gumption to check their bank statement by phone to see if that would provide a trail for him to go down. He discovered there was a pending charge on her debit card for a hotel out in Baton Rouge. With a glimmer of hope, he traveled the hour long ride.

Once G'Corey arrived at the Marriott, he personally walked the parking lot looking for her car. He even looked at the neighboring lots to see if perhaps she was slick about covering her tracks, but he came up with nothing.

"Fuck!" G'Corey yelled. He stared between his house and the dark of night through his windshield, wondering where the hell his wife was and what condition he would find her in once they reunited.

He peeled himself out of the car and dragged himself inside. Physically, he was void of energy, but his mind was restless. G'Corey resorted to the only thing he could think to do at that point. Dial Minnie's number relentlessly with the hopes she'd answer at least one of his calls.

Chapter 25

Between Minnie's tossing and turning coupled with her unconscious crying bouts plus Samiyah's own constant runs to the bathroom, it was impossible for Samiyah to sleep, thus she was forced to think. Think about how one day she was riding the stairway to heaven and the next she was on a highway to hell.

Samiyah got out of the bed. She opened the curtains and looked at the five a.m. view of downtown New Orleans.

When did life get so damn complicated? She had yet to figure that out.

On top of needing to make her degree in journalism make money so she can become financially stable, move out of Eli's house and start anew, she now was faced with going through with an abortion she didn't believe in or an adoption she wasn't sure she could follow through with.

She heavily exhaled. After losing her apartment and everything in it, one love of six years and another of one year, depleting her savings account to maintain necessities, and now carrying a baby for a man who denied the possibilities, at the least, that her child could be his baby made her wonder. *Does God have favorites?*

She walked over to her purse and retrieved her phone she powered off earlier once she saw Gerran was determined not to call.

The instant her phone restored itself, her notifications bar read she had two unheard voicemail messages.

Gerran: 1:41AM: You sending me to your voicemail, nah? Call me.

Gerran: 1:54AM: You tryna test me? See what I would do if you told me you were pregnant? And now you got the satisfaction of knowing I called, so you don't answer. {Gerran laughed} I see how you do, but look here, we still need to talk because if this pregnancy is real I need to know what you gon' do. And don't talk about if you're lying. {Gerran dropped the phone accidently and then picked it back up} If you're lying, there will be... End of call, the recorded operator said.

"Oh, *helllll* no! I'm not calling you back," Samiyah spoke below a whisper after hearing his messages. Ever since the day of Armageddon between Gerran and Cedric, he had treated Samiyah with the same courtesy he would his enemy. She wasn't in the mood to deal with his shit on top of her own.

Let him think what he wants about this pregnancy. I'm too drained to give a fuck.

Thinking about the little episode cured her need to talk to anyone. She silenced her phone this time and retired back to bed. She decided to see what would happen if she woke up again and tried her day over.

***

"Ummm." La'Tasha lifted her head off of the pillow and opened one eye just enough to see the time on the digital clock. It was 7:36AM. It wasn't her plan to stay the night, but it was something about the way the L went down last night that knocked her out cold. Feeling the aftermath of their greatest sex yet had her feeling higher than any drug.

Resting her head back against the pillow, she spiritedly stretched her arms and scissor kicked the sheets. She felt giddily good. So damn good because she could still feel Elias inside of her.

"Ooooh," she moaned. La'Tasha squeezed her legs together and ran her fingers over her thumping clit while the other hand traveled up her tightened stomach, over her plump breasts, and onto her neck. Then she stopped her sensual trace up her body abruptly. "What?" Her eyes shot open. She patted her neck and felt a necklace. It wouldn't have surprised her had it been hers, but this was clearly a gift from Eli.

She threw the covers back and rushed over to the mirror to examine it. The thin platinum necklace was beautiful and the diamond interlocking heart that rested in the middle was breathtaking. It took her breath away for sure.

Elias entered the room shirtless, wearing a pair of jogging pants, showing off what a strict upper body workout did for a brother. "You like it?" He smiled.

"Wooo," La'Tasha jumped, clutching her chest. "You startled me."

Elias chuckled, "My bad." He walked up on her and looked at her stand before him almost like she was uncomfortable about something. "You a'ight?" He placed a hand on her elbow.

She moved slightly away and nervously chuckled. "I'm good," she lied. Truth was she wasn't. She felt like the closeness they'd developed more so over the last couple of weeks were coming to bite her in the ass.

"You blingin', lil' mama. You like it?" he asked again since she didn't answer the first time.

"Oh—yea," she spoke truthfully. Elias' expensive taste was on point. It was the symbolism behind it that shook her up.

"Good." He prided himself on picking out a dope piece. He walked over to the bed and threw the covers back. "Did you see the card I left on the bed for you?"

Holy fuck! she thought. "Ah, oh, ummm." She began to fidget, rubbing her hand up the nape of her neck.

"Got it." He held the sealed card in his hand. "Read it." He passed it to her.

"Ummm, I don't think so, Eli." She tried to decline him gently.

Misreading her discomfort for being bashful, he pushed it into chest. "Read the damn thing, girl."

She clasped the envelope against her bosom and blew out long and hard like the task was a tedious one. La'Tasha opened it, then her eyes swept back and forth over each Hallmark word.

Goddamit, Eli. You just couldn't leave it at last night, could you? Fuck! she thought.

Elias was all teeth. Something the player in him would never do. He rocked his head side to side a little as he attempted to read her expression. Then his smile decreased in size. He knew she was finished reading, the card and the question he proposed weren't that long.

"Cat gotcha tongue?" He became nervous suddenly. "What's good?"

There was a side of her that imagined being boo'd up with Eli. Looking back at the question he wrote in her card, *Can we make this official?* made her want to say *yes* just because he was so adorable. Plus, she knew how hard it was for a prideful man like him to take a chance asking a girl like her to go steady. But what remained true despite his wonderful efforts was *he* fell in love, and she most definitely hadn't.

La'Tasha's face turned stone, she needed her actions to clearly communicate what was taking place so there would be no misunderstandings. She put the card down on the dresser and walked past him like he didn't just ask her a question, like he wasn't even standing there. La'Tasha began putting on her dress minus her underwear, she threw them in her purse.

Elias turned to face her, his arms folded across his chest with his hands latched underneath his armpits to secure the hold. His eyebrows drew inward, his eyes tightened, and his lips curled because she was telling him *fuck you* loudly in silence.

With a little struggle, she managed to unclaspe the diamond necklace and extended it to him, but he didn't reach for it. So, she dropped it at his feet. She turned around to walk out of his room, but Eli grabbed at her arm and jerked her as he spun her back toward him. He was boiling angry.

"What the fuck is wrong with you?"

The squeeze on her arm felt paralyzing, but she sported her infamous poker face as she pried his fingers off of her. "You caught feelings and you're asking me what's wrong? What? You thought because you did all of this, I was supposed to fall miraculously in love or something? All of it was cute, but—"

"*Cute?*" He bit his lip as she undermined his first attempt to ever show a woman a side he wasn't familiar with himself.

"Yes, cute. But I'm fine without love and as of today, I'll do fine without you, too." La'Tasha picked up her boots and walked out of his room.

Elias was flabbergasted. He literally felt the soul of his player ascend from his body and all that remained was a vulnerable man.

He followed behind La'Tasha and sped walk past her. Arriving at the front door, he widely swung it open. "Hurry the fuck on up out my house." He waved his hand like a traffic cop. La'Tasha heard him, but she first stopped off by the table. Eli frowned as he quickly swooped the flowers she picked up and began spitefully snapping them and mutilating the beautiful bloom. "You ain't taking shit of mine with you when you leave."

She shook her head and grabbed her car keys which were laying underneath the bouquet he thought she was taking. As she walked past him and out onto the porch, Eli was breathing lavatic heat in and out of his flared nostrils. She pressed the alarm button to her car, walking off seemingly unfazed.

Eli was feeling all kinds of fucked up, so her air of nonchalance didn't sit well with him. "Yo! Fuck you, Tasha!" he said passionately. "You didn't deserve shit I did for your funky ass. I wish I could take it back. All of it! Including the nut I gave you, too!"

Elias slammed his door and pounded one fist into the palm of his other hand as he let out a roar of regret. Regret for walking flat footed when he should have remained on his tippy toes.

In a salty mood, Eli turned toward his stereo. He slung those R&B shits out of the carousel and replaced them with N.O.'s late and great Tim Smooth. The moment the beat dropped, he zoned out and as soon as the chorus came on, he rapped along with the track so in the future he'd never forget it again.

You can't trust no hoe/Say what?/ You can't trust no hoe/You can't trust no hoe/You can't trust no hoe/Say what?/After you fuck that hoe, you 'posed to duck that hoe.

With the volume turned up like he was hosting a block party, he walked into his bedroom. He picked up the necklace and placed it in the box, he'd return it later. He looked at the card and felt foolish, so he tore it into shreds. He then reached for his cell phone and deleted her phone number, text messages, and any pictures of her.

He was done!

Coffee

Chapter 26

The smell of authentic Puerto Rican cuisine enticed Sleepy out of the bed and into the kitchen. His mother, Ava, was preparing a feast for the family. She had some Caribbean music playing as she moved her hips to the up tempo beat. At forty-seven years old, she still had the same moves when she was twenty something.

Ava was unaware Sleepy was standing in the doorway watching her groove jovially. He smiled as it brought back good memories from his childhood. Oftentimes, she would have either he or one of his siblings join her in Salsa all the while stirring pots.

He truly missed his mother and he hated that her visit was under such difficult circumstances. She'd been living with them for a month to be a support system, but as of today she would be returning home to New York.

Trying not to let her upcoming departure sour the time he currently had, he pushed those thoughts to back of his mind. "Bueno," Sleepy greeted his mom, hugging her snuggly from behind.

Ava pressed her cheek against his while puckering her lips. "Have a seat. Sit. Sit." She waved for him to immediately relax. "Are you hungry, Papi?"

"For your cooking? Always."

"Ummm, it smells great in here." Acacia walked in on their conversation, inhaling as she patted her rumbling tummy. She kissed Ava on the cheek and then stood behind Sleepy's chair with her arms resting on the back of the seat.

"Ma, in case we haven't said this enough, thank you."

"You don't have to thank me. I'm your mother. What else was I supposed to do?" Ava questioned seriously.

"It's just you stopped everything and came down on short notice. There was no way we were gonna be able to take care of everything by ourselves. That night when Diego—"

"What y'all talking about in here?" Diego appeared seemingly out of thin air. He slow strolled into the kitchen, pulling up a chair and gently taking a seat.

"Nothing much," Sleepy responded. "Thanking Ma for holding things down and helping Acacia out around the house."

"Yea. I'm gonna miss you when you leave, Ava." Acacia sincerely admitted.

Ava rinsed the spice seasonings off of her hands and turned around to face them. "I'm going to miss all of you. It's been so long since we've been able to sit around like family. It does my heart good to see my boys getting along." She walked over to Sleepy and cupped one side of his face. "Giving your brother a kidney to save his life was heroic. Te quiero mucho." She then picked up his hand, brought his knuckles to her lips and kissed them. Looking to Acacia, she smiled graciously. "We've had our differences in the past, but I couldn't be happier knowing my boy is in such good hands."

Diego looked over at his mother shower them with kisses, singing the praises of Saint Peter for Sleepy's nobility. Diego would have thought he was immune to certain jealousies having lived in his brother's shadow all of his life, but seeing his mother do everything but worship at his feet, for giving him a kidney he didn't ask for, almost made his top blow.

Once Ava was through appreciating Sleepy and Acacia, she kneeled down in front of Diego. "Dios mío. Diego, if I would have lost you, I would have died." She began crying into his lap.

Diego stroked her short cropped hair. "Don't cry, Ma. I ain't gone. Your son right here."

She looked up and wiped her flushed rose colored cheeks. "You're right, baby. Thanks to Sleepy you'll be here for many, many years to come."

She stood to hug Diego around the neck. Ava felt his arms wrap around her back, but what she didn't feel was the contempt he felt in his heart for her making Sleepy the centerpiece of everything.

Ava broke her hold and stood between both sons, grabbing their hands and standing them to their feet. "Promise me something." They both nodded their heads for her to go forward in her speech. Ava then joined Sleepy and Diego's hands together. "Promise me you two will never break this bond."

***

"Minnie?" G'Corey hysterically bolted up from his sleep and alarmingly called out her name when he heard a thud. He sprung up from the sofa and swung the front door open. He swiveled his head from side to side, but didn't see her. The sound he heard was the bang of the trashcans Waste Management were dropping alongside the curb. He dropped his head and shook it confusingly so, then he slammed the base of his hand against the frame of the door. "Shit!"

G'Corey turned to go back inside. He had no clue where to look next, but what he knew was he couldn't just sit idly by.

Pondering for a few minutes, he became hopeful and headed into the kitchen. Minnie kept her schedule on the freezer along with her field supervisor's phone numbers.

He snatched the paper from under the magnet and reached into his pocket for his phone. He dialed the number so quickly that he inputted it wrong twice before getting it right.

The phone rang. He tapped his foot intolerantly, waiting for Alverda to answer.

"Ms. Robertson speaking. How can—"

G'Corey didn't have the patience to hear all of that. "This is G'Corey, Minnie's husband."

"Good morning. I know who you—"

"My wife left with both set of car keys. Is she in the office or do you know what site she's at?"

Although G'Corey was sharp in his tone, Alverda remained calm and professional. "Sorry to hear that, sir, but Minnie hasn't come in this morning."

"Wha—what?" He stammered. "She left out this morning dressed for work, but she ain't there?" His voice went in and out of pitch as his emotions escalated.

Alverda shook her head *no*. "I'm afraid not, sir."

"Have you called her phone?" G'Corey grilled.

"Yes, but she didn't answer. Would you—"

G'Corey hung the phone up in her face. He walked into the bedroom and sat on his side of the bed and drank some of the medicine on the nightstand. He was still fighting the flu, but he couldn't afford to lay down like he desperately needed because he had to find his wife and child.

G'Corey looked over to the pot of cold, stiff grits in the bed and he became madder. He couldn't believe he was so close to making things right just for things to go wrong. He picked the pot up to carry it into the kitchen and not be reminded of the state of emergency he was currently in when he saw his second phone lying beside it.

"Son of a bitch!" G'Corey came face to face with the electronic diary of most of his misdoings. He moved the pot over to the dresser and then returned back to her side of the bed where it lay, mocking him for not destroying it when he had the chance.

He swiped the phone, squeezing it tightly as anger surged through his body and into the fingers that were coiled around it. G'Corey wanted to break it as if it would reverse the damage, but that would be futile. He balled his lip as he admonished himself, opening the phone. The battery was dead, so he plugged it into the charger. Once it restored itself, he scanned through it to see exactly what she saw.

It was without a doubt what all Minnie knew because in his sent box were several messages, pictures, and a videos she forwarded to her own phone.

"Muthafucka!" He began bouncing his leg in an antsy kind of fit. His nerves were shot. There was no way in hell she would want him back after all of that. But as sure as his name was G'Corey Arealious Daniels, he was going to get her back!

***

The sound of the hotel's phone ringing woke both Minnie and Samiyah. The clock read: 9:12 a.m. Only one person would be calling her. Minnie had text her second in command, Alverda, in the wee hours of the morning alerting her of what happened and how to reach her. She had to turn off her phone due to G'Corey's insistent calling, but she knew she had to be available for others.

Minnie answered, "Hello."

"Good morning, Minnie. This is Alverda."

"Good morning."

"I'm calling because your husband called here like you said he would." Alverda whispered so others in the office didn't overhear her conversation.

"What happened?" Minnie dispassionately inquired.

"He became irritated with me when he asked questions concerning your whereabouts, but I said nothing."

Minnie pursed her lips. "Good." She held the phone in silence for a moment so she could switch gears and handle business without the drip of negative emotions springing forth. "Well, here's the agenda. I will email the staff instructions they are to follow in my absence. I want you to filter what comes my way and only call me only if it's necessary, but other than that email me daily."

"I'm on top of it." Alverda's smile could be heard through her voice. "One more thing," she rushed. "If you need me for anything, say the word."

"Thank you, but keeping things quiet and telling him nothing is more than enough." Minnie mustered a smile of her own.

They said their goodbyes and ended the call.

"How you feeling this morning?" Samiyah asked the moment Minnie hung up the phone.

"I don't know. I'm so hurt I'm numb." Minnie's face mirrored the void she felt inwardly the instant she realized G'Corey's love was pliable.

Samiyah shook her head. She wanted to give her some type of advice because she too had been cheated on before, but similar shoes still weren't the same fit and since she hadn't traveled Minnie's relationship journey she remained silent.

Samiyah grabbed her phone to time check. She noticed some missed calls and a string of text messages from Gerran. She bypassed those to see the missed calls and one text from Eli.

7:59AM: Elias: This bitch played the fuck out of me. The longer I sit here and think about this shit makes me wanna get at this hoe. Man just come holla at cha boy.

She called him immediately, but he didn't answer. She called back a few times and still no answer. "Fuck!" Samiyah blurted.

"What's wrong?" Minnie snapped out of her woeful trance.

"Eli had been calling me and now he's not answering. I'm worried he's doing something stupid because of what happened with La'Tasha." Samiyah called his phone again.

"What happened between them?"

"No clue. We didn't talk, but based off of this text," Samiyah showed Minnie the message, "it ain't good."

"Go check on Eli. I'll be alright."

Samiyah felt stuck. Neither one of her friends needed to be alone, but she couldn't be in two places at once. "Let me see your phone." She reached out for it.

Minnie handed her *her* cell. "What are you about to do?"

Samiyah went through her contacts and pressed call under his name before she responded. Once the line was ringing, she replied, "I'm calling Yuriah."

"Samiyah. Don't." Minnie stood to her feet to take her phone back but it was too late. She heard Yuriah's deep voice through the tiny cell's speaker.

"Yuri? This is Samiyah. Did I wake you?"

"Nah, you good. Where's Minnie?" He was curious to know why she was calling him from Minnie's phone.

"Next to me. Listen, we are at the Omni because she can't go home."

"*Can't?*" Yuriah repeated and instantly became heated, but his tone didn't betray his inner feelings. "Put her on the phone." He firmly instructed. Whatever he was to find out needed to come from Minnie's mouth.

Samiyah handed her the phone.

"Hello," Minnie answered meekly.

"Tell me what happened—in person. What's your room number?" He spoke tenderly through the masculine strength of his voice.

Minnie paused to answer. She didn't want to see any harm from G'Corey or the police come his way for stepping in. "Yuriah, I don't want you to get involved."

"Too late. Room number?" He was immovable.

"Yuriah—"

"Minyoka!" He spoke in a no nonsense kind of way.

Minnie understood that attempting to reason him at this point wasn't an option. The few people who knew her full name never used it and the only time Yuriah would was when he meant business.

She replied, "Room 812."

"I'm on my way." He hung up the phone.

Minnie dropped her hand holding the cell into her lap and looked toward Samiyah, apprehensively. "It's about to be hell on earth."

Coffee

Chapter 27

An hour later, Samiyah pulled into an empty driveway. Elias' truck wasn't there. Without getting out of her car, she called him again.

"Hello," Elias answered unlike himself.

"Eli! Where are you?" Samiyah borderline screamed at him.

"Be cool. I just turned onto my street. Be there in a hot second."

Samiyah threw her phone on the passenger seat and stood outside of her car. She was so worried that she was pissed. The moment he pulled up behind her, she walked over to still moving vehicle. She was just about ready to chastise him for not picking up her previous calls, but when she saw his face she changed her mind.

"Eli," she called his name softly.

He didn't respond, all he did was wrap his arm around her neck and walked with her indoors. Elias separated himself from her and plopped down on the sofa.

Samiyah sat next to him, looked down at the dismantled flowers on the floor and then stared him in the face trying to piece his puzzling look together. But when she couldn't read him, she simply asked, "What happened?"

Elias folded his leg into the shape of a four and bridged his hands together, resting them at his sternum. He was almost too ashamed to speak of what he'd done, but Samiyah unlike Jacobi would never judge him.

"Long story short, that Cujo bitch turned on me. So, I did a one-eighty myself." Elias frowned.

Samiyah raised an eyebrow. "What did you do?"

Elias unclasped his hands. "A'ight. That lil' mu'fucka called herself blowing me down after I did all that romantic shit for her. You know you don't do no thuggah like that, ya heard me." He shook his head and became upset all over again. "That dog bitch left my crib, no doubt, feeling like the fuckin' man and to see her roll up out this bitch carefree and all did something to my soul. One minute I was in here confused as a muthafucka, questioning myself and then the next I was in front her house."

"Noooo," Samiyah bellowed. She was tripped out. As long as she knew Elias, he had always been too cold to be a hot head. But now the tides had changed, he was on fire.

"Yea, man. I leaned on my horn until that raggedy hoe came outside. I wanted to smash her damn face in, but instead I held up an ice pick and punctured every fuckin' tire on her BMW and scraped those costly rims up something nice."

"What she did?"

"She ain't do shit but clutch her damn pearls and watch from her porch. That was *my* money that had her rolling pretty and I'll be a muthafuck if she ride off in *any* sunsets on my shits. I would have saved myself the trip and done that shit in my driveway, but I didn't want her funky ass stuck over here at my house."

"So, what now?" Samiyah quizzed.

"Ain't shit up nah. I'm back on my *Bitches ain't shit but hoes and tricks* kick. Straight up. I'll never get burned like that again. I promise you that."

"Eli, I'm so sorry, baby. You showed your hand to the wrong player and lost, but I guarantee you *will* win with the right one." She rubbed his arm while looking at him as he looked straight ahead.

"I'm a'ight, yea." Elias gritted, blinking back tears of pisstivity that he would never let fall.

"No you're not," she countered. Samiyah placed a hand on his clenched jaw. "You're not alright and it's okay."

Eli knew he wasn't alright, too. He felt an unfamiliar weight in his chest and heard some very petty voices tell him he needed to fuck with her head since she fucked with his heart.

Elias leaned into the cup of Samiyah's hand. She stoked his low cut Caesar with her other to console him, then she pulled him into her embrace. She tenderly lifted his chin upward, so he would look her in the eye as she gently said, "Fuck her, Eli. If she can't see you, that's her bad."

The emotion in Samiyah's voice was reassuring, but the fire in her eyes was deadly. She was protective over Eli because she knew what others didn't. She was his ride or ride harder chick.

Eli felt like hell, but the lay against her breast was comforting and her skin smelled like Bath & Body Works. He also knew the shortest trip to heaven was the lay between her legs. So, he stretched his neck to kiss her and she obliged.

Their lip caress was soft at first and then it turned fiery.

"Ummm. Ummm." They both moaned as their tongues intertwined.

Elias began palming her breast hungrily and then in a lustful rage, he tore open her button down blouse. Samiyah's head fell back as he eagerly freed her breast from her bra and nursed on her hardening nipple.

"Haa. Haa," she panted.

Eli separated himself from her melons and stood to his feet. Crisscrossing both hands over his torso, he raised his shirt over his head and tossed it. He dropped his jogging pants to the floor, stepping out of them along with his boxers. Samiyah looked on in both admiration and desire. His dick was inflexible. It was as straight as an arrow and all it needed was a target to hit.

Déjà vu. They found themselves in the same space but both needing each other for the same reason *this* time. To feel wanted.

Elias bent down and peeled Samiyah's jeans and panties off. She slouched down on the sofa as he tugged at her pants. Once they were off, he lifted her to her feet and picked her up forcing her legs to coil around his waist.

She rested high above his head, peering down at him. With her arms wrapped around his neck, she dropped her head to kiss him. They had undeniable passion.

"I love you, Eli." She was breathing with anticipation to feel him again.

He supported her with one arm and reached for his throbbing dick and placed it at her wet center. "I love you, too."

Knock! Knock! Knock!

Right before the moment of penetration, both of their necks snapped in the direction of the heavy thud sound.

"Samiyah? Open up. I need to talk to you." His voice boomed from the other side of the door.

They shockingly looked at each other with screwed faces. "Gerran?" they mouthed in unison.

***

Knock! Knock! Knock!

"Minnie, it's me," Yuriah announced from outside of the hotel's door.

Born a Leo, it was his natural instinct to protect the pride and Minnie was definitely a part of his pack. So, it didn't take any convincing to be wherever she was in her time of need.

Minnie opened the door and before he could utter one word, she called out his name in a distressful manner and fell into his arms.

"I got you." Yuriah swallowed her within his embrace. Minnie's chubby stature against his thick, muscular build made her feel small in size and his six foot two inch frame made her a midget in height by comparison. After she released tears she didn't want to shed, Yuriah pulled away and held her at bay. "Tell me what happened."

She walked him over to the bed and she sat down. Yuriah remained standing, sucking in his bottom lip. He did that to refrain from speaking his mind because he already knew her pain had G'Corey written all over it.

Minnie hung her head low, but he lifted it back high. "Don't do that." He shook his head. "You don't have to be embarrassed."

She bobbed her head up and down to acknowledge what he told her. She attempted to open her mouth and tell the nightmarish story, but instead tears formed two perfect streams down her round face. Yuriah headed into the bathroom, retrieved the box of Kleenex hotels customarily placed on the sink for their patrons and sat down beside her, dabbing her face dry.

The longer it took her to speak, the more concerned he was becoming, but Yuriah didn't rush her to talk. He simply massaged her shoulder.

Minutes passed before Minnie was able to finally open up. "G'Corey has had multiple affairs with strange women, some I personally know. He has a baby on the way with Tracie. And he never worked *a* day off shore. Everything I believed was a lie. I had no idea the prince charming *and* villain of my fairytale was the same man. I'm such an idiot." Minnie began sobbing into Yuriah's shoulder.

"Never dat! You just loved the wrong man." Those words were soothing and believable, but the ones he kept imprisoned under his tongue were scorching.

Yuriah was a man of few words by nature, so G'Corey would just have to *feel* his wrath.

Minnie closed her eyes and cried on and on. Her head was hurting, her heart was hurting, and now her stomach was hurting.

Without looking to examine herself, she pulled a pillow from off of the bed and covered her lap. Minnie felt a surge of wetness involuntarily soak between her legs. "Oh, crap. Yuri, look away." She sniffled, groaning from sudden discomfort. "I accidently peed on myself."

Yuriah removed the pillow when he saw twisted agony cover her face. "That's not urine." He withheld his alarm. "You're bleeding. It looks like you might be miscarrying."

***

Gerran waited a minute before he knocked again. "Samiyah! I know you're home. I see your car. Listen, I'm not gonna piss you off. I just want to talk to you."

"It's whatever you want," Eli spoke with her body still suspended in the air.

"I'ma talk to him," she decided.

Samiyah slid down the length of Eli's body slowly, coming into contact with his still very hard muscle. Once her feet were planted on the floor, she scrambled to get her things quietly as Elias put his clothes back on. She retreated upstairs to get dressed while Eli cracked the door open.

"What's up Eli? I need to talk to Samiyah. Can I come in?" Gerran asked.

Elias looked at him with the same displeasure he would a pesky door salesman's. "Nah, you good where you at. She'll be out to holla atchu."

"Dawg, it's like that?" Gerran's face housed a look of confusion.

Elias closed the door and locked it. *That should answer his question.* The way he saw it Gerran had been acting like a broad, so he found no fault in treating him like one.

Five minutes later, Samiyah came downstairs redressed in different clothes. "Where's Gerran? Did he leave?"

"Nah, that buster still on the porch." Elias booted up. Samiyah was about to walk past him and step outside, but Eli stopped her. "Listen, Yah. I don't have nothing against Gerran as long as he stay in line. If he get out of pocket once, leave that muthafucka guessing, ya heard me. You don't have to eat nobody's shit."

Samiyah stared him in the eyes and pressed her hand flatly against his chest and over his beating heart. "ASAP."

"Fo'sho," he responded.

The last time Gerran took the initiative to reach out to Samiyah was Christmas of last year. And the last couple of encounters they've had since then, all ended ugly. She wasn't sure if this visit would be any different, but she was on her way out of the door to find out.

Chapter 28

Yuriah snatched the folded blanket from off of the sofa and wrapped Minnie in it. He scooped her in his arms and rushed out of the room and down the hall, standing in front of the elevator pushing the down button repeatedly.

University Hospital was just minutes away. Yuriah hoped he would be able to get her there in time to spare her at least one heartache.

"Ahhhh," Minnie cried as stronger cramps coursed through her abdomen. Her voice quaked with uncertainty. "Yuri, I'm scared. Am I losing my baby?"

He held her tighter as the doors opened. "Let's hope not."

***

G'Corey had been calling Kawanna all morning, but she hadn't picked up any of his calls. That infuriated him even more because now he was super convinced she was the culprit behind his wife locating his phone. She was dodging his calls which was something she'd never done before. She reeked of guilt in his mind.

He was fuming. A full twenty-four hours had passed and he hadn't heard from Minnie. The blame had to lie with someone and he would be damned if it be him.

He called Kawanna one more time and her pattern remained the same. She was giving him the silent treatment. G'Corey snapped his phone shut. "That bitter bitch!"

He angrily grabbed his keys and his Glock. He wanted to see how quiet she would be when he showed up, putting that thang in her face.

***

"What's dude's problem?" Gerran asked the moment Samiyah stepped outside. "He act like y'all—" Her eyebrows drew inward and she immediately spun on her heels to go back inside. Samiyah was not going to allow Gerran to degrade her. He reached out for her arm. "I'm sorry. I'm sorry."

Samiyah turned to face him. "What do you want, Gerran?" She didn't hide her displeasure through her tone.

He looked at the mix emotions that danced in her eyes. He could tell she was hurt, confused, and fed up. But the fact she was talking to him at all, considering the jerk he had been, spoke volumes. Gerran knew she still loved him and as quiet as it was kept, he still loved her too.

"It's kind of chilly out here. Do you wanna go for a ride and we talk?"

"No." She shook her head.

"How about we sit in my car and I turn the heat on. I know you're cold."

"What *I am* is curious. What do you want?" She grew defensively impatient. "Did you come to remind me that I ain't shit in your book?"

He reached for her hands. "Nothing like that. I came because I wanted to apologize. I've been wrong. I mean, finding out about dude cut me deep and I ain't healed from that, not by a long shot. But since yesterday when you told me you're pregnant and the baby's mine, I couldn't stop thinking about us."

Samiyah saw him soften before her eyes. It had been so long since he had talked to her without a chill in his voice.

"If you're certain this baby is ours, I will find a way to get past the past because *this* will be our future." He unzipped her jacket to press his hand against her stomach.

Samiyah's spent countless nights thinking his hatred would be eternal and they would never be an item again, but there he was making plans.

She lowered and shook her head, closing her eyes to bridge back the tears. She was becoming overwhelmed. First her lips quivered, then her body trembled.

"What's wrong?" He swept her locs from her face, so he could see her fully.

"Aww I wannid wah anodha chance." Samiyah cries altered the pronunciation of her words.

Gerran pulled her into his embrace and she cradled her head against his chest. "I want another chance too," he co-signed. "We have a lot to talk about. A lot. But I do want another chance."

Samiyah cried until she couldn't and then pulled back from his hold. "Why now?" She sniffled. "Is it only because of the baby?"

Gerran looked off to the side as if the answer was laying on the concrete. "I can't lie. Yea." Samiyah stepped back until she bumped into the siding of Eli's house and then drooped her eyes in disappointment. Gerran bridged the gap between them. "Let me explain. You lost three of my babies in the past and all we ever wanted was to raise a family together. And the way I see it, if the Most High saw fit to bless you with my seed, I need to be there to nurture it and you, regardless."

"But that's the only—"

"No. It's not the only reason." He cut her off and finished her thought. "You hurt my heart and I'm still fucked up 'bout that, but I never stopped loving you because of it. It was my pride that wouldn't let me tell you I missed you."

"You missed me?"

"Come on, Yah. You been a thuggah's best friend going on seven years, nah. You held shit down when I couldn't. And aside from that lame you was fuckin' with, you been loyal to me."

She ran the side of her hand under her nose to wipe away the dripping snot. She looked up at him, then back down to her feet. Samiyah had so much on her mind, but couldn't think of one thing to say.

"Are you hungry? Can we have lunch? Go anywhere or do anything that would get me up out this weather?" The sixty degree temperature was chilling his bones.

Samiyah nodded her head. "Okay," she spoke softly. "Let me get my purse."

She headed inside and Gerran retreated to his car.

"Eli?" Samiyah called out for him as she walked to his bedroom, assuming he was in there. "Where you at?" She didn't see him.

"Bathroom," he responded through a strain.

She tapped slightly on the door and then opened it. "Good gawd!" She pinched her nose.

"No one told your ass to come in." He flashed a smile. Funny, but even on a toilet, he still looked flawless.

"Why do you take all of your clothes off just to shit?"

He hunched his shoulders. "Gotta get comfortable, ya heard me."

"Well, I was just letting you know I'm 'bout to step off with Gerran. I don't know what time I'll be back, but I will. Do you need something aside from air fresheners and incense?"

Eli fanned his funk her way with the wave of his hand. "This ain't roses?" They both laughed. "Nah, I'm straight."

"If I take too long to return and you need me before then, call me."

"Fo'sho," Eli grunted. Samiyah closed the door and prepared to step out of his room. "Oh, Yah." Eli called her back into the bathroom.

She opened the door. "What?" She held her breath, responding in a nasally tone.

"Remember what I told you 'bout ole boy."

Samiyah walked all the way inside and gave him a kiss on the cheek. "I remember every word you speak." She faintly smiled at him before departing, yet again.

Elias wasn't sure, but he began feeling some type of way about Samiyah leaving with Gerran.

***

G'Corey showed up at Kawanna's apartment. He knew she was there before he knocked on her door because he had pulled alongside Delight's car.

He jumped out with his gat in the front of his waistband, taking her steps two at a time until he was on the third floor in front of N-303.

G'Corey pounded slow and methodically, "Open up, Kawanna." It took everything in him not to go ham off top, but he was seconds away from doing so the longer the 36 x 80 inch wooded contraption didn't swing open.

Kawanna put her finger tips up to Delight's lips, ceasing her conversation when she heard G'Corey from out of her bedroom which was right off of the front door.

"What is he doing here?" Delight whispered.

"I told you he has been calling me nonstop." Kawanna jumped off of her bed when she heard him bang a little louder this time. "Holy shit! He is pissed because I told Minnie the truth when she came over here. I didn't know how she knew, but she did and I opened up. And now he's gonna kick my ass. I can hear it." She began to tremble.

Fed up with Kawanna's avoidance, G'Corey lifted his size twelve and kicked her door.

Boom!

That jolted both ladies out of her bedroom and into the front room. Kawanna panicked as she reflexively scrambled to search and secure a sharp object.

"He can snatch that from you and use it on us. We need something else." Delight frantically looked for another defense. They were going to need it. He was adamant about getting in and they were petrified for their lives.

Kawanna began hyperventilating. "Oh, my God. I'm gonna die! He's going to kill me because she knows," she cried.

Delight rushed over to her and held her face. "Look at me. You not gonna die." Delight embraced the weapon she found in the kitchen's cabinet.

G'Corey kicked the door again and this time the door gave way to the force and it flew open.

Boom!

Kawanna yelped and Delight scurried off. G'Corey walked through her house, pausing briefly when he saw Kawanna standing there shaking with a butcher's knife in her unsteady hand. He raised his shirt and pulled out his gun. Kawanna's fingers uncoiled from around the handle, releasing her protection. Fear rendered her motionless as he began walking toward her.

"Bitch! You thought you could fuck up my life without me fucking up yours?" G'Corey gritted.

Kawanna's mouth moved, but no words formed.

Just as he raised his piece, Delight came from behind the wall and sprayed wasp spray which acted as mace, but more effective.

"Aaahhhh!" G'Corey covered his burning eyes and immediately began choking as his asthma flared up from the excessive amount of repellent Delight shot his way. He was blinded and unable to breath, grabbing at his throat.

"Let's go! Let's go! Let's go!" Delight wildly dragged Kawanna by the arm past G'Corey who was now on his knees, gasping for more air.

Even in the midst of an asthma flare up, G'Corey managed to threaten them as they scurried to get away.

"I'm gonna kill you bitches!" he hurled.

Chapter 29
Later that evening…

Yuriah pulled up to his five bedroom, creole-style, three level town-home in the City Park, back of town area.

Minnie sat emotionless in the passenger seat with her head damn near in her lap. She felt so twilight, she didn't even recognize Yuriah had opened her door with his hand extended, reaching out for hers.

"We're here," he said with more tenderness than ever before.

The sound of his voice caused her to slowly look in his direction before she returned her head to her lap again, allowing a fresh batch of tears to fall like heavy raindrops. "My baby is gone." The moment the last word left her lips, her whole body vibrated to the wails of her violent cries. Her eyes were clenched tightly as she released her anguish, her confusion, and her loss through her emotional waterfall.

Yuriah stooped down at curb level, looking up at her and feeling helpless to stop her pain. He wanted to get her inside and comfortable, but her mind had her too stuck to move. Allowing her the room to feel, he closed her door and got back in his car and sat silently until she finished.

After two hours had elapsed, the evening sky had turned the color of dark night. Minnie finally spoke, "I'm ready to go now."

Yuriah turned off the engine, turned off the low heat and exited his vehicle. He walked over to her side and reached for her hand again. Placing her fingertips in the palms of his hand, she dizzily stood to her feet. The anesthesia the doctors administered still had an effect on her.

"I got you." He closed his door, then gently swooped her into his arms as he carried her up the fourteen steps that led to his porch.

She groaned as a result of the painful cramps rushing through her body. The physician told her the dilation and curettage procedure, also known as a D & C, would leave her with discomfort for up to two days.

Once inside, Yuriah disarmed the alarm and walked her into the only bedroom on the first floor, his. Cutting on the light to see his path, he then carefully laid her on the bed. "I'll be right back."

Yuriah retreated to his car to retrieve the items he picked up from CVS. He hit his alarm and rushed back inside. He stopped off in the kitchen and grabbed a bottle of Kentwood water and headed back into his room.

He sat the items in his hand down with the exception of the bag that had the Ibuprofens in them. Yuriah sat next to her, then helped her to a seating position. "Here, take this." He handed her the two pills. He then twisted the cap off of the bottle and placed it in her hands. "This should help with your discomfort."

"Thank you," she spoke softly.

"Relax yourself while I get you prepped for bed." He grabbed the box and bags off of the floor, went into his master bath attached off of his suite and started the shower. He pulled out the bath seat he just purchased and placed it inside of his walk-in shower.

He pulled out all of the personal content in the bag and aligned it on his counter. There was a nightie and a pair of underwear. He also picked up on toiletries he knew she'd need including a box of Always overnight for the hemorrhaging. Yuriah set a fresh wash and dry towel along with a bar of unscented Dove soap, per the recommendation of the nurse. She was all set up.

Yuri headed back over to Minnie and assisted her into the bathroom. "Everything you need is in there already. I'll be right outside this door if you need me for anything."

Minnie shook her head and thanked him with her saddened eyes.

***

Gerran pulled up to Elias' house and parked behind his truck. "You sure that's what you want? 'Cause there won't be no turning back." He advised, imploring that she choose wisely.

Samiyah reviewed their emotionally charged conversation, both the mountain highs and the valley lows and concluded that she was certain of her choice. "I'm sure." She wore a straight face, then got out of his car.

She walked inside and the first place she headed was Eli's bedroom. She found him kicked back, relaxing in his recliner with a glass of Crown to his lips. "Can I talk to you?" She needlessly asked.

He nodded his head, welcoming her to do so. "Penny for your thoughts."

She decided to give him the short version. "After a lot of talking, fussing, arguing, and apologies, we decided to give each other another try."

Eli raised both eyebrows in a surprised reaction. "Word?" He sat upright in his chair. "You sure he's who you want?"

She almost felt out of order answering him. It sort of felt like he was challenging her to truly consider her decision. "Yea. I want him."

Elias bobbed his head while staring into his drink. "So, what's your game plan? I know you have one."

"Ummm, I'm going home with him tonight." She felt strange all of sudden. It seemed like she was breaking his heart although she was only following hers. "Are you okay with that?"

"I'm straight, ya heard me. You like it, I love it." Eli felt salty. He wasn't sure if it was because she was leaving his house or because she was leaving *him*.

***

Twenty-five minutes later, Minnie emerged out of the bathroom to discover Yuriah on the bed with two bowls on the bed tray before him.

"You haven't eaten all day, so I reheated some yakamein I made last night."

She sat down next to him. "It smells good, but I'm not hungry." She declined.

"You need to eat something, Mouse." She shook her head defiantly. "Try. For me," he reasoned.

"Okay," she surrendered.

The steam was bristling off of the noodles in beef broth with roast cubes, hard boiled eggs, garnished with green onions. He chopped off the length of the noodles against the bowl and filled the spoon with its soupy deliciousness. "Open up."

She accepted the first bite and chewed gradually. She ate another spoonful, but by the time he lifted the utensil to her mouth again, she rejected it. "I don't want no more. I'm sorry."

"You did good." He removed everything off of the bed and pulled back the covers. "Climb in." He tucked her in, turned on the side lamp and turned off the room's light as he took a seat in the dark corner.

Yuriah sat in deep thought as he waited for Minnie to fall asleep before he exited to give her *her* privacy. After thirty minutes of quietness when he thought she finally drifted off, the silence was broken with her crying outburst.

Yuri jumped up and headed to the bed. "I'm right here." He rubbed her back as she sat up. "Talk to me."

She whimpered before doing so. "Yuri, I feel so empty inside. How did I go from two heartbeats to just one?" Minnie dropped her forehead into his chest and boo-hoo'd. She was in mourning.

He was certain her question was rhetorical. He surely couldn't answer if it wasn't. He held her until she lay down on her own and eventually fell asleep.

He was blistering as he reflected on the warning he'd given G'Corey awhile back. *If any of your shit comes back to hurt her, I will hurt you!* He wasn't sure if G'Corey had taken him seriously, but what G'Corey would learn tonight was that a man's word was most definitely his bond.

Yuriah soundlessly left out of the room, careful not to disturb her. He entered into his hallway and stopped in front of wall shelving that doubled as one of several stash spots for his artillery. He grabbed his infamous .44 and headed out of the door.

***

With Samiyah gone, Eli's didn't have a desire to be home alone. He was still throwed off by the fake ass way La'Tasha handled him and now he was missing his round. The house felt too big for only him. He had to get out.

Eli chose not to go to Top Notch because he didn't want to run the risk of seeing that no good, low down trick whose name he vowed never to let cross his lips. He ended up in New Orleans' East on Lake Forrest Blvd. at The Bar at Aqua Blu. Jacobi swore it was a nice little duck off that jumped off. And tonight Eli was looking for a *jump off.*

Soulja Slim's *Straight 2 the Dance Floor* was playing the moment he walked through the double doors. The building was moderately sized, accommodating a dance floor, several pub tables and chairs scattered around the place along with a few pool tables. But what stood out front and center was the extremely long bar with the name of the business outlined in a fluorescent blue color.

Eli stood at the bar top waiting for service. There were three female servers behind the counter and out of those bar maids working, a very beautiful one flashed a smile and took his order. It was always the same beverage for him.

"Crown. Two cubes."

She tapped the wooded top and poured him a glass. He handed her a Franklin. "Run me a tab."

"Sure thing, baby," the bartender replied.

Eli held on to her hand as he placed the money in her palm. "What's your name?"

She pointed to the embroidery stitched on her shirt. "Blu," she smiled. As she prepared his drink, she made small talk. "Are you enjoying your night so far?"

"That depends if you're tryna be a part of it," Elias sized her up.

Blu wasn't the style of woman he'd typically go for, but tonight wasn't about types. Pussy was pussy and she was looking smashable. She wasn't stacked, but she was working with something nonetheless.

She was five feet three inches and very slender. She had long, cold black, thick natural hair with blue colored tips that matched her blue fingernails. A smile that could warm the iciest heart, but her most appealing asset was the chocolate coat of skin she was giftwrapped in.

Elias was fond of all browns, but it was something about a dark skinned woman that turned him on.

"Sorry, but you're not my type." She shook her head.

That was a first for Eli. It surprised him enough to question her preference. "If I'm not, who is?" He chuckled.

She leaned on top of the partition and Elias got a whiff of her erection provoking sweet scent and captured a bird's eye view of her B cup bites before he followed her pointing finger.

"Get the fuck outta here. You like girls?"

"Guilty," Blu lied. Elias was most definitely her type. Tall, caramel, ripped, and overall sexy, but he was guy number five that night who attempted to talk under her apron. She wasn't about to entertain them or him if that was the way they were coming.

"Shit. That just means we have something in common. I like girls too."

"And *I* like my job. Let me handle my business. We'll talk later if you're around." She skated off to tend to the other patrons pouring in.

Got damn me and this chase, Elias shook his head and smirked as he watched her little booty switch. Taking a sip of his Crown, he knew she'd be his next hit.

***

Yuriah parked one block away from Minnie's door. His adrenaline was coursing rapidly through his veins as he replayed every roller coaster-ish emotion Minnie experienced at G'Corey's hands. He put a light jog in his step as he walked the short distance down the poorly lit street that would seal G'Corey's fate.

He took his fo-fo from out the small of his back and bashed G'Corey's window with the butt of his gun before he secured it in his pants.

G'Corey woke up out of his sleep at the sound of his alarm blaring. Not sure what triggered the security system, he grabbed his keys and disarmed the sound before swinging his door open to investigate what activated it.

Yuriah could have shot him and got in the wind, but that was too easy. G'Corey needed to be stomped out and humiliated because of it. Yuri planned on showing him first hand why the streets crowned him Drop.

Yuri stepped from out of the shadows and into the dull light that shined from the street post. G'Corey narrowed his eyes, attempting to make out the image. When he identified it was Yuri, there was no need to talk. Judging from the menacing scowl on his face, G'Corey already knew what it was.

G'Corey grimaced and reached for his piece, but forgot that he had removed it. Those seconds wasted would prove to be at his detriment.

Yuriah rushed toward him at top speed. G'Corey instinctually lifted his foot to kick him and use Yuri's momentum against him, but Yuriah side stepped and grabbed his suspended leg. Yanking him forward, G'Corey fell backwards hitting the back of his head against the concrete steps. He didn't have time to come out of his slight daze because in one quick motion, Yuriah straddled him and began delivering relentless blows to his face.

G'Corey began swinging wildly, but his hits were more of a nuisance than an assault. Yuriah pinned one of his arms with his knee to weaken his defense as G'Corey starting bucking, kicking, and moving more riotously to get out of the compromising position.

Yuriah then mercilessly grabbed G'Corey around the neck with his left hand, choking him to the point where it felt like his windpipe was on the verge of collapsing under his applied pressure. G'Corey struggled to free the vice grip Yuriah maintained all the while eating each brain rattling punch.

Eventually, G'Corey's kicks became slower and his clawing to free his throat, less powerful as his eyes literally began to bulge out of its sockets.

Yuriah cocked back his bloody fist one last time and landed a punch so devastating that G'Corey's glass jaw was heard cracking under the hit.

G'Corey then gagged and grumbled as Yuriah got off of him, looking down on him while shaking his head in disgust.

"Minnie is dead to you and if she ain't," his growl turned sinister, "you will be!"

"Arrrggghhh," G'Corey groaned unable to formulate a word. The only thing preventing his jaw from laying on the ground was the skin and tissue connecting the bones.

"Ole pussy ass," Yuriah spat before he casually strolled to his car, leaving G'Corey leaking on his front steps.

Coffee

Chapter 30
Six weeks later...

Since Sleepy had requested family medical leave of absence two and a half months ago, he hadn't been back to work. He was in no threat of losing his position at his job but short term disability, which was a fraction of his check, would soon stop. And with Acacia only working part time hours at her job to be his caretaker, Sleepy was growing agitated and concerned with how they would maintain things without running through their entire savings.

His post-recovery issues still managed to complicate the simple everyday rituals of driving, using the bathroom if his bowels were too hard, and sleep still didn't come easily. It drove him insane and unfortunately Acacia suffered the brunt of his anguish.

But to add insult to injury, the greater thorn in his side was that his brother recuperated without any health hiccups. The success of the transplant for Diego didn't bother him, but his body's poor response to it depressed the hell out of him.

Things needed to change and soon because the dichotomy between Sleepy and his girl was taking a severe beating.

***

Slowly but surely, Minnie was coming out of the funk she'd been in for weeks. Although she remained filled with disbelief that rendered her speechless at times, she was nonetheless making progress. Yuriah was a major factor in her process. At times, he was the only person capable of penetrating her shell. His constant support made it impossible for her to slip into a coma, cocooning herself from everyone.

Minnie was lying across her bed in Yuriah's master suite. It had now become her room since she had moved in as he took up occupancy in a separate sleeping quarter.

She rolled over to her side and saw her silent cellular phone light up with an incoming call. Today was a *do not disturb* kind of day, but she had been neglectful recently and she knew it was wrong, so she answered.

"Hey, Yah."

"It's about time you answered one of my calls. How have you been, stranger?"

"I know. I'm a bad friend, huh?"

"Never dat. I know you're going through something, but like you told me earlier this year *don't shut out those who love you.*"

"Funny thing about advice, it's easier said than followed." She sighed and then smiled to pick up her mood. "How have you been? How's your bud? How's Gerran?" Minnie asked.

Samiyah held back some of her elation when she spoke of her growing joy because she knew Minnie was still reeling over her own loss. "We're good."

Minnie frowned at her short response. "You don't have to be stingy with your news. Tell me whatever you're holding back attempting to spare my feelings. Let me live vicariously through your happiness."

With much hesitancy Samiyah opened her mouth to share, still choosing to hold back in the name of being considerate. "Me and baby are doing great. I just turned twelve weeks and my doctor said I should no longer experience morning sickness going into my second trimester. I hope she's right. Now, as for Gerran, he's good. It's still an adjustment for him taking me back, but he said he will work through it. All in all, our good days are great and our bad days are hmmm so *so*. We gon' be just fine, though."

"I trust y'all will be better than fine." Minnie paused for a second before she spoke again. "I'm so happy you crossed over the scare of the seven week hump." Minnie referred to Samiyah's painful past of miscarriages that didn't surpass her seventh week of gestation. "Do you know anything that will help me make it past my pain?"

Samiyah was slow to answer although she knew her response. "Time. Let it run its course and you'll be okay. It won't erase the memory and nor should it, but you will gain peace—in time."

Minnie's moping could be heard through her short inhales. She sighed and shakily repeated, "Time."

They held the phone with no words passed. It was as if they both chose to have a moment of silence out of respect for Minnie's misfortune.

Deciding to change the wind of the sail and off of the trauma surrounding her unborn, Samiyah reopened conversation. "Well, enough about me. Tell me what's good and positive on your end?" Samiyah cradle the phone against her cheek and shoulder as she began washing dishes.

"I don't know if this is good, per say, but it is a positive, I guess. Ummm, that *no fault* divorce petition I filed last month was finalized as of today. So, now I am back to being plain ole Minnie Mitchell."

"Well, Ms. Mitchell, you did what was right and there's nothing wrong about that."

"I know, but it still doesn't stop the depression. I lost everything, Yah. Husband, baby, home—gone. If it wasn't for Alverda stepping up to take care of my business at work and Yuriah being my rock in every sense of the word, I would have lost my mind too. I just can't believe this is my life," she sighed.

"My friend, T. Michelle, told me this once. *In order to construct, you must first destruct.* Meaning, this is your opportunity to rebuild on a stronger foundation, using better bricks and insulation. It may be a disastrous mess right now, but oh once you're done, it will be beautiful!"

"I needed to hear that." Minnie's voice crackling could clearly be heard.

"Know what else I think you need?" Samiyah questioned.

"What's that?"

"A sista hug and if it's alright with you, Acacia and I can come over later and love on you."

"That's a plan, my sista."

Minnie hung up the phone and smiled genuinely. She may have been robbed of her childhood dream which was to have the ideal marriage followed by a baby's carriage. But with sistas like Samiyah and Acacia, and a friend like Yuriah, the world still had a bit of sweetness to it.

***

Tracie ran her hands over her beach ball stomach excited at her baby's constant kicking as she waited in the lobby of the doctor's office. A sonogram she had weeks ago confirmed she was having a boy, just like she'd hoped. She already knew his name. What she didn't know was who he would come out looking like.

"You'll be tall like your daddy but have my nose." She was twenty-one weeks, but had been talking to her son ever since her OB told her he could hear outside of the womb at sixteen weeks.

"Ma'am." The nurse called Tracie. "The doctor would like to see you."

Tracie stood to her feet and with a slight wobble, she moseyed through the door the lady held open. The doctor offered her a seat, but she opted to stand at G'Corey's side and listen to whatever instructions the oral surgeon had.

"Mrs. Daniels?" The doctor questioned. G'Corey shook his head *no*. "Sorry, Ms.—" He waited for Tracie to fill in the blank.

"Terry. Ms. Terry for now." She had mistaken G'Corey purpose for getting her to come home and misunderstood her pawn position on his chess board as finally being his queen piece.

"Okay, Ms. Terry. I've explained this to him already, but I wanted to ensure that you were also aware of the maintenance after the wire removal."

The doctor proceeded to explain everything to Tracie. She rubbed her stomach, glancing at G'Corey from time to time as Doc continued telling her the do's and don'ts.

G'Corey mentally checked out. He couldn't hear anything except the voices in his head and every last one of them were pissed the fuck off! He was in a very dark place.

For six weeks, his wired mouth was a reminder to knock Yuriah's block off. It didn't matter the length of time it would take to touch him because he was definitely getting touched. He also vowed to make good on his death threats to Kawanna because had she not exposed shit, his life would be perfect with Minnie.

Minnie, he thought. He missed her so much his chest held a perpetual tightness to it. It was foul how she cleared their bank accounts, leaving him with zilch but he charged that to the game. He was willing to move past her transgressions as long as she was willing to do the same.

G'Corey had reached out to her, but she changed her number. She hadn't been reporting to work on any of the spontaneous days he'd showed up. He never saw her car parked by her parents and she even stopped attending church services. It was like she turned into a ghost.

The only thing that kept his mental faculties in order was the idea that he could still make it right. Their baby, who according to the calendar he'd marked every week, was still baking in the oven at eighteen weeks now. That gave him hope that he could get his wife and his life back.

G'Corey glared over at Tracie soaking in every word the doctor was dripping as he shook his head dissatisfied with life. He was displeased that Tracie was the one who remained when the dust settled. He detested her. And that baby he thought he took care of still didn't change the fact that he intended on toe tagging her when the time was right. But for now, he once again needed her. After much convincing through text messages, she finally came from out of hiding a few days ago. It irked him to give her the pleasure of feeling she had the ups on him, but he was penniless and damn near desperate without the stash she still held hostage. So, he had to bite the bullet—for now.

Coffee

Chapter 31
Yuriah & Minnie...

Minnie had been in her room all morning, but it wasn't until the smell of something too divine distracted her enough to pull away from the work she had been doing for her Home Health agency and step outside of her room. She opened her door and the heavenly aroma strongly infiltrated her nose and commanded her feet to follow the scent.

"Yuriah?" She called his name as she headed straight toward the kitchen. He wasn't there. "Yuriah?"

"In the den," he called out from the back of the house.

She walked down the long hallway, bypassing the stairs that aligned the right side of the wall and her room that was a few feet down but on the other hand side. Once she walked down the three steps leading into the sunken lounge area, she gasped.

There was a thick quilted blanket sprawled over the chocolate hardwood floors and on it was an assortment of goodies. She placed her knuckles over her lips, supporting her elbow with her other hand as she took in the scene.

Yuriah walked over to her. "Come here." He led her to have a seat in front of the seventy-two inch wall projector. "Get comfortable and relax with me. Today I thought you'd take a trip down memory lane with me. You cool with that?"

If her smile had gotten any wider, she wouldn't have been able to see a thing. "Yea, I'm cool."

"What does this remind you of?" He shifted through the snacks he picked up from the corner store. "I bought some Hubig lemon pies, Elmer's Chee-Wees, Zapp's Cajun Dill chips and pralines."

"All of this reminds of the zoo—zoos we'd munch on while you helped me study or when we would be in my dorm room watching—" Her attention was diverted to the sudden sound.

He pressed play on the remote to the DVD player as she was speaking which automatically resumed the disc.

"*The Jefferson's!*" she continued. "We would always watch the Jefferson's," she reiterated. Oh, my God," she laughed. "Oooh, remember the Valentine's episode when George had sung to Louise?" She recalled one of the favorite scenes.

"Fo'sho, I do. It was one of the best ones."

Then they both sang.

Weezy, it's so easy, to be in love with you.

Minnie cracked up and Yuriah was happy to see her shining. He was glad to know his mission to raise her spirits was working.

"I also have the entire season of *Gimme a Break* and *Sanford & Son*, but it don't stop there," he noted.

"What else could there be?" She gushed.

"Catered lunch is what that be," he ebonically charmed.

"Really?"

"Oh, yea!"

"By whom?"

"By moi," he pointed at his chest. "I fried up some shrimps, oysters, and catfish nuggets to make us some po'boys. And I picked up your favorite Big Shot Pineapple cold drink to wash it all down."

"You're too much but also just what I needed. Thanks for being here."

He bobbed his head slowly and brought her snugly into the fold of his arm. "That will never change."

***

G'Corey & Tracie...

G'Corey stared at Tracie who was staring at him from across the dining room table. "What?" He looked over at her annoyed.

"I had given you a couple of days to bring this up, but you hadn't. Mind telling me if you were going to choose me, why did you beat my ass when I was only going to set the record straight with Minnie that night?" She stared intently for an answer.

"I got other shit on my mind, yea." He flippantly spoke.

"And this is all that's on mine. I have always had your back, pretty much like I do now. Each time those skank ass *wanna be down* broads kicked you, I picked you up. Yet and still you break my heart. Just tell me why?"

G'Corey knew saying the wrong thing would have him permanently S.O.L. with getting his stash and cash, so he choose his words carefully. "I'm an asshole and I shouldn't have put my hands on you. I don't think sometimes, you know that. But I'm sorry." He hoped his smile covered his insincerity because he loathed being there with her and he was only able to perpetrate happiness for so long in one sitting.

"How do I know I can believe you?"

"You can't. But I'm here, ain't I? Took me a minute, but I know where it's good at, nah." It ate G'Corey's insides to front that hard, but he had to make a believer out of her. "On some real shit, where's my product?"

"That's what this is about?" She pushed herself away from the table, animatedly, and stood to her feet. "You stuntin' so you can get your hands on your precious powder, then you gon' get ghost?"

"Hell no! Look, if I'm not able to make money soon, I won't be able to take care of me nor this family. You *really* wanna be a thuggah's Bonnie, then give me my issue,"

Tracie didn't want to rock the boat too hard. Her disability check only covered so much, so she digressed but not before firing off a few questions. "We a team for good, right? No more Minnie, ever? No more games?"

"We good on all of that?" G'Corey lied. He was going to use Tracie until she had the baby, send her to her maker, and he'd leave his seed at the fire station because he didn't want him.

Tracie watched his body movements like she was a trained human lie detector, looking for any reason to pull back on her end of the bargain they discussed by phone a few days ago. But she believed him when he said they were in it to win it this time. "Alright. It will take a week or so because it's in Indiana by my peoples."

"What? What the fuck it's doing way out there?" His nerves snapped like a thin twig.

"Ummm, calm down. The dope could have been flushed and the money spent but it ain't, so don't trip. I will get in touch with my cousin, King, and when he comes down for Mardi Gras I will tell him to bring that back."

This slick, bitch! G'Corey hissed under his breath.

King was a quick tempered D-Boy out of Gary, IN and there was only one reason Tracie allowed him to hold his shit down. *Insurance.* If she would have never requested the dope be returned to her, King would have known what time it was.

G'Corey clenched his fists underneath the table as he hid the derision on his face as best as he could. "Get on the horn with that boy, ya heard me. I got moves to make with no time to waste."

She pulled her phone from her back pocket, but instead of making the call, she placed it on the table. She walked over to the side where he sat and tenderly ran her hand across the broads of his shoulders as she stood behind him. Tracie leaned down and began nibbling on his ear.

"Make love to me. Let me know it's real." She moved her hands up toward his head as she ran her fingers over the waves of his hair.

G'Corey eyes rolled like marbles. This cornered position he was in was messing with his mind. He had a priority list that was sky high and fucking Tracie wasn't on it.

"I'll meet you in the bedroom." He gritted through a fake smile.

"Okay, baby." Tracie obliged with no back talk.

G'Corey wasn't able to rise from his seat, let alone the occasion. His fella was lifeless. He was going to need time he didn't have to coach himself into an erection because she brought out the limp dick in him.

Focus on the mission, he thought. *Do what you gotta do now, so you can get what you need later.*

On that note, he man'd up and headed into the room where Tracie already lay naked, squirming on top of the sheets waiting for him to do her. The sight of her exposed pussy pissed him off.

"Fuck me," Tracie panted.

Fuck, me, G'Corey miserably mouthed.

Chapter 32
Gerran & Samiyah...

"Two large hot chocolates, please." Gerran ordered cocoa drinks from Café Du Monde for him and Samiyah.

After getting their beverages, he walked her across Decatur St. and over to the horse and carriage that awaited them for their romantic evening ride.

Gerran climbed in first, taking their cups and placing them securely on the seats before grabbing Samiyah by both of her hands, helping her inside of the buggy. "Watch your step," he smiled down on her.

Gerran opened up the thick blanket he brought with him to wrap them inside of with the purpose of warding off the cool whip of wind that chilled the city.

The man who identified himself as Mr. Theriot took off from in front of Jackson Square and onto an intimate ride through the Quarters.

"Are you warm?" He had her snuggled in his embrace as he took a sip from his drink.

She looked up at him admirably. "I'm perfect."

He rested his free hand on her swollen belly and kissed her temple. "This may not seem like the right time, but if you think about it, it is."

Samiyah's smile turned and she closed her eyes briefly with the hopes he wasn't going to bring up—

"Cedric. What made you get involved with that cat?"

Samiyah's shoulders, countenance, and head dropped all at the same time. "I told you everything already. Why are we doing this again?"

Gerran placed a finger under her chin and shifted her face toward his. "I never listened to your answers. I only reacted to what I heard." She lowered her head into her chest and Gerran picked it up again. "Yah, I want to move past it but in order to do that, I need you to tell me while a thuggah paying attention with his heart."

She sighed and reluctantly spoke, "We were just friends in the beginning and *us* happening wasn't intentional. Things just took a different turn the less you made yourself available. He stepped up and began giving me *the more* from you I was missing. Look, I really don't want to talk about this. We have a future I much rather concentrate on. I've already apologized a thousand times and I am not doing nothing like that again. Can you leave the past in the past, please?"

"Mr. Babineaux," Mr. Theriot addressed Gerran. "I do believe we made ah first stop of tha night, suh," he spoke in a Cajun rhythm.

Gerran stretched his neck to see where they were and bobbed his head with approval. "Thank you, my man."

Once the carriage came to a complete stop, Gerran made his exit. Samiyah confusingly looked at him. He just asked her to reopen the chapter on Cedric, but he didn't respond. He reached out for her to assist her down. She extended her hand. "Can you answer my question?"

"Yes, but after you answer mine."

"Huh?"

"Walk with me?" Gerran led Samiyah a few feet down from where they were dropped off at, front and center amongst a small crowd that was gathered around a young male singing group consisting of four teens recently signed to his label, Raw Music Entertainment.

When the fellas known as the Crescent City Boyz saw Gerran, their manager/producer, they ended their current melody and began singing a cover song from New Edition.

Gerran stood behind Samiyah and wrapped her inside of his arms, rocking to the acapella tunes coming from his dynamic R&B sensation.

Sunny days/Everybody loves them/Tell me baby/Can you stand the rain/Storms will come/This we know for sure/Tell me baby/Can you stand the rain?

The crowd grew larger, but despite all of the women gathered around, the charismatic young men performed strictly for Samiyah. The spotlight was intentionally on her. Gerran wanted to know if she could handle the bad weather moving forward, so he decided to ask in a very unique way.

When the song concluded, Gerran stood in front of her and asked, "Well, can you?"

Samiyah wiped away the sentimental tears that welled in her eyes. "Yes. Yes, I can, baby." She shook her head rapidly.

On cue, the young men began singing Michael Jackson's *I Just Can't Stop Loving You*. Gerran wanted to make tonight memorable. It was his way to show Samiyah he could be there for her in ways he was absent before because he knew his life wasn't much without her in it.

Gerran leaned his head onto Samiyah's and again they began a lover's rock. But midway through the song, he pulled away from her.

"What?" Samiyah reactively questioned and reached out for him, but he only stared at her.

You know how I feel/I won't stop until/I hear your voice saying "I do"

The group paused their singing and hummed the melody as Gerran took one of the mics.

"Samiyah, you've hurt me but only out of reaction to me hurting you. To answer your earlier question, I am ready to put that in the past because what's in store for our future is much *much* greater. So, all I want to know is will you walk with me in it?"

Samiyah giddily, happily shook her head *yes*.

Gerran dropped to one knee. The crowd roared. Samiyah's eyes bulged with surprise as she covered her hanging mouth. "Will you do it as my wife?" He pulled out a five carat, antique, princess cut diamond and held it up high for her to see.

With no hesitation, she blurted, "I do." Samiyah began crying profusely as Gerran placed the ring on, kissing her hand afterwards.

He stood to his feet, swirled his finger into the air and the Crescent City Boyz resumed the bridge of the song.

I just can't stop loving you/I just can't stop loving you/(And if I did now) And if I stop/Please tell me just what will I do/I just can't stop loving you.

When Samiyah zealously tongued Gerran, sparks flew. He knew without doubt while interlocked in her kiss that *their* love was indeed stronger than *his* pride.

Coffee

Chapter 33
Sleepy & Acacia...

Acacia stood in her bathroom doorway wearing a crotch-less nightie. It was creeping on three months since she felt Sleepy's intimate touches, but that was all changing tonight. Their visit to the nephrologist, his kidney doctor, informed them that Sleepy had sexual clearance to rock her world.

She was barely able to hold herself up. Desire coursed through her body so strongly it made her knees feel shaky. She stared at Sleepy realizing that without him even trying, he looked hella sexy.

After drooling over the *man* meal she was about to consume, she moseyed over toward him. Although he was lying flat on his back looking up at the ceiling, she still opted to cat walk his way.

She climbed onto the bed. "Is there room enough for me?" Acacia spoke with much Latina spice.

Sleepy rotated his head to face her, then back at the ceiling. "Of course, Acacia."

She scrunched her nose. "That sounded dry, but I know something that isn't," she seductively cooed, placing delicate kisses on his exposed chest.

Disinterested, Sleepy rolled his eyes and heavily sighed. Acacia paused but decided to disregard what she felt was him blowing her off and continued to pursue turning him on so he could turn her out. "Acacia," Sleepy called out.

She was tonguing his ear and breathing softly on his neck. "Yes, Papi."

"Not tonight."

Acacia kept going. She was determined to convince him that he was just as ready to make love as she was. She needed tonight to happen. Sleepy had been intimately distant and rightfully so, but now there was no conceivable reason in her mind that he couldn't show her she was more than his cook, maid, on-call nurse, and comforter. She needed to be his woman. The one he couldn't keep his hands off of.

She lowered her kisses to his abdomen, sensually traveling to his man jungle. And just as she placed her fingers on his Python, he grabbed her by her shoulders and roughly pushed her off of him. "I said *not tonight!*"

Acacia hurriedly jumped off of the bed. "If not tonight, when? How long are you gonna feel sorry for yourself and how long will I have to pay for it?" She hit herself across the chest.

"I have other things on my mind right now." His voice maintained a level of cool that further pissed Acacia off.

"Clearly," she smarted, squinting her eyes at him. Acacia grabbed her robe off of the hook from behind the bathroom door, angrily threw it on, and left out of the room.

She stomped off into the kitchen and reached in the cabinets, seizing a bottle of Gin by its neck. She twisted the top off and took a huge swig to the head. The liquor burned going down her throat just as the tears scorched a trail going down her cheeks.

She leaned against the counter, crying, thinking, and drinking.

Day in and day out, week after week, I catered to every nagging, simple and tedious task you asked me to do. But the one time I ask for something—something you could enjoy, you shut me down? Tsss. I can't fuckin' believe you. I can't fuckin' believe it!

Moments later, Diego strolled into the kitchen. His intention was to a get a few pieces of fruit and head back into his room, but he checked on Acacia when he saw how displeased she looked. "What's up, Ma? You a'ight?"

"Do I look it?" Attitude resounded from her voice.

Diego bit into the peach he pulled from the crisp bin out of the refrigerator and then he stepped to her. "If you need an adjustment," he grabbed at his crotch, "you know which door is mine."

"Fuck off!" she spat.

He slid his hand in her robe, touching her stomach. "Nah, fuck with me."

She shook her head and moved him away. Diego didn't put up a fight as he backed up. He just rolled his tongue over his top grill and cooly walked out of the kitchen.

Acacia refastened her robe and took her bottle into the living room where she sat in the dark, griping at how he casually dismissed her. At the very least, he could have placated her emotions and made her feel like she was his woman in the sensual sense. But he didn't.

She took a swig. Another. And another. Two hours had passed and she nearly finished the bottle. Now on her level, she convinced herself she should take what she wanted. Permission wasn't needed.

She slowly got up from the sofa and walked down the hallway leading to the bedroom. She stepped inside of the room, locked the door and then cut on the light switch. He was asleep like she expected, but he was going to wake up, get up, and serve her up.

Acacia removed her robe, allowing it to fall to the floor. She pulled the blanket off of him and snatched his pajama pants down.

"Acacia?" He was startled out of his sleep.

"Ssshhh," she put a finger to her lips. "Don't say shit. I want to be fucked and you're going to fuck me. Understood?"

Diego's dick stood at attention, agreeing with her demand before his head had the chance to.

The sight of his erection coupled with her raging hormones forced Sleepy completely out of her mind. She wanted to feel good and if her man wasn't going to do it, he had a brother who would.

Diego licked his lips as he watched her come out of her negligee. He then stood to his feet, she turned off the light and with caution thrown in the wind, they hungrily devoured each other.

*K*awanna & Delight...

"Stop calling me!" Kawanna screamed into the phone before she ended the call. Her bad nerves made her entire body tremble.

"What did he say this time?" Delight balled her mouth angrily.

"He said I can only hide so long before he finds me." She blinked her eyelids rapidly in an effort to bridge back tears.

It took Kawanna some time to finally feel comfortable enough to go home for more than a few minutes at a spell after G'Corey's initial threat to her and her cousin, but now after several weeks he was harassing her and threatening to make good on his promise if she didn't tell him the truth about Minnie and her whereabouts.

"Look, I am gonna get more of your clothes and personal items and you need to make the call and get his no good ass locked up." Delight shoved her cell phone into Kawanna's hand. "Take your life back."

Fear pitted in the bowels of Kawanna's stomach forced tears to push past her eyelids. She couldn't believe how drastically he snapped on her. Was the decimation of his life with Minnie worth taking hers? She wasn't sure how much of his intimidations stemmed from hurt or hatred, but as Delight preached to her several times before, she couldn't roll the dice on that one.

Kawanna shook her head in understanding. She dialed the number to the police precinct, placing the call on speaker.

The line rang a few times, but then a gentleman answered. "Headquarters."

"Ah," her voice shook, "I have information about illegal activities I wish to report."

"Okay. What's your name, sweetheart?" The detective could hear the nervousness through her tone.

"I have to?"

Delight nudged her cousin's shoulder and got her attention. She mouthed, *Tell him your damn name.*

"You're there?" he asked.

"Ummm, yes. Ah—ummm," she cleared her throat. "My name is Kawanna. Kawanna James."

"Alright, Ms. James. I'm Detective Ellis. Would you be willing to come down to the precinct and speak with me in person?"

Kawanna looked to Delight who shook her head yes as rapidly as a bobble head. "Yes."

"Can you be here in the hour?" He further questioned.

"I can." Kawanna stated.

"Grab a pen and paper." After the detective provided Kawanna with directions downtown, he termed the call.

Thirty minutes later, Kawanna and Delight stood outside in front of the address they were given.

Delight looked at how frightful her baby cousin was, so she placed her arm around Kawanna's shoulder. "You'll be okay. Let's go inside and get this over and done with."

An hour later, they emerged out of the building. She didn't want to dime him out, but if speaking with the police was the only way she'd get peace from him, then so be it.

*E*lias & Blu...

It took Eli a minute to convince Blu to go out with him. After several weeks of charming her on her turf at The Bar at Aqua Blu, she finally agreed to see him outside of her job.

It was highly unusual for Blu to leave work early, but she entrusted her best friend, Kanari, with locking up the place.

"I'm out," Blu looked over her shoulder as she headed out of the door.

"Cla-clank," Kanari double tapped her crossed wrists. It was their way of reminding each other to keep the lock secure on the vagina vault.

"Cla-clank," Blu repeated as she laughed.

Eli was leaning against his truck when he saw Blu stepping out. He couldn't see her fully, but her big, wild and curly hair was unmistakable.

Blu had a style he was digging. In some ways, she reminded him of Samiyah which was why he kept coming around. He found himself missing his round, but he respected the reasons they hadn't been kicking it lately.

"So, this is what you look like out of uniform," Eli onced her over before giving her a hug.

Blu wore her signature color blue at all times and tonight was no different. She sported a matching velour jacket and pantsuit with a pair of white G Nikes. Eli approved of what he saw, but shook his head at the same time. She was too damn cute to be playing for the same team.

"Is that a good thing?"

"Oh, yea. Now, check it. I've seen what you look like in your work and casual clothes. Now I just need to see you in your bedroom attire."

"*Ha. Ha. Ha.* Good one," she laughed while shaking her finger to say *no*. She then looked at her watch. "It's midnight. Where do you want to go? What do you have in mind?" Elias had a lustful look in his eye and was about to answer, but she quickly spoke up first. "Don't you dare say it," she warned, faking a mean face.

"Wasn't nobody gonna suggest going to Eli's." He paused for a second. "Unless, you *want* to go to Eli's." He threw his hands up as if to say what's up.

"Couldn't resist yourself, huh? Boy, you cracks me up. But be serious, where to?"

"On some real shit, we can walk Bourbon St. Grab a couple of them Hand Grenades from Tropical Isle and get twisted. But I'm 'bout freesylin' this night."

"I'm down for that."

They got in Eli's truck and as he started the ignition Lil Wayne bumped from the stereo.

"Ooh. Uhn. Uhn. Put on something else," Blu scrunched up her face.

"Who you wanna hear? B.Gizzle? C-Murder?"

"None of them," she shook her head.

"You must like Bounce?"

"No," she giggled. "I like FM 98's Quiet Storm."

"Who listens to the radio?"

"Us. Now, turn it on," she pointed to his dash.

"Blu is bossy, huh?"

"When I need to be." She folded her arms tightly, pretending to be a snob.

"It's all good lil' mama." He flashed a smile that made her look away otherwise he'd know how much she was feeling him.

Norman Connors' *You Are My Starship* invaded their eardrums and Blu began singing along as she swayed in her seat.

Elias put his truck in gear and pulled out of the parking lot. "Need me to stop at Walgreens before we hit that I10?"

"She stopped grooving, "For what?"

"The Chloraseptic spray you clearly need for that horrible scratch in your throat."

She playfully punched him. "Don't be talking about my singing like that. I can sing the man off the moon."

"Or keep him up there permanently, ya heard me." He ribbed her.

"Oooohhh," she curled her lips and tightened her eyes before she broke out laughing.

Initially Eli's purpose for pursing Blu was to change her sexual preference to Elias. It would appease the predator part of his nature, but after weeks of vibing with her, he discovered her friendship wasn't half bad. However, his agenda didn't waiver, he was simply willing to enjoy the play of his pussy until he demolished it.

Old habits die hard, he thought.

Electricity briefly sparked between them when they caught one another's gazes. "Fuck around and keep lookin' at a thuggah like you want the D and I'ma change your whole life."

"You wish," she teased.

"I will," he exuded confidence.

Coffee

Chapter 34
Four Months Later...

The ladies were scheduled to meet at Frankie & Johnny's on Arabella St. in the uptown area for their customary get together and to dine on some of the best alligator pies on that side of the Mississippi.

Samiyah picked Acacia up and they were the first to arrive. They sat parked inside of her car as they waited for Minnie.

Acacia placed her hand on Samiyah's huge, round belly. "You're kicking 'cause *other mommy* is here, huh, Lil' Acacia? You know I can't wait to meet you, right? I'm going to spoil you and love you up." Acacia lit up as she spoke to *her* baby.

"Ah, sista gurl. Is this your child or mine?"

"Mine," she said with attitude. "All you're doing is carrying her for me."

Samiyah had to laugh. "Listen to me slowly. I need you to prepare yourself right now. Her name will be Swayze. Swayyyy-zeeee. Umm-kay?"

Acacia sat back in her seat with her lips pooched and her arms folded.

"What's the matter?" Samiyah questioned when she saw genuine sadness wash over her face.

"I know it's your pregnancy *and* your baby, but giving my name to a lil' girl I already love is the closest I'll ever come to having a child of my own since I'm not capable of conceiving." She began a fight to withhold her selfish tears from falling. "But Swayze's a cool name too." She steadied her voice as she told a small untruth.

Samiyah's heart ached for her because she knew how desperately she wanted a little one. "You know you gon' be the na'nan. And being the godmother is just like being the mommy."

Acacia was still feeling some type of way, but to christen her bebé was the next best thing. "I guess you're right."

She touched the side of her face until Acacia's vexation softened. Seconds later, she saw a vehicle pull up. "There she goes." Samiyah spotted Yuriah getting out of his truck and opening his passenger's door.

Minnie climbed out with his assistance and then she stood on her tiptoe and pecked him on the lips. As she attempted to walk away, he pulled her back by the hand and kissed her like he'd never see her again.

"Goddamn, is she gonna have a face when he's through?" Acacia angled her head sideways to fully see the passionate lip lock.

"I refuse to get jealous," Samiyah joked, watching the show.

"Bye, baby. See you later." Minnie waved. With her head in the clouds, she turned around to walk toward the entrance of the restaurant almost bumping into her girls who were blocking her path.

"Lucy, you got some splainin' to do," Samiyah placed a hand on her hip, faking an attitude while holding back her laugh.

Minnie blushed, "What?"

"No *whats*. Give us the juice. When did Yuriah leave the friend zone?" Acacia inquired giddily.

"Ummm, I don't know. It sort of just happened," Minnie hunched her shoulders.

Samiyah mimicked Minnie's move sarcastically. *"It sort of just happened?"* she repeated.

"Yes," Minnie giggled. "Let's go inside and discuss things over lunch. She walked to the door and held it open, ushering them inside.

Samiyah and Acacia gave each other funny faces before they went in.

They grabbed a seat and the waitress immediately took their drink and food order. Once the server left the girls to themselves, they went in on Minnie.

"Spill it," Samiyah was anxious to know the details.

"Yea, come on with it. Did y'all do it yet?" Acacia leaned across the table to get closer to Minnie who was sitting directly in front of her.

"No we have not," she shyly dropped her eyes to the floor.

"Tsss. I don't believe you. The way he kissed you looked like steamy, hot, vertical sex," Acacia analyzed.

"Seriously, we haven't. Now, don't get me wrong, I have been emotionally vulnerable and I wanted to physically erase the hurt with sex, but he wouldn't allow it. He refused me and although I felt rejected, I understood. Besides, I want a relationship groomed outside of the bedroom first. It'll mean we can sustain our bond without sex being the glue." Minnie glanced over at Samiyah eating packaged Saltine crackers while making faces. "What? What are you snickering about?"

"You and him. I remember you shutting me down when I told you Yuri was the man you should have married, but nooooooo," Samiyah teased.

Minnie chuckled, "You did, right? I wore rose colored glasses then, but I have perfect vision now. I most definitely know it's good with Yuriah. I mean who better to be with than your best friend?" she asked, rhetorically. "So how is married life with yours, newlywed?" Minnie took the spotlight off of her.

Samiyah dove right into her answer. "I am so high right now. Things couldn't be better between us. He's still very busy, but he's giving me the attention I need by including me when he can't make it about me. He hasn't missed one doctor's appointment. And don't let me get started about how the sex has improved. I can't seem to get enough of his ass." Samiyah gave them the *umm hmmm gurllll* look.

"How do you like your new house?" Acacia inquired.

"It's too big for me, but Gerran insisted we get all the room and space we have because he wants a large family." She stretched her arms out widely.

"Speaking of marriage, yours is only a few weeks away. Are you excited or are you excited?" Samiyah was overjoyed that each of their storms passed and they all received a rainbow as a gift for their endurance.

"Oh, god!" Acacia threw her head back and closed her eyes. "Y'all don't want to keep talking about y'all?"

That raised immediate concern for both Minnie and Samiyah.

"What's the matter?" Samiyah reached out to touch her arm.

"What's wrong?" Minnie's question overlapped Samiyah's.

She sighed heavily. "Fact: Me and Sleepy's love has been written in stone years ago, so when he asked me to marry him, it was a no brainer. Problem is…" she fidgeted in her seat. "…what started off as my problem ended up being my answer."

"I know you not saying what I think you saying," Samiyah tilted her head and gave her the *I'm waiting* look.

"Take your time," Minnie took a different approach when she saw the strain on Acacia's face as she tried to address Samiyah's question.

"Ummm, one night in an angry and extremely horny state of mind, I sexed Diego like there was no tomorrow."

"Okay, it just happened one—"

"One of several times," Acacia swiftly corrected Samiyah. "I have been sleeping with him for months. There's no excuse for being a slut bag, I know. But the accidental sex only became an affair because Sleepy pushed me away constantly since the surgery. I know it's still wrong and if the shoe was on the other foot, I'd kill him!" Her face transformed from a pitiful sorry expression to a menacing glower. She shook her head in disbelief of her double standard and continued. "But the *strap up your seatbelt* part is—although I never uttered these words, especially to him but I think I love Diego, too."

Samiyah coughed out her peach ice tea, spitting some onto the table. Acacia gently patted her on the back. "You what?" She choked on her words.

"You heard right," Acacia clarified. "Listen, nothing about my love for Sleepy has changed and I swear I am gonna end this shit with Diego regardless to what that lil' hoe below says."

"Don't go criticizing yourself, Acacia. No one is judging you. It just took me by surprise, that's all," Samiyah spoke sincerely.

Acacia exhaled deeply. "I don't know why I kept it a secret from you guys. Maybe I was afraid because I didn't want to admit how much I enjoyed the way he made me feel. He hungered for me while Sleepy was on an Acacia diet. I guess I craved the forbidden fruit more than I despised it."

Minnie remained silent, but there was no judgment in it. She just couldn't relate to her plight, so she didn't try.

"And if y'all are wondering, I will mean my vows when I say them."

"I trust you will. Look, I know the dilemma of loving two men. All I can say is the drama isn't worth the pleasure it brings. So, if you know without doubt Sleepy is who you want, cut ties with his brother ASAP. That protects everyone in the end."

"Oh, Sleepy is who I want. Can't see myself living without him. That's why I don't understand how I even let it go there." Acacia was truly puzzled. When a feasible answer didn't come to her, she simply looked at both of her girls, agreed with Samiyah and then promised both herself and them that she would.

Tomorrow, Acacia thought.

***

Elias and Blu were stretched out on his sofa, laying on opposite ends listening to FM 98's Quiet Storm while singing each of the songs in broken harmony. Elias wasn't sure how cuddling and conversation became their late night ritual but it had.

Alexander O'Neal went off of the radio and Cameo's *Why Have I Lost You* came on.

"I love this song." Blu snapped her fingers and jammed for a second until she realized Eli's was in a different zone. "What's the matter?" She sat upright.

"I'm straight." He quickly blew off her question.

"No, you're not."

"Who knows *me* better than *me*?" he snapped.

"Well, I've been around you practically every day going on six months, so I would know when your demeanor has changed. I mean that doesn't make me a Samiyah, but I would like to think it doesn't make me a stranger either."

"It really ain't shit, ya heard me."

"Good. That should make it easier for you to tell me." Blu was adamant for Elias to give her more than a surface response.

They stared one another down, neither person budging. But after minutes of intense exchanges, Elias threw his hands up. "Fuck it," he conceded. "A girl from back in the day broke a thuggah's heart and I used to play this song over and over until the cassette popped. Happy, nosey ass lil' girl?"

Blu gave him the side eye and pursed her lips. "There's more to this story. I can see the disgust on your face." She took notice of the boot in his mouth. "How about this. You let me in and I will reveal something of my own. Deal?"

"Whatever," he sighed. "Her name was Celeste. She was older than I was, so we didn't run in the same circles but we used to always see each other at Hunters Field Park. Years passed by without us speaking, but the summer I turned twelve, my parents died in a wreck and that changed our status."

"Awww, I'm sorry to hear that." She rubbed his forearm.

"Yea," he shook his head. "Well, shit wasn't the same for me and everyone in the hood knew why. So, one day she made it a point to holla at me."

"Hey, E. Can I sit next to you?" Celeste asked.

Elias didn't bother looking up. "It's a free country."

She sat beside him on the steps of his Uncle Flint's home. "Sorry about what happened to your people. I know how you feel." Celeste attempted to rub his back, but Elias jumped up.

"You don't know shit! Nobody does," he balled his mouth to stop his lips from trembling.

Celeste rose to her feet as well. "You're wrong. I do. I lost my daddy five years ago when I was ten. Trust me, I know your pain."

Elias lessoned his defense. "Sorry."

"You good." She smiled to show there was no offense taken.

Celeste left that day, but she returned many days afterwards to check on him over a period of weeks. One day passing his house on N. Rocheblave St. he wasn't sitting on his porch like he usually would be, so she knocked on his door. It took a few persistent knocks, but he answered.

"I'm not coming outside," he groaned.

"Well, can I come in?" she asked in her high pitch voice.

Elias leaned on the door. He rubbed his eyes dry and then he opened the screen door to let her in.

They sat on opposite ends of the sofa. There was silence between them and an awkward cloud hovering over them because of it. Each time Celeste tried to make conversation, she was met with a grunt or a head nod, furthering the weirdness in the room. But she knew the secluded place he was in, she stayed there for a long time after her father was killed.

She stood to her feet and stretched out her hand. "Come here." He ignored her. She repeated herself when he didn't budge. "Come here," she spoke with more demand. He stood up and then placed his hand in hers. "Where's your room?"

"Huh?" Elias was dumbfounded. "It's down the hall."

Celeste walked him into his bedroom and she cut straight to the chase. "Take off your clothes."

For the second time, Elias repeated, "Huh?"

She shook her head. "Take off your clothes as in in get naked."

"Why?" Elias wasn't totally clueless to Celeste's advances, but he never gone where she was trying to go.

"We're gonna do it. It'll make you feel better. So, get naked." She began unbuckling her shorts and Eli hesitantly did the same. Now, both in their underwear, she instructed, "Kiss me."

Elias did so timidly, but at fifteen she was no stranger to the block she was walking him around. She pushed her tongue into his mouth as she sucked on his lip. Still engaged in their kiss, she removed her panties and slipped his drawers down as well. Then she climbed on his twin sized bed and coiled her finger, beckoning him to get in with her.

She raised her bra over her breast and Eli became flushed with embarrassment as his penis hardened.

"Don't be shy. That's what supposed to happen. Now just climb on top of me and put it in."

"And then what?" he questioned.

"Hump."

"Every day for the remainder of that summer, she let me pop that coochie. I even thought that made her my girlfriend. But one day, she was done with no explanations. I should have known she wasn't shit, but she had my lil' young ass open. Come to find out, she got with some thuggah a few years older than her and she was throwing the pussy his way. Shit fucked me up real good. But that was then."

"Wow, Elias. Do you realize your intimacy issues stem from that moment in your life? It's super clear the *that was then* still bothers you now."

"I ain't gon' stunt you might just be right. But its dog bitches like Celeste and that ratchet, man-eating hoe I told you about that sealed the deal on a thuggah giving his heart away. I don't know what type of broads you fuck with, but the ones I run across ain't worth a paper food stamp."

"Hmmm, well, here's my confession." An uncomfortable window opened for Blu to share something she'd been holding her tongue on. "Speaking of broads, I don't have any."

"That's your great reveal? That you're single."

"No. The fact that I'm not gay is, though."

"What? Wait a minute. Let me get this straight. You straight?" She shook her head *yes*. "But you intentionally led a thuggah to believe you wasn't tryna get poked."

"Actually, I never embellished on the *being a lesbian* lie. I just said it and never set the record straight afterwards. And you're right. I'm not tryna get poked. Look, I'm sorry, for real. I wanted to tell you that I really liked *you*, but answer me honestly. Would you have taken the time to know me as a person with a pussy or a pussy who's a person?" Elias said nothing. "Exactly my point."

He shook his head, slowly. "Be happy I like yo lil' ass. Otherwise—"

"Otherwise what?" She curled her lips.

"Your faces don't scare me, thuggette. Like I was saying, otherwise, yo ass would know what boot to booty feels like."

"Oh, really?" she laughed. "Real talk. Everything I've shared with you has been on the up and up, so if it's all the same, I still want to see what can happen between us as friends."

"Friends with benefits, right?" Elias already had an *off limits* friend in Samiyah. He didn't need a second one.

"This has the potential for more—if you play your cards right."

***

"I'm out of bags. I'm 'bout to run to the corner store real quick." G'Corey announced.

"Ooo, pick me up a bag of hot fries, a banana moon pie, a Delaware Punch, a hot pickle, and a handful of wine candies."

"I'm walkin', yea. I ain't 'bout to be carrying all of them bags."

G'Corey was heading to the living room when he heard a knock at the door. "Shit," he said below his breath. He turned around and walked to the back of the house. "Trace, catch the door. That's probably my sister and I ain't tryna talk to her right now. She on some other shit."

"What you want me to tell her? Your car's parked outside?"

"Tell her I stepped off with one of my boys and you don't know when I'll be back. I'ma just kite out through the backyard and hit the store up that way."

"Alright. Since I'm doing you this favor, get all my stuff. Me and Junior are having cravings."

"A'ight then," G'Corey stepped out of the back door, hopped the fence and walked the short trail leading to the store.

The visitor knocked again. Tracie yelled as she approached the door, "I'm coming." She looked through the peephole and saw it wasn't Renee. She didn't know who it was, but in G'Corey's business it could have been anyone. "Who is it?"

"Damon," the young man responded.

She didn't register the name, but Tracie would tell him the same thing that she told everyone else when they'd come by unannounced, *Call him first!*

The moment Tracie opened the door, a narcotics team of four men rushed inside almost knocking her down.

Police! Police! They chimed.

"What the hell? Y'all can't barge in here like this!" Tracie hysterically flailed her arms.

The plain clothes officer who identified himself as Damon held up a piece of paper. "This search warrant says we can. Step aside."

She snatched the legal document from out of his hand and tore it up. "I don't give a shit about this. Get the fuck out my house!" Tracie ignorantly demanded, standing as close to his face as her nine month belly would allow.

"Once we're done here, we will." The officer pushed her back.

"Don't be putting your fuckin' hands on me, bitch." She shoved him back. He then barricaded Tracie from moving freely as she angrily cursed him out.

"Calm down!" he screamed in her face.

Tracie yelled to the top of her lungs, telling each person rummaging through her home how they could all kiss her ass on the way out.

"Is he here?" one law enforcer asked.

"No, but his jackpot is," the narc announced, holding kilos of cocaine in the air.

Seeing the dope silenced Tracie's ranting.

"You're gonna need to come with us."

"I don't need to do shit!" Tracie rolled her neck in protest.

Meanwhile, G'Corey was on his way back to the house when a lil' knucklehead ran up to him. "My dude, the block is hot." He pointed toward Tracie being sat in the back of an unmarked vehicle.

Tracie's screaming could be heard from up the block, "Y'all planted that shit in my house! Fuck y'all! Fuck all y'all!"

"Fuck!" G'Corey spun around quickly and dipped off on the side of the nearest house where he watched on from a distance. He witnessed a man carrying a duffle bag out of Tracie's house and he knew they got him for his entire stash. "Goddamn! I'll be a muthafuck!"

Chapter 35
One Month Later...

"**H**appy birthday! It's your wedding day! I'm so freaking thrilled you're joining me in the wives' club," Samiyah yelled as she wobbled over to Acacia doing the cabbage patch. "Look at the beautiful Mrs. Angel Santana."

Acacia gave a quick smirk, but her lack of energy was noticeable. "Can you ladies excuse us?" She asked each of her cousins who were congregated in her dressing room to step out.

Acacia's dry tone struck her as odd. So, once the last lady left, she immediately questioned. "What's wrong?"

"This guilt is killing me, Yah. You know ever since my brother was killed on my birthday, I've dreaded today coming. But because of Sleepy," she dropped her head, "this day will have renewed meaning." She began to snivel. "Why did I cheat on him and of all people with his brother?"

The expression on Acacia's face was heartbreaking. Samiyah placed her hands on her cheeks and lifted her head until their eyes met. "Don't beat yourself up for a past you can't change. Come here." She pulled her into her arms, kissing her forehead.

"It's hard not to. Sleepy has no idea who he's marrying and as much as I want to come clean, he'll leave me for good and I can't have that." Acacia released shameful tears. "You know instead of being understanding of Sleepy's depression, I used it to justify my actions. And even when Sleepy apologized, explained his frustrations, and begged my forgiveness, I still allowed myself to drown in lust with Diego. The way I handled things you would have sworn I didn't love Sleepy, but I do. Tsss. The nerve of me to be pissed off like it was his struggle alone. I should have never carried on a relationship with his brother," she scoffed.

"True, but that's over now." Samiyah wiped her face with the palms of her hands. "Stop crying, otherwise people are going to think something is wrong." Acacia looked away. "Look at me," she brought her attention back to her. "All you can do now is not repeat the past and start forgiving yourself so you can move forward with your husband."

Acacia allowed the word to swim in her head for few seconds. "You're right," she agreed. "Sorry. I just needed to get that off my chest, I guess."

"Chile, as many times as you were there for me, this ain't nothing." Samiyah made light of her venting. "Well, since you're good, I need to pay this water bill. This lil' girl stay sitting on my doggone bladder."

"Do me favor, please. Check on the guests and make sure everything is going smoothly. Drop in on Sleepy, tell him I love him so much. And—"

"Ahh, nervine, I'll handle the guests, but you can tell your man yourself once you see him at the alter. Now, let me go." Samiyah bounced on her foot.

"I am nervous, huh?" Acacia laughed at herself. "Go 'head and use the bathroom, go," she shooed her out of the door, giggling before she closed it.

Acacia sat down and stared at herself in the mirror. She watched herself breathe slowly. "Smile. You're getting mar—" The sound of the door opening caught her off guard, but the reflection startled her half to death. "Diego, what are you doing here?"

"I should be asking you the same question." He shut the door and locked it.

Acacia rose to her feet and pointed past him. "You have to go. Right now!" She headed in his direction to kick him out, but he blocked her and attempted to kiss her instead. "Stop it, Diego! Shit!" She backed away from him, wiping her mouth.

"This lil' fight we do is the animal attraction you crave, so why are you frontin', Ma?"

"Diego, I told you it was over between us. No more flirting, kissing, sexing, anything that puts me in the same room as you. We are through. I am getting married—today! "Why are you even doing this?" Acacia questioned in a pleading kind of way.

"Sleepy's my brother and I know this is fucked up, but this is real life and I want you in mine. You know he doesn't make you feel alive like I do. So, I don't even know why you buggin', Ma."

"Listen, we took things too far. We should have never—"

Diego angrily cut her off. "You wasn't saying all that shit when I was making you moan *my* name."

"Diego. Don't!"

"Don't what?" The volume of his voice escalated. "Don't tell the truth? Don't say how you fell in love me and somewhere in all of this I fell in love with you?"

"Lower your damn voice," she admonished.

He ignored her demand and angrily shouted. "Am I lying?"

"Hell yea, you're lying, to yourself and to me. Now, go!" She shoved him. "Go!" Fearful tears brewed in her eyes. Their back and forth was sure to draw unwanted attention, but Diego was looking as if getting caught in her room, alone, was what he wanted when he refused to move.

Diego protested that he wasn't the only one to see the shift between them. What started off as a forbidden fuck, turned into her confiding in him as he confided in her. He hadn't felt a connection like that since Isa. He regretfully let her go too easily, so he couldn't imagine doing the same with Acacia.

They continued their heated debate for another five minutes before Diego looked at her sternly. "If I walk out that door, you will never see or hear from me again, yo." He pulled out his plane ticket and held it up to her face to show her that he wasn't bluffing. "My plane leaves *today*."

The fire they made was unforgettable, but she chose to be true to her heart, not her loins. "Well then go and never return," she spoke weakly although she meant it with all her strength.

Diego could see the conflict in her eyes, whether she admitted it or not. However, it was obvious his presence would only prove him to be a fool. There was no way she would leave Sleepy for him. The ivory wedding dress that clung to her curves perfectly confirmed it.

"You're gonna regret me leaving," he spat in his final attempt to threaten her with his departure.

"Actually, I regretted you coming."

"It's like that?" His feelings were crushed. He hesitated briefly but firmly adios'd her. "A'ight. I'm out." He picked up his pride and stormed over to the door, swinging it open, leaving as quickly as he came.

Acacia clutched her chest and trotted off behind him, stopping at the door only to see if anyone saw him leave. *Whew! The coast was clear*, she observed.

She took another seat in front of the mirror and began fixing her makeup. *Lord, let this day go smoothly*, she dabbed a Kleenex under her eye.

A knock at her door caused her to jump again, but immediately recognizing the voice of her mother from the other side calmed her instantly.

"Come in," Acacia put on her happy face. Isabel looked worried and it caused Acacia's expression to drop. "Don't tell me something's wrong."

"Hopefully not, but we can't find Sleepy."

"You can't find Sleepy!" She sprung up from her seat. "What you mean you can't find Sleepy?" Acacia became instantly alarmed.

Her mother hunched her shoulder and threw up prayer hands. "He was supposed to be at the alter twenty minutes ago, but he's not there."

Acacia became weak and stumbled backwards, supporting herself with the table she bumped into. "Oh, God!"

"What, baby?" Isabel moved closer.

That sick son of a bitch told him! Acacia thought. "Oh, God! She thundered. "Move out of my way, Ma." Acacia damn near mowed her down while moving past her. She hiked up her dress and headed through the back doors of the cathedral. She began a panic stricken search for his truck. When she didn't find it, she rushed through the parking lot and over to her limo driver who was leaning against the vehicle. She opened the back door and in one quick breath she blurted, "Take me home, now!"

***

"Ms. Terry, I'm Ms. Fontenot, the prosecuting attorney working on this case." She cleared her throat and retracted her hand once she saw Tracie had no intentions on shaking it. "Very well. I'm here to offer you a plea deal in exchange for information that will lead to the whereabouts of G'Corey Daniels. Are you willing to cooperate?"

Tracie sat slouched with one arm thrown over the back off a raggedy wooden chair. "Do I look the least bit interested?"

"You should be. Being a first time offender isn't going to give you the leniency you might be hoping for. We found five kilos of cocaine and thirty thousand dollars. That's a drug trafficking charge with intent to distribute. Now, we know it belongs to Mr. Daniels but if you insist on taking his charge, you will be looking at fifteen years. That means that precious little boy you just had won't even know who you are. He'll be calling your aunt his mommy and by the time he realizes you're his mother, he will probably end up hating you for choosing a man over raising him, *your* flesh and blood."

Tracie buckled on the inside. There was no greater pain than being separated from her son minutes after she delivered. But in her heart she believed that by doing right by G'Corey Jr.'s father she was indirectly doing right by her son. Besides, she knew as soon as G'Corey could get his hands on ten percent of her bail he would bond her out.

Tracie was fearful of the outcome but she smiled on the inside because she knew this would solidify her position with G'Corey. He would see her ultimate sacrifice and love her for it. "Do what you need to do, miss. I'm ready to go to my cell."

Ms. Fontenot stared at Tracie, waiting on her to break because she could smell uncertainty emanating off of her. But true to Tracie's stubborn nature, she kept it together and remained firm in her resolute.

"Have it your way," she said. She bammed on the glass window signaling the guard to open the door. "Once you step out of this room, I will prosecute you to the fullest extent of the law," she threatened.

Tracie stood to her feet, turned around and placed her hands behind her back so she could be handcuffed.

Ms. Fontenot shook her head. "St. Gabriel Women's Prison is full of ladies just like you," she sneered.

"Well, get my bed ready."

Coffee

Chapter 36

As the driver was pulling onto Acacia's street, she saw Sleepy's truck parked in the driveway. Her heart rate sped up and caused her to breathe irrationally. *He knows*, she thought. "You can leave and return back to the church," she said hurriedly.

The chauffer looked at her through the rearview mirror and nodded his head. As he slowed up approaching his destination, he was unable to bring the limousine to a complete stop before Acacia opened the door to rush out of it. He shook his head as he watched Acacia trip over her dress trying to get inside. But once she disappeared inside of her home, he pulled off like he was instructed.

***

Family and friends of both Sleepy and Acacia were becoming restless and rumors of their disappearance started swarming around as gossip usually does.

Searching for Acacia, Minnie stepped outside of the church. She located Samiyah standing at the bottom of the steps, so she approached her. "What's going on? Where's Sleepy and Acacia?"

Samiyah knew just as much as she did. "I don't know. She wasn't in her dressing room and I've tried calling her phone, but it just keeps ringing."

"I've tried calling myself and I'm getting nothing."

Samiyah gasped and then covered her mouth. "When we last talked, she was telling me how guilty she felt about her involvement with Diego. She was pretty upset about it, but she swore to me she was fine before I left her alone."

"Oh, my goodness. Do you think she confessed?" Minnie questioned.

"I hope not. I surely told her not to, but knowing her she may have."

"That would explain things, Maybe Sleepy left when she told him, but if that be the case. Where's she? She doesn't drive." Minnie was becoming agitated.

"Wasn't her limo parked right here?" Samiyah's pointed to the curb. "It was," she answered herself. "Call Gerran out here. Tell him we need to leave, now!"

***

Acacia rushed inside and ran directly to their bedroom. Her momentum came to a complete halt when she saw Sleepy throwing his clothes into a suitcase. "Sleepy, what are you doing?"

He paused for a moment without turning around to address her, thought to respond but then decided against it.

She frantically walked over to him. "Tell me what happened. Let's talk about it," she spoke timidly. He remained deathly silent as if he heard no one speaking. Acacia began removing his clothes as he put them in. "Talk to me," she whined. "Papi, please."

He angrily broke his silence. "Don't you dare try to sweet talk me as if you're innocent." He snarled in her direction before he returned his efforts to packing.

Acacia knew for certain he knew. *Diego refused to just let me be happy*, she thought. She was too frightful to utter his name, but there was no way not to. "Is this about Diego?" She held her breath as she waited on his answer.

Sleepy clenched his jaw and his fist and turned her way. "Nah, this is about *you* and Diego," he spoke harshly.

"Papi, please let me explain. I—I," she fumbled over her words.

"Acacia hold onto your dignity and step aside. There's nothing you can tell me right now that I haven't already overheard while you and my brother were having y'all lover's quarrel."

Acacia clamped her eyes shut and recalled hearing noises outside of her dressing room's door, but she didn't phantom it was Sleepy, at least she hoped it wasn't. "It isn't what you think," she attempted to reason. "I stupidly, foolishly allowed myself to be with him only when I felt you didn't want me." Sleepy looked at her despicably. "No, no, no, I'm not saying it was your fault. I'm just saying," she searched for the right words, "I was wrong. Baby, please understand me."

He angrily wiped away tears that fell from his eyes. "For years I put up with your mood swings, jealous ways, and sporadic behavior because I loved you." He poked her shoulder. "I go through a serious life changing event and slipped in a little bit of a funk and you abandon ship? And with my brother? You're a new kind of low."

"Sleepy, I'm sorry."

"You are that," he confirmed. "I just wish I would have found out before I spent all this money trying to give you your dream wedding and a diamond to brag about." Looking at Acacia groveling only enraged him. "Move out of my way. I'm done talking."

"Sleepy!" Acacia jumped in front of him, trying to barricade him from leaving out of their room. "You have to give me a chance to make this right." He ignored her and pushed her aside. She staggered off, but regained her balance. "You can't leave me!" Acacia was hysterical. She snatched the luggage out of his hand and threw it to the floor.

Sleepy grabbed for his luggage and she reached for it at the same time. They stood in the middle of the hallway tussling for possession of it until he finally let it go. "Keep it"

"Sleepy, stay!" she screeched.

There was no chance in hell Sleepy would allow her tears and theatrics to stop him from setting her free and she knew this. Sleepy continued through the house, but stopped dramatically once he got to the door. For Sleepy, things began moving in slow motion but Acacia felt time suspend altogether. Her heart beat echoed outside of her chest and acoustically boomed in surround sound. She felt so outer body that she wasn't aware when she ran into the kitchen, pulled out a butcher's knife, or the moment when she lunged at Sleepy until she heard a heavy thud hit the floor.

"Urggghhhh!!!" Sleepy loudly roared in gut wrenching pain.

His screams jolted her into the now. Acacia was petrified as the crimson colored diameter grew larger, staining his white tuxedo. "Oh, my God! What did I do?" She kneeled down beside him, placing her trembling hands on his back inches away from where she drove the sharp blade into his spine.

Sleepy's legs faintly twitched as he attempted to get up, but he was losing sensation much too rapidly to energize his movement. He was trying to speak, but his fight for air took precedence. The only audible sound was the gurgling noises he made through the blood spilling through his lips.

"Hold on, Papi. I'ma get help." She dashed into the living room and snatched the cordless phone. She hurried back to Sleepy's side and frantically dialed 9-1-1.

"9-1-1, what's your emergency?" The dispatcher spoke.

Acacia cries thundered through the receiver. "I stabbed my fiancé and he's dying! I need help, please! My address is…" She anxiously paced the floor until she concluded her call. Finally, she hung up. "Sleepy, help is on the way. I'm gonna fix this," she said through tears.

Agony registered in his eyes as he painfully stared at Acacia, moving his mouth slowing as a fish would out of water.

"What are you trying to say, baby?" She dropped down to his face, placing her ear by his lips trying to capture what he was saying. "I can't understand, baby." She looked back at him.

A tear fell from the crease of his eye as he strained to speak again. "I," was the only word that parted from his lips before he crossed over.

"Sleepy? Sleepy?" She shook his lifeless body. She called his name repeatedly, but when she took notice of his soulless eyes staring off into nothingness, Acacia freakishly screamed, "Noooooooooo! Noooooooo! Noooooooooo!" Acacia went ballistic. She stood to her feet, pulling at her hair and screaming a gut curdling roar. "Sleepyyyyyyy!" She belted over and over until something snapped in her mind and then she went morbidly silent.

Once again, she found herself in the kitchen. She fumbled through the drawer unable to see clearly for the tears that hazed her vision. She wiped her eyes with the back of her arm and located a sharp knife.

In a zombiefied manner, she walked back up front by Sleepy's body and stood over him, tears dripping on his face. "I'm so sorry, Sleepy." She held the blade to her wrist and then looked up at the ceiling, "Forgive me, Father."

Acacia deeply sliced one wrist causing an immediate spill of blood and with the remaining strength she had, she cut the other. The knife slipped from her grip and two red pools formed on each side of her. She woozily stood on her feet until she collapsed on the floor, lying at her lover's side.

Staring him squarely in the eyes, she chanted, "I love you. I love—you. I—lov…" Acacia's words faded to black.

***

"Oh, shit!" Samiyah's forehead creased with worry lines when she saw police cars and yellow tape blocking Sleepy's and Acacia's property.

Gerran parked across the street from their house. Samiyah attempted to open the door and step out, but he advised her not to. "Stay in the car. I'll check to see what's going on."

But his words traveled through one ear and out of the other because the moment she saw a body with a white sheet draped over it being carried out of the house, her impulses jolted her out of the car. She carelessly ran across the street oblivious to Yuriah and Minnie's approaching vehicle.

"Oh, no, no, no, no, no," Samiyah continuously chanted as she tried to breech the *do not cross* tape.

"You can't go in there," the officer said, blocking her.

Samiyah pointed past him. "Those are my friends in there," she balled.

Gerran made his way to her and held her from behind. He tried to spin her around, but she was adamant about observing the scene. "Gerran, let me go." She tried to pry out of his arms. "I have to check on Acacia. Let me goooooo!"

Minnie never crossed the street as she watched from a distance, crying. Yuriah cradle her against his chest, telling her that it would be alright.

"Oh, my God. That can't be my people," Samiyah yelled. "Where's Acacia? Acacia?" She bombastically screamed her name. "Acacia?" Samiyah shouted and cried so much, she started to choke for air.

"She's hyperventilating. She needs oxygen." An EMT alerted a nearby technician.

"Breathe, baby. Breathe." Gerran coached Samiyah as the mask was placed over her nose and mouth.

Samiyah fought off the help. "Move! Where's Acacia? I gotta get to Acacia."

After minutes of arguing back and forth with Gerran who was trying to calm her along with the EMT's, she finally quilled her fussing only to fixate her eyes on a second stretcher being walked out of the house, then in a sudden outburst Samiyah screamed at the top of her lungs," Noooo!"

Gerran bear hugged Samiyah even tighter, preventing her from falling to the ground. Once she was back on her feet, she fought even harder to get out of his hold and over to Acacia. "Calm down, baby."

"She can't be dead! She can't be dead!" Samiyah jumped up and down, getting more excited with each passing second. In the midst of her hysteria, Samiyah's felt her water break along with a spasm like pain that felt likened to a kidney punch. "Ohhh, nooooooo," she cried, grabbing her stomach. "I'm going into labor!"

***

Later that night...

Waaaaa... Waaaa...

"Your special delivery came four weeks early, but you have a healthy, beautiful baby girl, Mrs. Babineaux." The delivering doctor informed the exhausted mother.

Samiyah was too drained to smile. She was overjoyed that her baby arrived, but underwhelmed at her friend's departure.

After the baby was cleaned, the nurse attempted to place the tiny bundle in Samiyah's arms but she was too weak to hold her. Instead, Gerran grabbed his daughter and held her close to her face.

"Hey, baby girl." Her voice trembled as tears streamed.

After she kissed the baby's rosy fat cheeks, Gerran placed her in her nursery bed, walked into the waiting room and informed everyone that his wife delivered successfully. Elias, Blu, Minnie, Yuriah, and Samiyah's parents all followed him into the delivery room to see the new addition.

There wasn't much chatter amongst them although the occasion was joyous. It was just too hard to truly celebrate that moment in lieu of the grim events that took place earlier that day.

***

A week later...

Friends and family of Acacia De La Rosa were departing as her coffin was being lowered into the earth.

Minnie cried as she tossed roses upon her friend's casket. "This isn't how your story was supposed to end. Sleepy's gone. You're gone. This is all wrong!" She shook her head in disbelief and then without warning she collapsed. She would have plundered to the ground if it had not been for Yuriah standing behind her to catch her fall.

A few bystanders waved their hands to give her air as she came to. Yuriah lifted Minnie into his arms. "I need to get her home. I'll have her call you later." Yuriah informed Samiyah as he cradled against his chest, walking out of the cemetery.

Tears spilled out of Samiyah's eyes like a leaky faucet. She wanted to check on Minnie, but she was stuck. She couldn't even utter a response to Yuriah but she managed a slow head nod to signal her understanding.

"I'll step back to give you a little time alone," Gerran sweetly offered.

Samiyah bobbed her head agreeing with his gesture. She stood mummified at the gravesite of her beloved friend, holding her sleeping daughter.

Samiyah choked on unspoken words, but after a few inhale/exhales she was able to speak. "I have good news. I had your baby on your birthday. She came at 9:08 that night. Were you in the room to see it?" She took a few short rapid breaths as she fought the urge to let out a full fledge wail before she continued. "Guess what, best friend? Her name is Acacia and her middle name is Rose, kinda like your last name." Samiyah dropped her head and began bouncing impatiently on her feet as her thoughts centered on the way she had to introduce her little girl to her best.

Gerran sensed Samiyah was coming unglued, so he stepped to her and wrapped his arms around her shoulder. "You're ready to go?" Dazed, she shook her head *no*. He then reached for his daughter. "Give me the baby and I'll leave you to your conversation." She shook her head and passed Acacia off to him. He kissed her gingerly on the fore-head and stepped away to give her *her* privacy.

"Why you had to leave me, Acacia, bruh?" she groaned. "Who gon' ride for me like you, huh? What about that lil' girl back there you told me was yours? You were gonna teach her Spanish, remember? Mannnn, I need you and you ain't even here," she whined. "What am I supposed to do now? Huh?" Samiyah slowly dropped to her knees and clutched the earth in her palms. "What now?"

Gerran walked over to her again. "Come on, baby. It's time to go." He placed his hand underneath her arm and gently encouraged her to stand to her feet.

Samiyah remained dumbfounded as she waited to hear an answer to the many questions she put out there for Acacia to answer. But after another nudge from Gerran, she stood up weakly.

She wiped the fresh batch of tears away from her puffy eyes with the sleeve of her jacket. She attempted to say her final goodbye, but she couldn't. Only her lips moved. She shook her head remorsefully and turned to walk away, occasionally looking over her shoulder at what would forever stain her heart as the day a piece of her died on the inside.

Chapter 37
Three Months Later...

"**I**s everything okay? Is Acacia doing better? I called as soon as I got your message." Minnie hurried her words in a panic the moment Samiyah answered her phone.

"We're still at Children's Hospital and have been all morning. They informed me that she has severe anemia which explained her loss of skin color and the jaundice. Right now they are giving her fluids intravenously, but she is going to need a blood transfusion."

"My poor pudding." Minnie was upset at the news. "You can do that, though. "Can't you?"

"If I wasn't pregnant, I would have been able to."

"You are?" Minnie was happily surprised by the news of her pregnancy.

"Yes and as a result I'm not able to donate. So, now Gerran is giving them his blood to test against hers. Once all things check out, we will be able to get our little girl back to health."

"You sound exhausted." Minnie detected the sleep in her voice.

"I am. I thought my tiredness came from adjusting to motherhood, but all along it's because I'm expecting. Then I haven't had any real sleep dealing with my baby's medical issue."

"How long before you hear anything?"

"Well, Gerran just came back from seeing the phlebotomist. Once everything comes back from the lab, I suppose it should be a few hours before we know the next steps to take. But I can't call it right now."

"You know I can postpone my honeymoon and come straight to you once we have our ceremony."

"You'll do no such thing. Acacia will be fine. Once this transfusion is performed her body will be able to produce the red blood cells she needs on her own and with a little monitoring, all things will be good." Samiyah comforted Minnie into feeling things would be alright.

"Are you sure? Because me and Yuriah will be out of the country for two weeks and if you need me, I want to be here." Minnie made it known that nothing including her honeymoon mattered more than her godchild.

"I'm positive. Knowing you have my back is good enough for me."
Samiyah smiled upon her friendship. "Well, I wish I could be there to
welcome you into the folds of the wives' club, but—"

"But you have something more important than that on your plate
right now." Minnie finished her sentence. "We hired a photographer,
he'll take plenty pictures. It'll be like you were there for the whole
thing."

"It's so not the same, but please send Yuri our love. Let him know
that he couldn't be marrying a better woman."

"Awww, I love you, Yah."

"I love you, too. Now, go on and get ready for your big day."

Minnie just about shrilled at the thought of seeing Yuriah in his
tux. "I'll call and check on you before we board our plane, okay?"

"That works."

"Okay, kiss my baby and tell Gerran stop stressing. God got it."
Minnie advised her friend before she hung up the phone.

Samiyah closed her eyes. *Acacia, I need you to be our lil' girl's
angel and watch over her, okay?*

***

A few hours later...

November provided the perfect fall weather. The autumn leaves on
the trees provided the flawless back drop to the outdoor wedding being
held in City Park for the soon to be Mr. & Mrs. Leblanc.

Minnie wanted something small and quaint, so only a handful of
people were invited, five from his side and five from hers. She experienced the big hoop la of a wedding and she didn't want that this time
around, but she did agree to Yuriah sharing a half page publication in
the lagniappe section of The Times Picayune announcing their wedding. He wanted her to have a special memorabilia of the day he made
her his wife.

Minnie stood in her bedroom, applying the last of her mascara to
her lashes. "You look beautiful, baby." Minnie's mother complimented
her.

"I feel beautiful, Ma. He makes me feel beautiful. Oh, God," she gushed. "I never knew love like this before and now that I know what it feels like to be treated as a Queen, it makes me see just how low I'd set the bar before him."

"Well, baby, this moment here is all that matters now," Naomi smiled.

Minnie looked at the time. "Oh, Ma, it's almost time."

"Oh, yes. We need to head on over. Can't have my child late to one of the most special events in a girl's life."

Her mother helped her gather everything she needed from her house before Minnie locked up. Naomi carefully lifted her train and helped her inside of her truck.

When they arrived at City Park, Yuriah had a chariot waiting on her and her mother. They were to take the five minute ride to the secluded spot they picked out to share their vows.

As Minnie drew near to the small congregation waiting on her to make her entrance, she couldn't contain the burst of energy that made her shout. "Woooo! I just had to get that out of my system." She stomped her feet in excitement.

Once the two white horse drawn carriage came to a stop, the driver assisted both mother and bride out of the buggy. "Enjoy your day, Miss." He took off his hat and bowed before Minnie.

She bowed like a Southern Belle and giggled. "Thank you, sir."

A gentleman escorted Naomi as Minnie's father waited at the beginning of the make shift aisle with an extended hand. She placed her hand in his. "You look amazing, baby girl."

Minnie blushed, "Awww, daddy."

"I've always knew you would marry him," pride bounced off of his words.

"Really?" she beamed.

"Oh, yea, baby girl. Everyone could tell how much he loved you ever since y'all were teens. You were the only one who didn't notice. Glad you see it now, he's a good man."

"He is, daddy. He's one of the good ones."

Ribbon in the Sky played queuing Mr. Mitchell to begin his walk with his daughter.

Don't cry. Don't cry. Aww, shucks, you're crying, Minnie tried to talk herself into keeping dry eyes.

Her father gave her his handkerchief when he heard her whimpers. She dabbed at the wetness and then straightened her face as best as she could. But it was hard for her. Seeing Yuriah stand there proudly awaiting to take her hand in matrimony did something to her.

"Who here before us gives this woman away to be married?" Reverend E. Willis asked the ritualistic question.

"I do," Mr. Mitchell spoke as he passed her hand to Yuriah's.

The men both gave each other a gentlemen's nod and then the reverend proceeded with the ceremony.

"...Is there any among you that object to the marrying of these two standing before me today?" He questioned the few people in attendance. "Speak now or forever hold your peace."

Minnie gushed with overflowing love as she stared at Yuriah who emoted her same happiness. The Reverend was seconds away from continuing with the nuptials when a disturbing voice boomed with animosity.

"I object, muthafuckas!" G'Corey came from behind an oak tree, approaching them slowly and with caution.

Yuriah whipped his head toward the sound of the disgruntled man, instinctively maneuvering his bride-to-be behind him. When Yuri saw it was G'Corey, his expression turned stone in the face of his enemy.

There was no need for any speeches in G'Corey's mind. Yuriah should have known he was going to strike back. G'Corey raised his .9mm and aimed for Yuri's chest. "Die slow, bitch!"

Boc! Boc!

***

Later that evening...

"Why is meeting your people so important? I'm dating you, not them." Elias felt weird parked in front of Blu's family home, staring at it like it was the house on Elm St.

"Eli, quit acting all nervous. My folks won't bite. Well, maybe grandma, 'cause she's a bit freaky, but no one else." She cracked a small joke to lighten his tension.

He smiled her way. "What is it about you, huh? You started off on my *hit it* list and now I'm meeting your people. Shit never work out like you plan."

"Well, that's a good thing. And it's not so much what's special about me as it is what's special about *us*. We had chemistry that worked great as friends and although the man whore in you resisted the change, it was only inevitable you became a one woman's man because you were ready to love someone who was willing to love you back."

"Is that right? Is that what your associate's degree at DeVry taught you?" She play punched him in the shoulder. "I'm just kidding, Blu. Damn," he chuckled. "But you right. You hit a thuggah's soft spot."

She looked out of the window of her car and noticed both her mom and pop's vehicles along with her sister's newly painted BMW was parked in the driveway. "Looks like the gang's all here."

Elias wiped the moisture accumulating on his hands on his jeans. He looked at the house and then to her. "I'm getting some cutty tonight, goddamn." He pointed his finger downward to express that he meant *tonight.*

She shook her head and laughed his statement off. Their first time making love wasn't going to be a tradeoff. *He gets my vaulted treasure because he met The Cormiers? I don't think so,* she thought. However, she wasn't going to discount the huge step he was making by having family dinner. She knew he was out of his comfort zone.

"In due time," she responded to his demand. She looked at the time. "Come on, scary. You stalled enough." They got out of her car and walked up the steps leading to the porch.

"Wait!" he stopped her. "What am I walking into? I've never met nobody's folks before and the only mothers I've met were MILFs."

Blu touched him on the cheek and let out a giggle. His honest sense of humor made him so attractive to her. "Be yourself, baby. They'll love you. You'll do fine, okay?"

When Blu rang the doorbell, Elias grabbed her hand and squeezed it. She found his shyness adorable and confirming of his feelings he tended to put a cap on.

"Baby," her mother greeted her with open arms. "Come in."

"Hey, mama. Let me introduce you to my boyfriend, Elias. Elias, this is my mama, Lauryn." He gave her a church hug.

"Nice to meet you, sugar." Lauryn warmly welcomed him.

"Same here," he replied.

Still hand in hand, they walked further into her childhood home until she spotted her father watching a football game. "Daddy-O, come over here. Come meet my guy." He clicked the off button on the remote and headed out of the den and into the living room. "This is my daddy, Langston. Daddy, this is Elias."

"Mr. Cormier to you," he extended his hand, giving Eli a very firm and long handshake. "Who's your people?" he sternly inquired.

"Daddy, be niceeee." Blu tiptoed and kissed him on the cheek. He softened under his baby girl's warmth.

"The Duprees out the seventh ward, sir," Elias answered respectfully.

Blu switched gears and redirected Eli's attention to her Grams, sitting in her wheelchair.

"And this sweet ole lady is my Grandma LuLu." Blu winked her eye at Eli, reminding him about her Na'na's fresh hands. He leaned over and hugged her. "My oldest sister, Langley, is out of town, but I'll introduce you to the brat, my other sister, when she comes downstairs." She leaned over and whispered into his ear. "She can be a bit of a pill, but she can be a'ight when she wanna."

"Cool," he bobbed his head.

"Well, I hope everyone brought their appetites because Mama has cooked enough to feed the block," Lauryn happily announced.

She wheeled her mother and directed everyone into the separate dining area. Langston took his seat at the head of the eight chair dining room table. Blu and Elias filed suit.

Before them was a spread to feed the gods. "We have seafood gumbo, stuffed bell peppers, potato salad, homemade mac n cheese, two types of vegetables. You name it, I made it," she chuckled as she grabbed a chair.

"Blue Diamond, go call your sister from up there. Don't make no goddamn sense how she comes over here just to alienate herself," he grumbled.

Just as Blu was excusing herself from the table, she heard the click of her sister's heels descending the hardwood stairs. "Here she comes now."

"All of this smells good," Elias complimented the chef, making small talk of his own. He took another deep inhale, but what he registered this time wasn't the hot, steamy buttered rolls sitting before him. It had been nine months, but he still recognized the soft lingering scent of J'adore. *If I turn around and it be that bitch*, he thought.

"Eli," Blu tapped his shoulder. "I'd like for you to meet my sister."

Before Elias could turn around fully, he venomously spoke her name right as Blu introduced her.

"La'Tasha," they said.

***

Meanwhile...

"What's taking so long?" Gerran paced the floor in the nurse's office.

"Baby, keep calm. You're making me nervous." Samiyah sat on the edge of her seat.

"I don't understand how your bloodwork took only a couple of hours, but it seems as if we have been here all damn day with mine." Gerran was antsy and anxious to hold his little girl in his arms to let her know that everything was going to be just fine.

"The technician has a lot to do, I'm sure. But our baby is being cared for in the midst of all this." Samiyah shared her dwindling optimism. She too was growing concern with the amount of time they'd been waiting.

"You're right." He finally sat down and gave her a kiss on the lips. "I'm just ready to get this over with and I know you are too."

"Indeed, I am." In an effort to give them a more positive vibe, she changed the topic. "How did you feel when the doctor told us earlier about this new baby?"

Gerran smiled for the first time since being there. "It felt great. I want you having as many of my children as you can carry. I'm kinda hoping for a boy this time, but as long as it's healthy, I don't mind what we have." He placed his hand on the small pooch Acacia left behind.

For a tender moment, they relished in the bliss of the new bundle until the door creaked open and snapped them back to the reason they were there. Both Gerran and Samiyah shot up from their seated position.

The nurse stepped into the room. "Thank y'all for being so patient with me. I have the result here in my folder." She took a seat behind her desk. "Have a seat," she offered.

"We're good. Just tell us what do we do now?" Gerran was anxious to set things in motion.

Fifteen years of being a nurse still wasn't enough preparation to deliver bad news to her patients or their care takers. She sighed and then clasped her hands together. "After reviewing everything twice, I'm afraid you won't be a candidate to donate blood for baby Babineaux, sir."

"Why not? What's wrong?" He felt a pang in his heart.

Samiyah was in a state of shock. She needed to know what was really going on with the treatment of their baby. "What are you talking about?" Confusion rested firmly on both her and Gerran's faces.

The nurse looked very uncomfortable but then she spoke, "Tests came back and the results show you're not a match."

"What are you saying, lady?" Gerran's initial woeful look turned menacing.

"Sorry to say this, sir, but you're not the father."

To Be Continued...
Love Knows No Boundaries III: *Pandora's Box*
The Finale
Available Now!

Author's Note

Hi _____ (insert name here)

I struggled mentally to complete this novel because of a tremendous loss that occurred, but it was with my pressing desire to honor my daddy *and* to give you all what I felt was an explosive read that I pushed forward.

The end is near and true colors will come out in the sizzling conclusion: Pandora's Box. I do hope you're ready.

Also, if I may request one more thing, I ask that you leave a review on Amazon regarding your reading experience. It's so important to me to know if I have served my purpose as a writer by giving you a quality product and an entertaining read. Hope you have enjoyed and thank you in advance.

Peace and Blessings,
Queen Coffee

Coffee

TORN BETWEEN TWO
By **Coffee**
LAY IT DOWN **III**
By **Jamaica**
BLOOD OF A BOSS **IV**
By **Askari**
BRIDE OF A HUSTLA **III**
By **Destiny Skai**
WHEN A GOOD GIRL GOES BAD **II**
By **Adrienne**
LOVE & CHASIN' PAPER **II**
By **Qay Crockett**
THE HEART OF A GANGSTA **II**
By **Jerry Jackson**
TO DIE IN VAIN **II**
By **ASAD**
THE BOSS MAN'S DAUGHTERS **II**
By **Aryanna**

Available Now

RESTRAING ORDER **I & II**

By **CA$H & Coffee**

LOVE KNOWS NO BOUNDARIES **I II & III**

By **Coffee**

LAY IT DOWN **I & II**

LAST OF A DYING BREED

By **Jamaica**

PUSH IT TO THE LIMIT

By **Bre' Hayes**

BLOOD OF A BOSS **I II & III**

By **Askari**

THE STREETS BLEED MURDER **I, II & III**

THE HEART OF A GANGSTA

By **Jerry Jackson**

CUM FOR ME

An **LDP Erotica Collaboration**

BRIDE OF A HUSTLA **I & II**

By **Destiny Skai**

WHEN A GOOD GIRL GOES BAD

By **Adrienne**

A GANGSTER'S REVENGE **I II III & IV**

THE BOSS MAN'S DAUGHTERS

A SAVAGE LOVE **I & II**

By **Aryanna**

WHAT ABOUT US **I & II**

NEVER LOVE AGAIN

THUG ADDICTION

By **Kim Kaye**

THE KING CARTEL **I, II & III**

By **Frank Gresham**

THESE NIGGAS AIN'T LOYAL **I, II & III**

By **Nikki Tee**

GANGSTA SHYT **I II &III**

By **CATO**

THE ULTIMATE BETRAYAL

By **Phoenix**

DON'T FU#K WITH MY HEART **I & II**

By **Linnea**

BOSS'N UP **I & II**

By **Royal Nicole**

I LOVE YOU TO DEATH

By Destiny J

I RIDE FOR MY HITTA

I STILL RIDE FOR MY HITTA

By **Misty Holt**

LOVE & CHASIN' PAPER

By **Qay Crockett**

TO DIE IN VAIN

By **ASAD**

BOOKS BY LDP'S CEO, CA$H

TRUST IN NO MAN
TRUST IN NO MAN 2
TRUST IN NO MAN 3
BONDED BY BLOOD
SHORTY GOT A THUG
IN LOVE WITH A CONVICT
THUGS CRY
THUGS CRY 2
TRUST NO BITCH
TRUST NO BITCH 2
TRUST NO BITCH 3
TIL MY CASKET DROPS
RESTRAINING ORDER
RESTRAINING ORDER 2

Coming Soon
THUGS CRY 3
BONDED BY BLOOD 2
BOW DOWN TO MY GANGSTA

Stay Connected with Us!

Text **LOCKDOWN** to 22828 to stay up-to-date with new releases, sneak peaks, contests and more…

Thank you!

www.ingramcontent.com/pod-product-compliance
Lightning Source LLC
Chambersburg PA
CBHW070842250626
47159CB00003B/899